CN
CARTOON NETWORK

OVER THE GARDEN WALL™

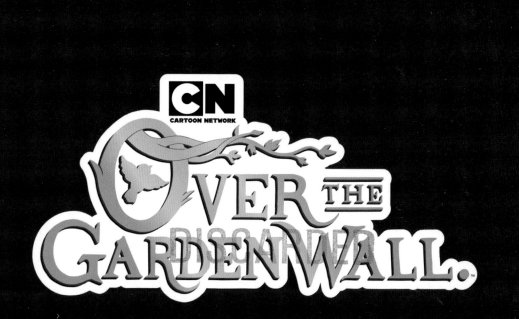

VOLUME FIVE

OVER THE GARDEN WALL **Volume Five, September 2018.** Published by KaBOOM!, a division of Boom Entertainment, Inc. OVER THE GARDEN WALL, CARTOON NETWORK, the logos, and all related characters and elements are trademarks of and © Cartoon Network. (S18) All rights reserved. Originally published in single magazine form as Over the Garden Wall Ongoing No. 17-20. © Cartoon Network. (S17) All rights reserved. KaBOOM!™ and the KaBOOM logo are trademarks of Boom Entertainment, Inc., registered in various countries and categories. All characters, events, and institutions depicted herein are fictional. Any similarity between any of the names, characters, persons, events, and/or institutions in this publication to actual names, characters, and persons, whether living or dead, events, and/or institutions is unintended and purely coincidental. KaBOOM! does not read or accept unsolicited submissions of ideas, stories, or artwork.

BOOM! Studios, 5670 Wilshire Boulevard, Suite 400, Los Angeles, CA 90036-5679. Printed in China. First Printing.

ISBN: 978-1-68415-242-1, eISBN: 978-1-64144-104-9

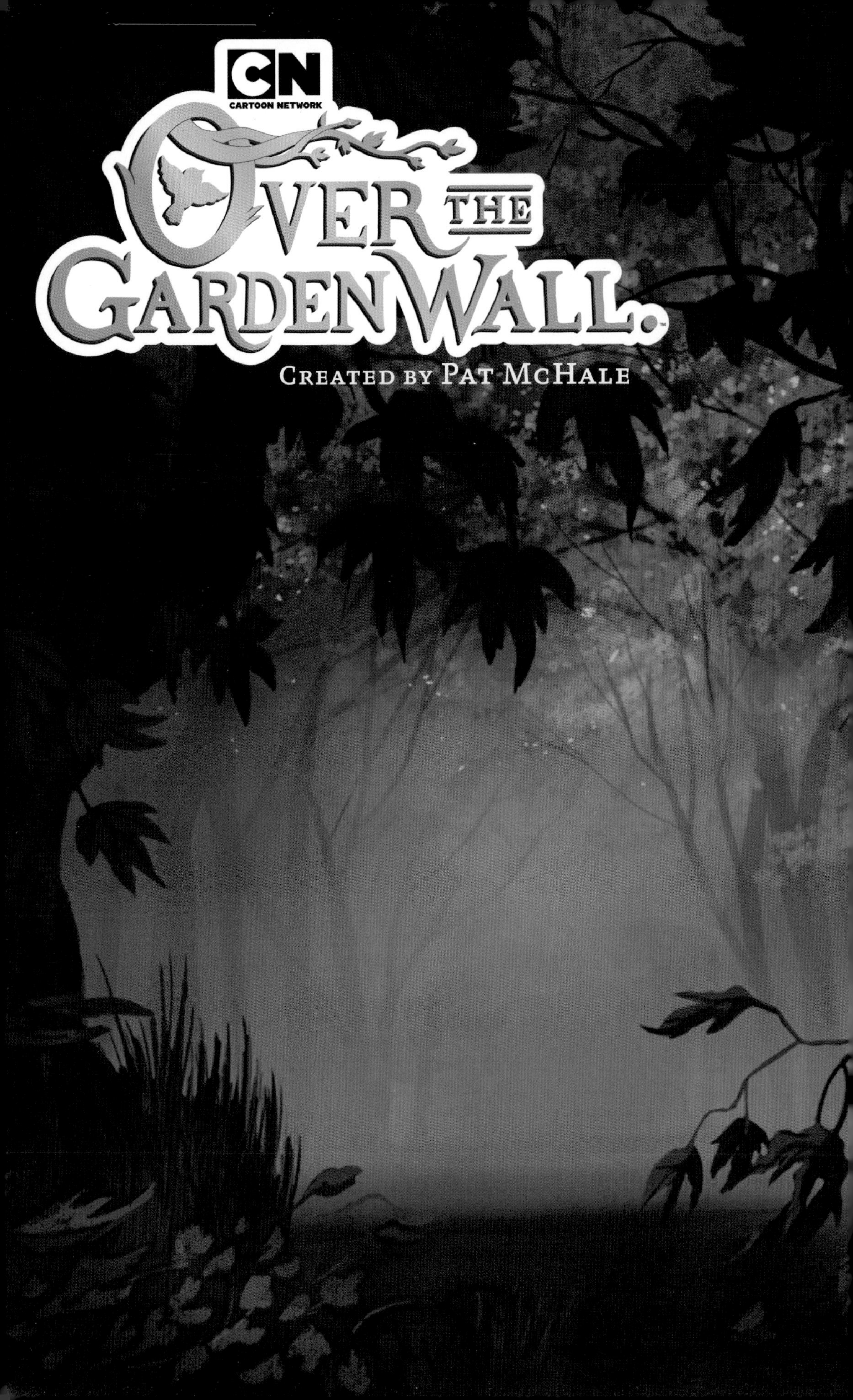
CN
CARTOON NETWORK
OVER THE GARDEN WALL.
CREATED BY PAT MCHALE

WRITTEN BY
KIERNAN SJURSEN-LIEN

"THE CAT AND THE FIDDLE"
ILLUSTRATED BY JORGE MONLONGO
COLORS BY WHITNEY COGAR
LETTERS BY WARREN MONTGOMERY

"TURKEYS AND TURNKEYS"
ILLUSTRATED BY KIERNAN SJURSEN-LIEN
COLORS BY EMILY SATTERFIELD
LETTERS BY WARREN MONTGOMERY

"GO FISH"
ILLUSTRATED BY CARA MCGEE
COLORS BY WHITNEY COGAR
LETTERS BY WARREN MONTGOMERY

"TEA'D OFF"
ILLUSTRATED & LETTERED BY
JIM CAMPBELL

COVER BY DIIGII DAGUNA

DESIGNER KARA LEOPARD
ASSOCIATE EDITOR MATTHEW LEVINE
EDITOR WHITNEY LEOPARD

WITH SPECIAL THANKS TO MARISA MARIONAKIS,
JANET NO, CURTIS LELASH, KATIE KRENTZ, PERNELLE
HAYES, ADRIENNE LEE, STACY RENFROE AND THE
WONDERFUL FOLKS AT CARTOON NETWORK.

The Cat and the Fiddle

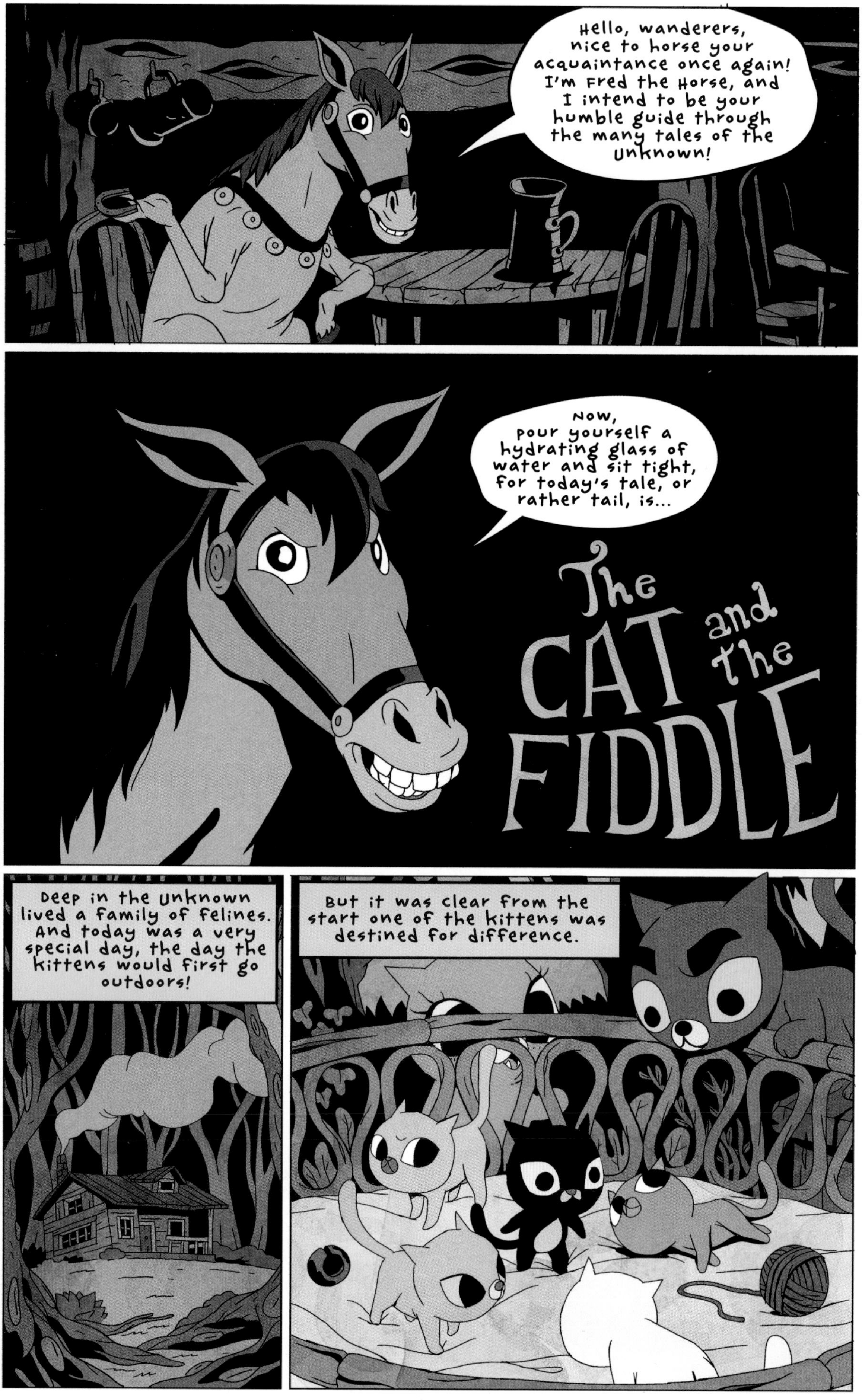
Hello, wanderers, nice to horse your acquaintance once again! I'm Fred the Horse, and I intend to be your humble guide through the many tales of the unknown!
Now, pour yourself a hydrating glass of water and sit tight, for today's tale, or rather tail, is...
The CAT and the FIDDLE
Deep in the Unknown lived a family of felines. And today was a very special day, the day the kittens would first go outdoors!
But it was clear from the start one of the kittens was destined for difference.

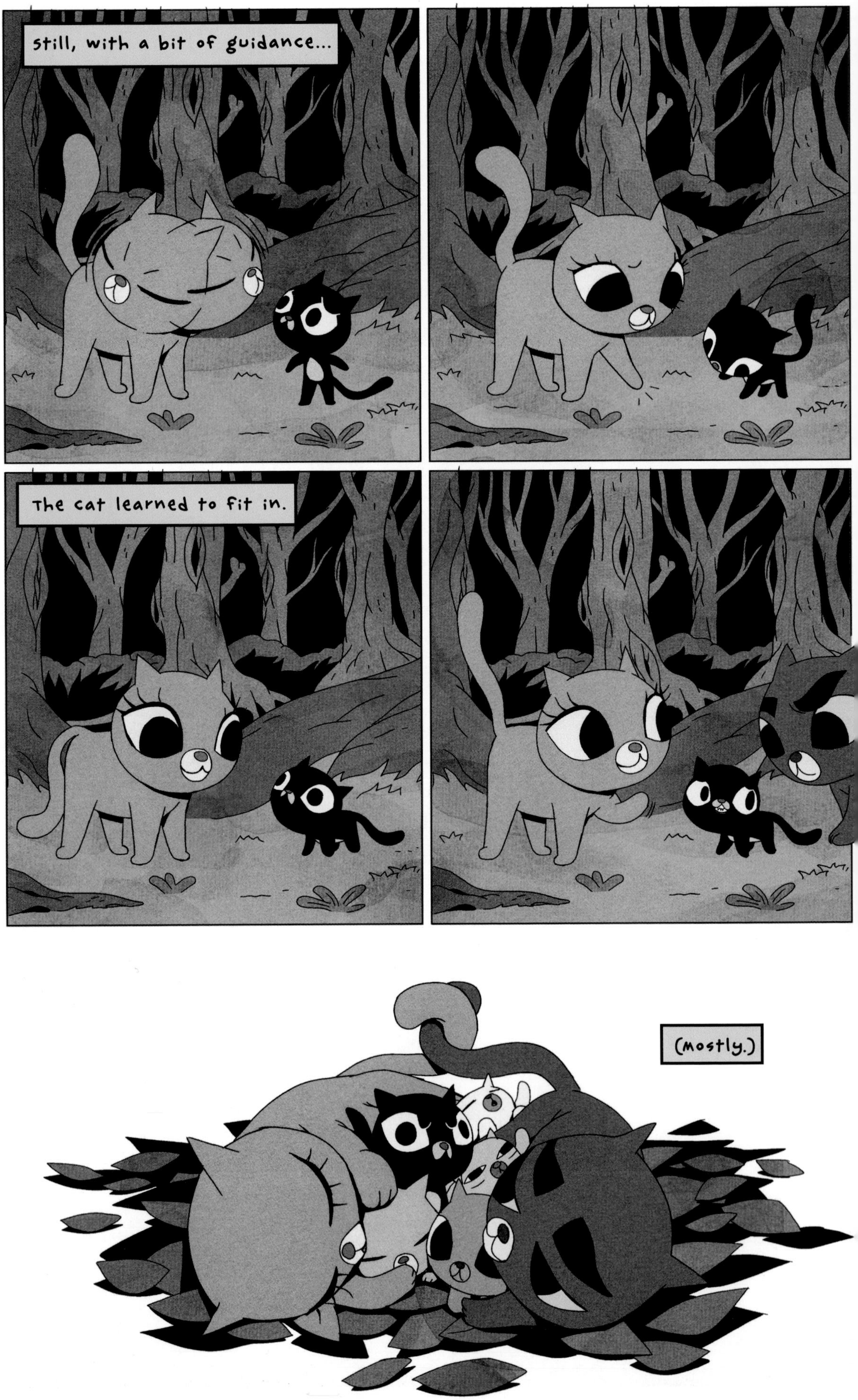
Still, with a bit of guidance...
The cat learned to fit in.
(mostly.)

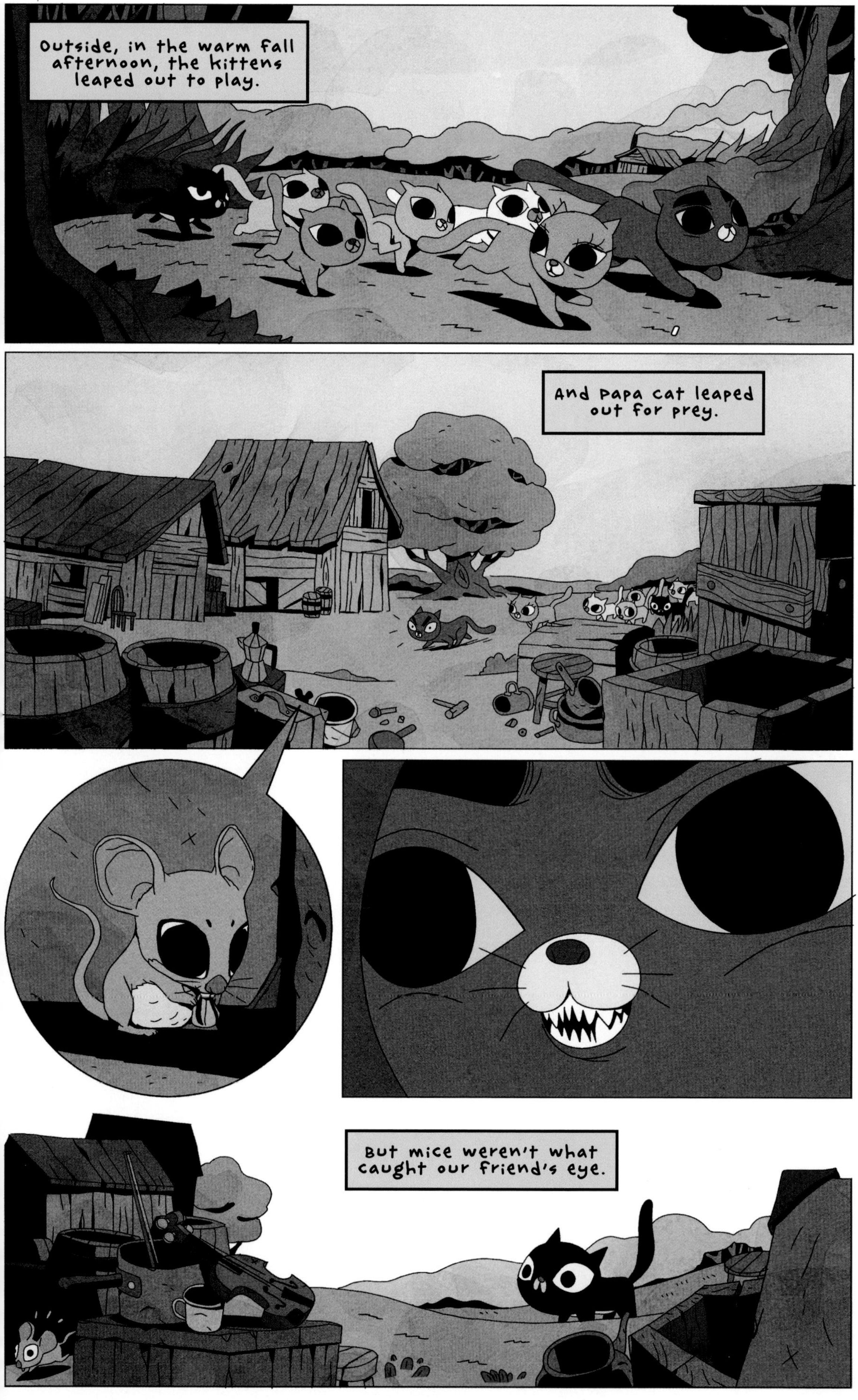
Outside, in the warm fall afternoon, the kittens leaped out to play.
And papa cat leaped out for prey.
But mice weren't what caught our friend's eye.

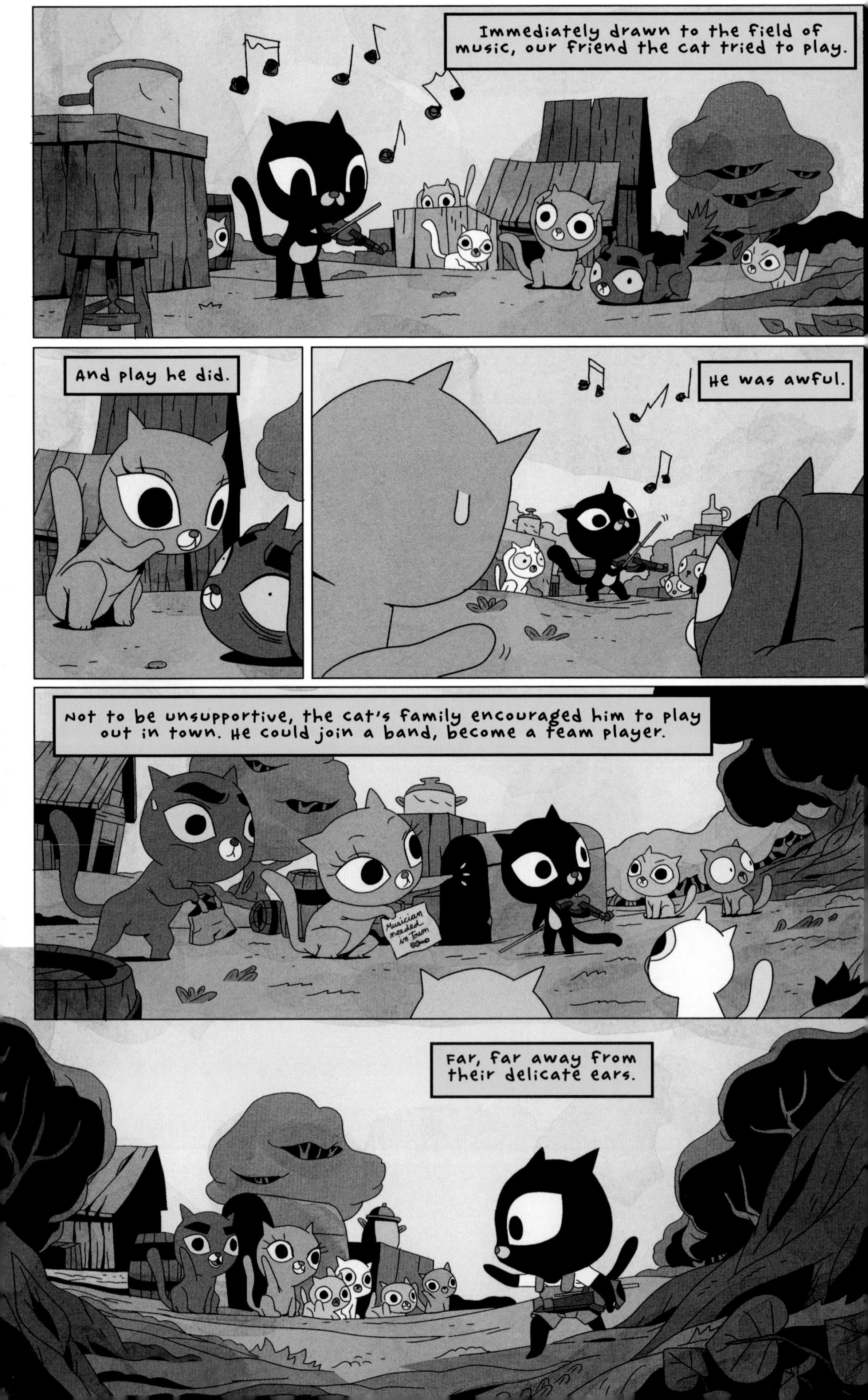
Immediately drawn to the field of music, our friend the cat tried to play.
And play he did.
He was awful.
Not to be unsupportive, the cat's family encouraged him to play out in town. He could join a band, become a team player.
Musician needed in Town
Far, far away from their delicate ears.

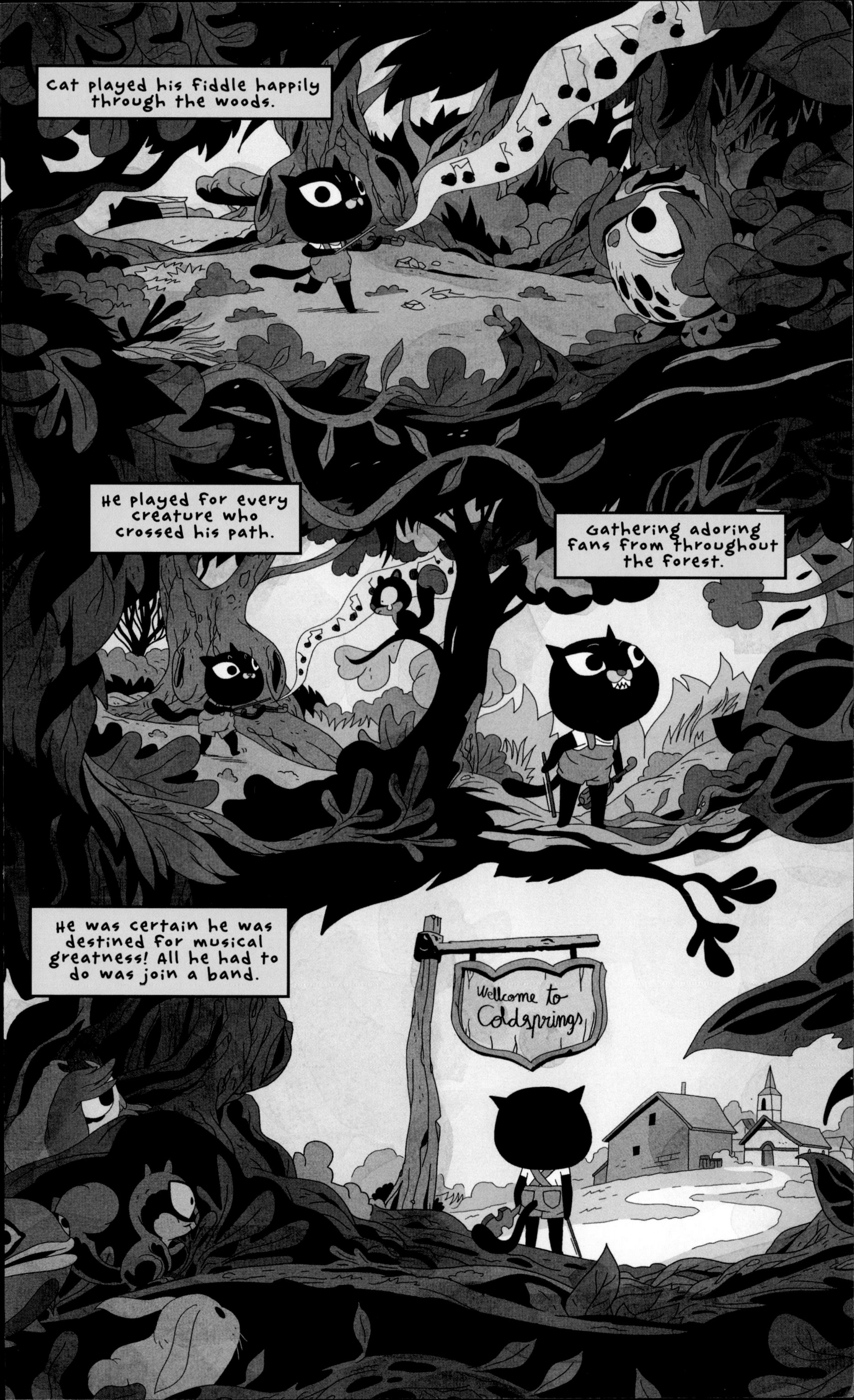
Cat played his fiddle happily through the woods.
He played for every creature who crossed his path.
Gathering adoring fans from throughout the forest.
He was certain he was destined for musical greatness! All he had to do was join a band.
Wellcome to Coldsprings

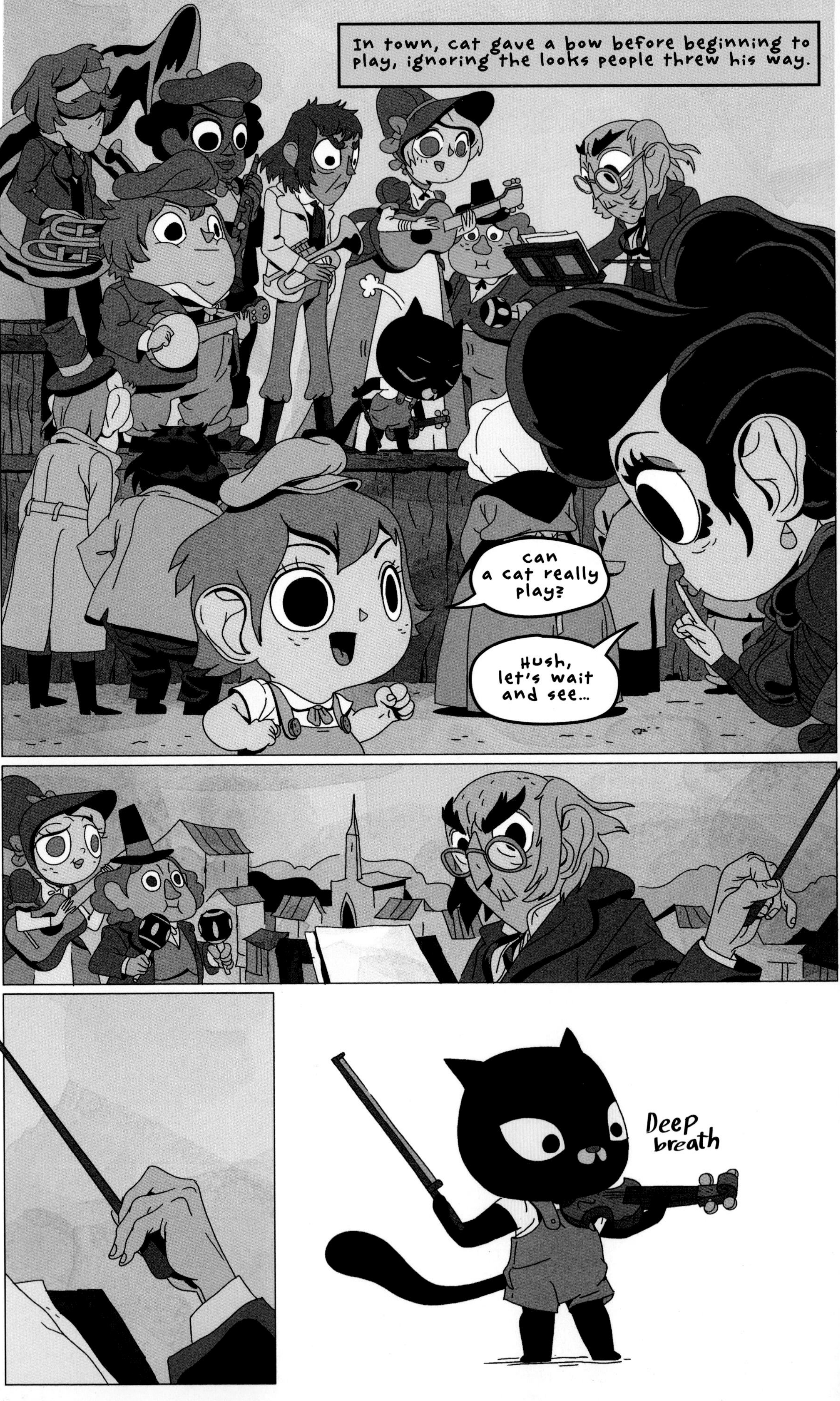
In town, cat gave a bow before beginning to play, ignoring the looks people threw his way.
can a cat really play?
Hush, let's wait and see...
Deep breath

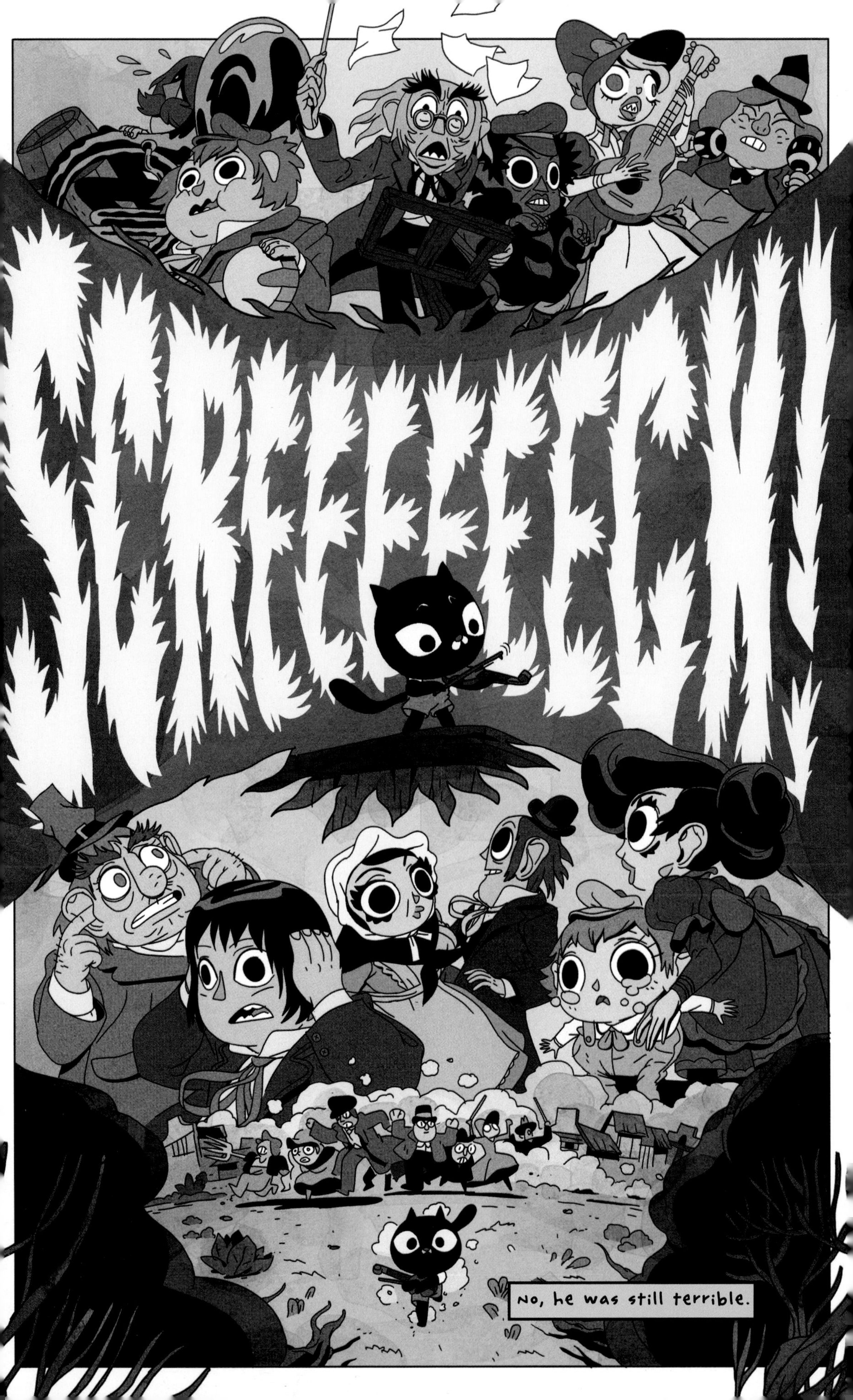
No, he was still terrible.

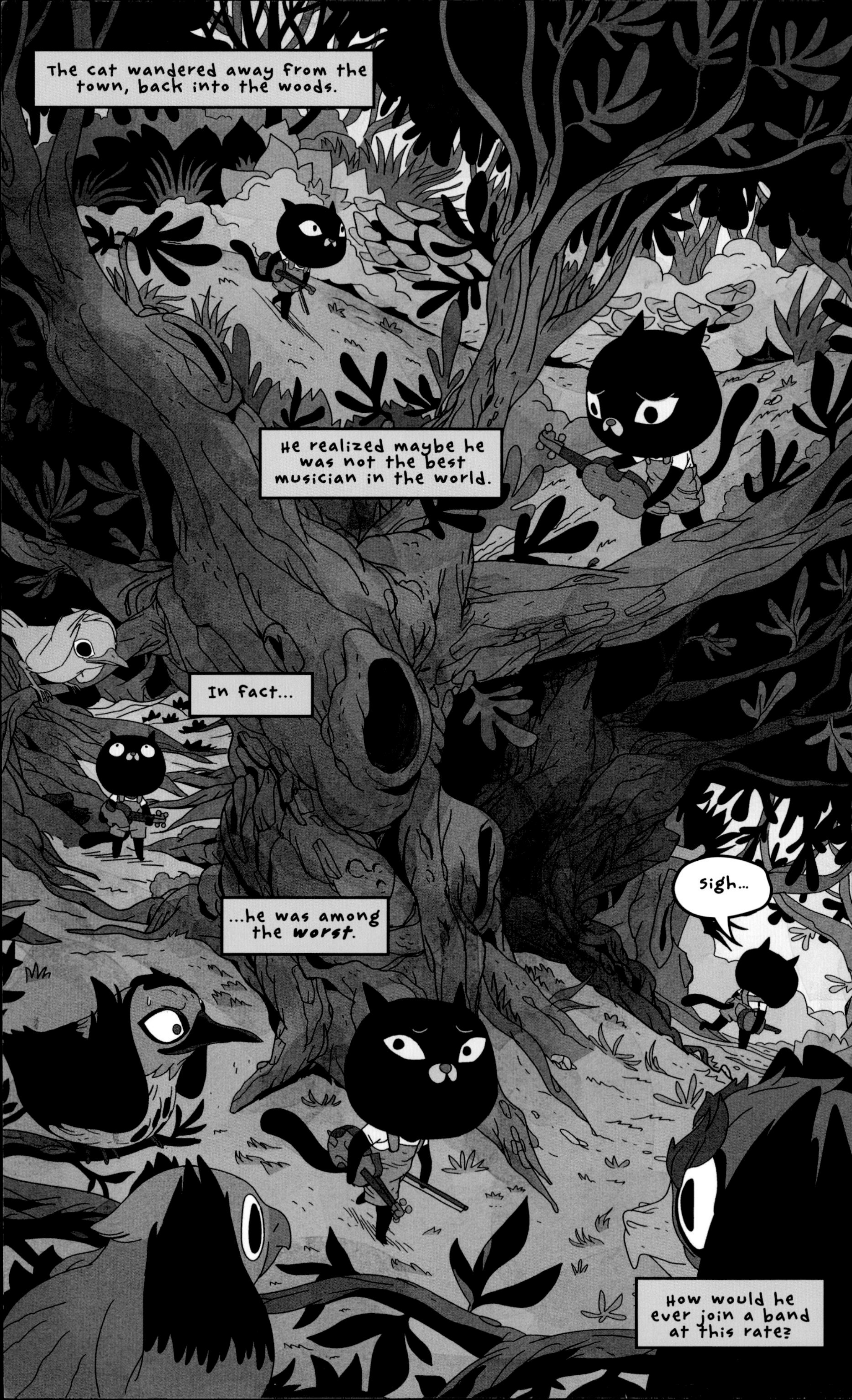
The cat wandered away from the town, back into the woods.
He realized maybe he was not the best musician in the world.
In fact...
...he was among the *worst*.
Sigh...
How would he ever join a band at this rate?

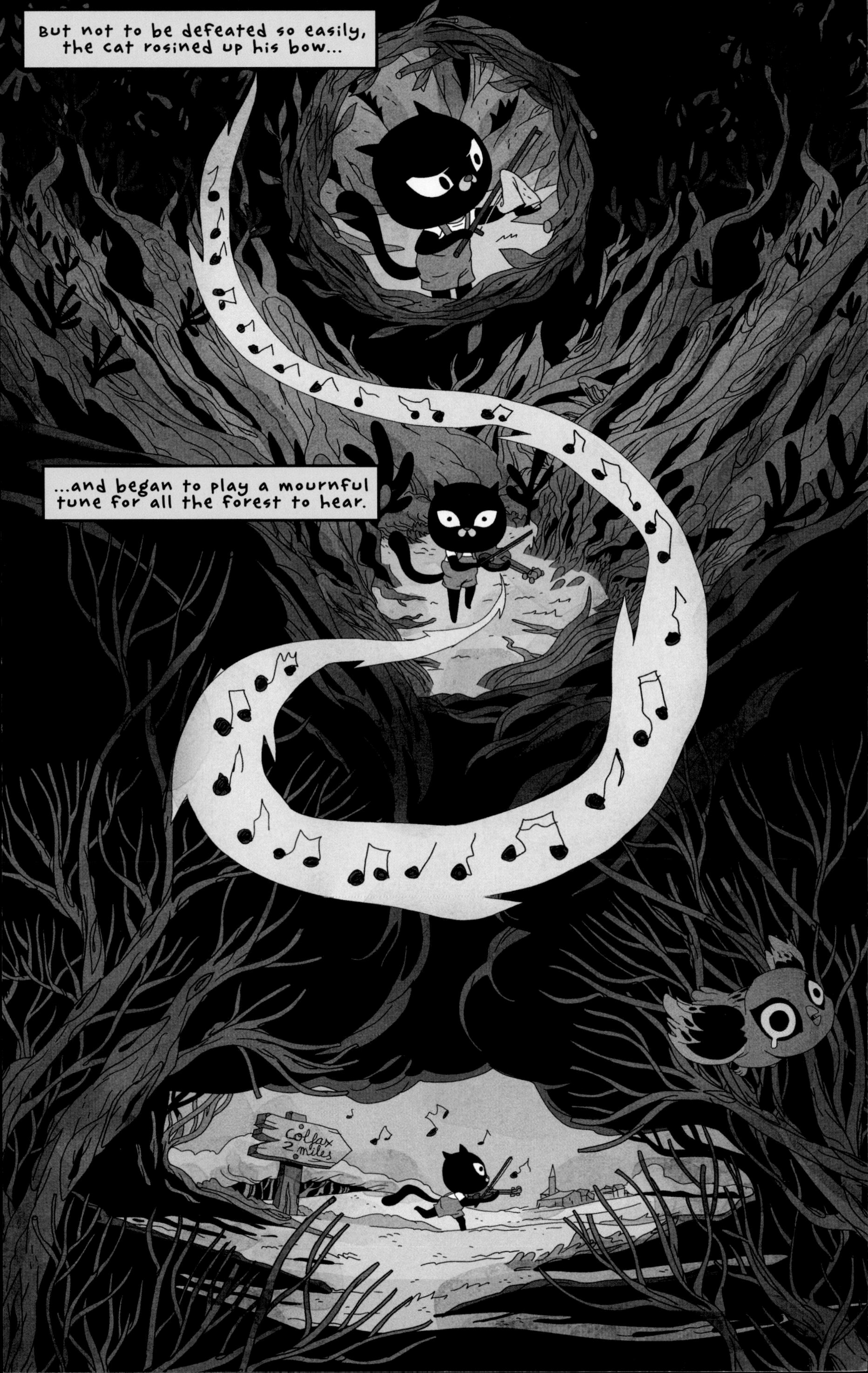
But not to be defeated so easily, the cat rosined up his bow...
...and began to play a mournful tune for all the forest to hear.
Colfax 2 miles

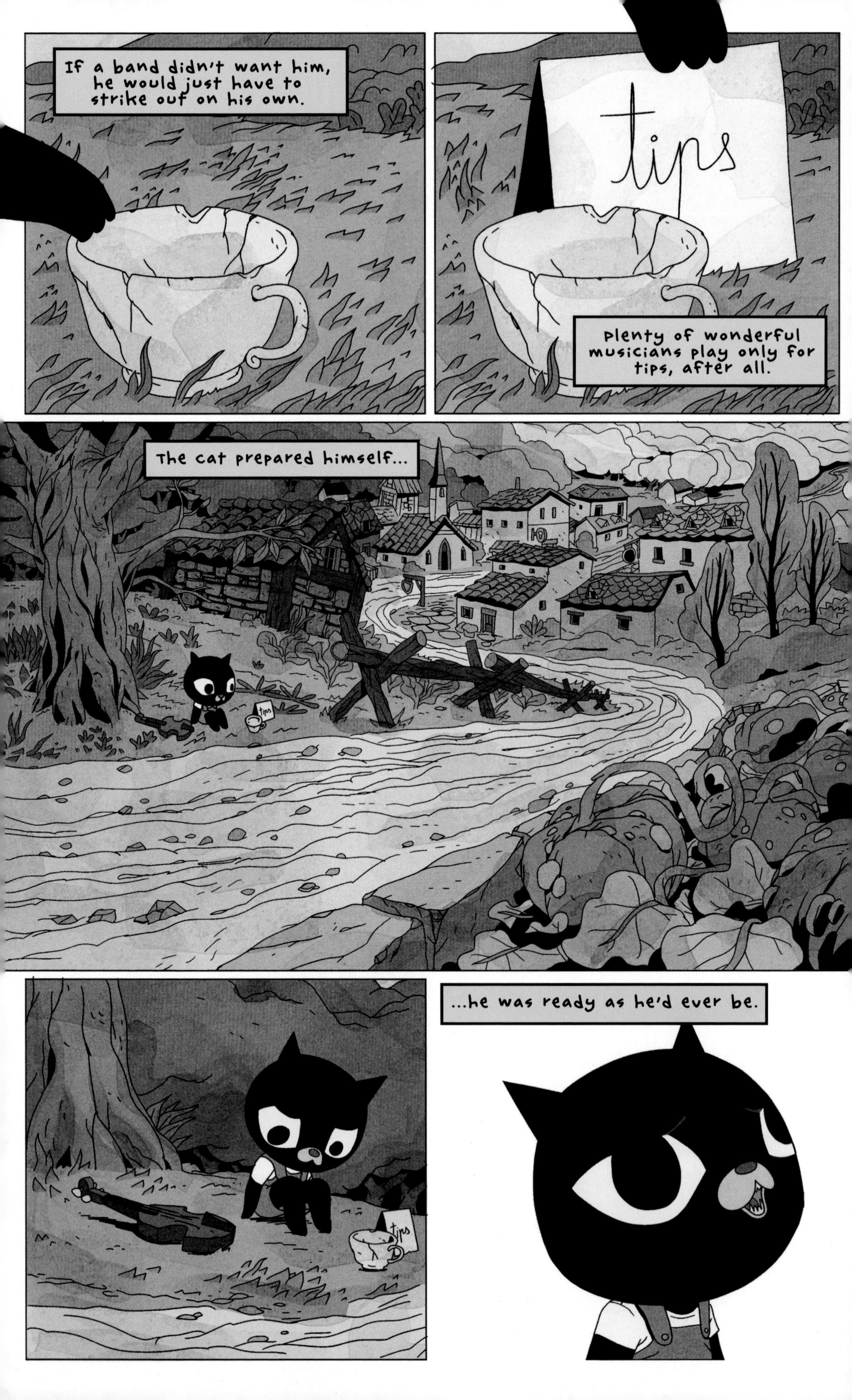
If a band didn't want him, he would just have to strike out on his own.
tips
Plenty of wonderful musicians play only for tips, after all.
The cat prepared himself...
tips
tips
...he was ready as he'd ever be.

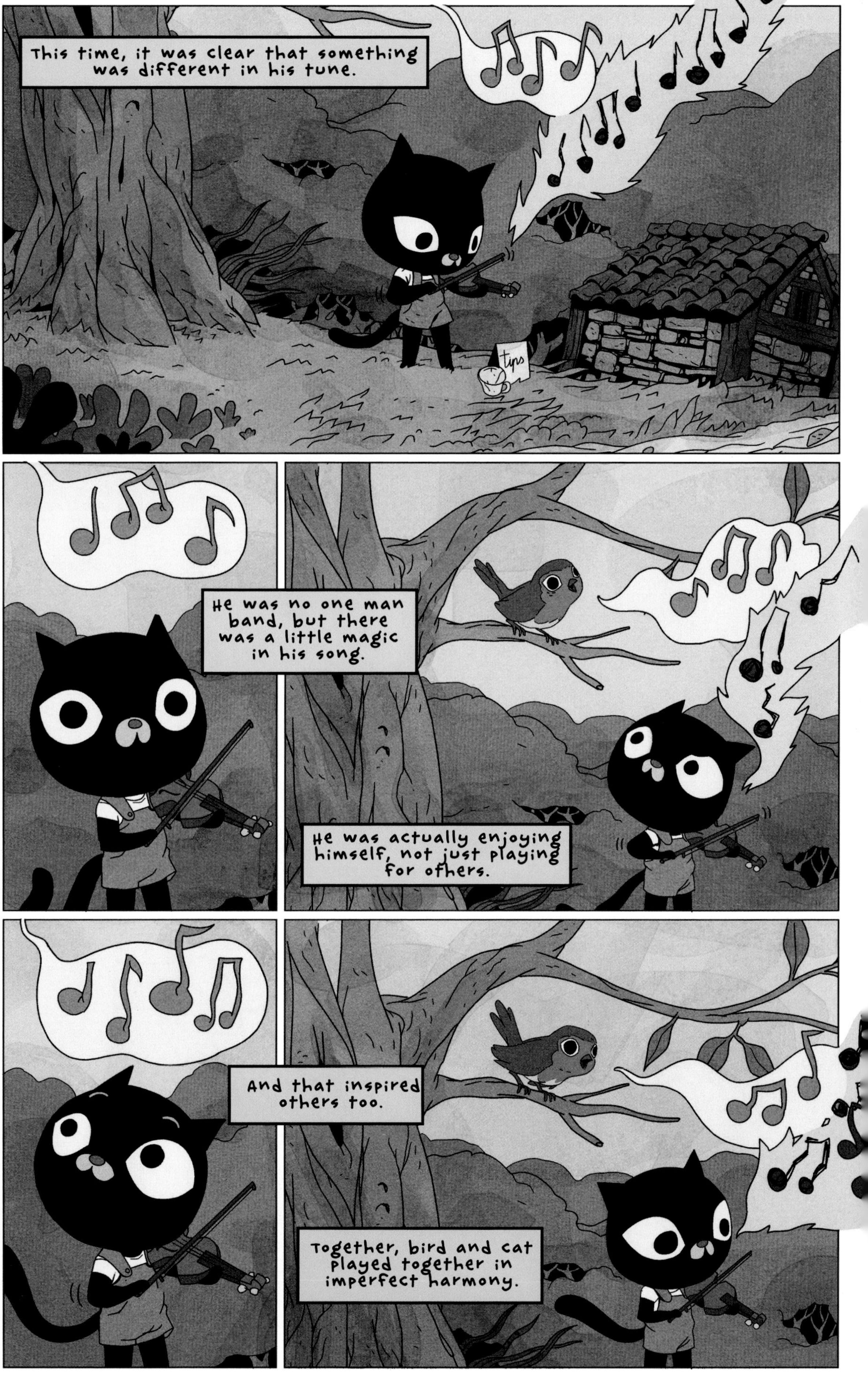
This time, it was clear that something was different in his tune.
tips
He was no one man band, but there was a little magic in his song.
He was actually enjoying himself, not just playing for others.
And that inspired others too.
Together, bird and cat played together in imperfect harmony.

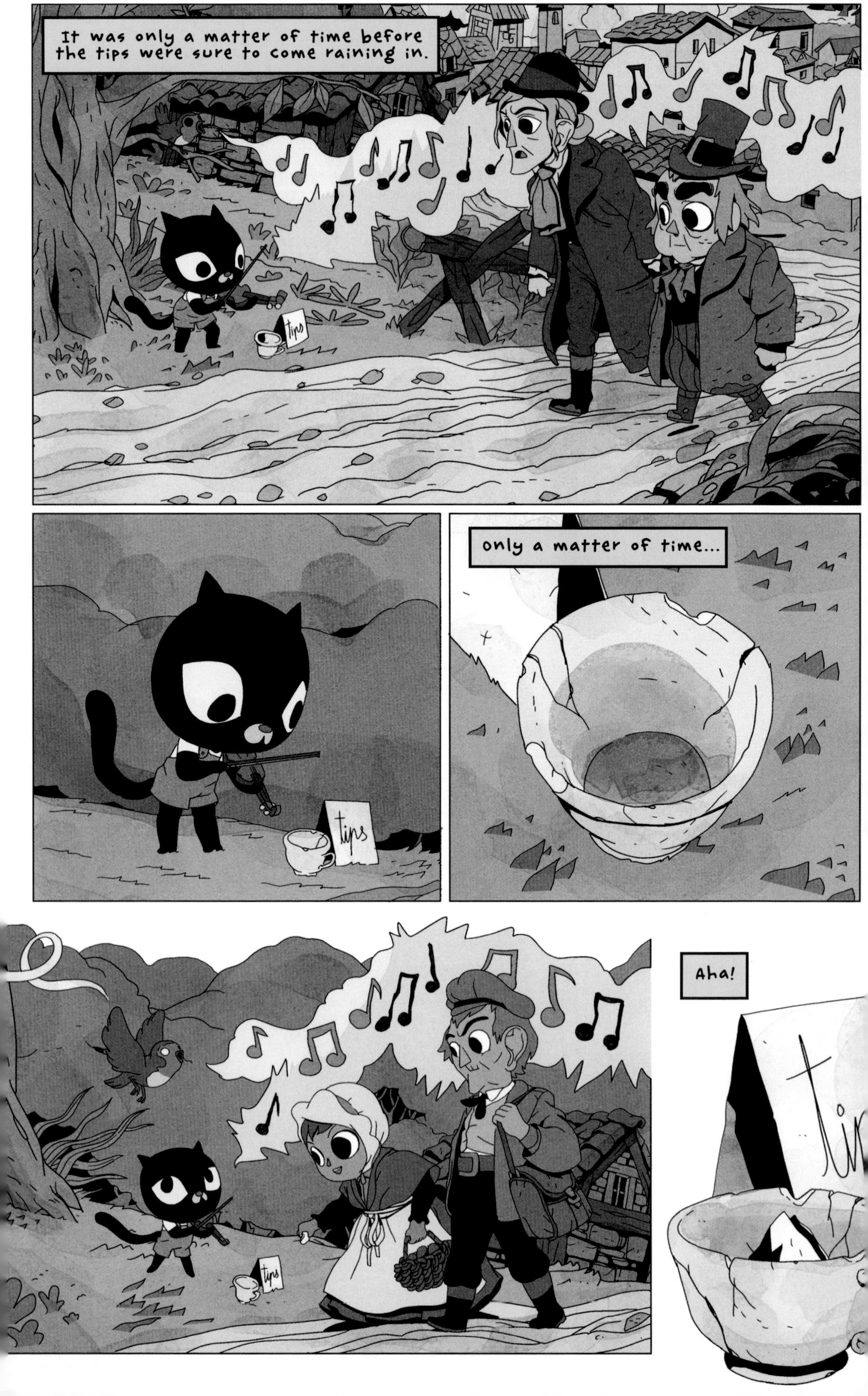
It was only a matter of time before the tips were sure to come raining in.
tips
tips
only a matter of time...
tips
Aha!

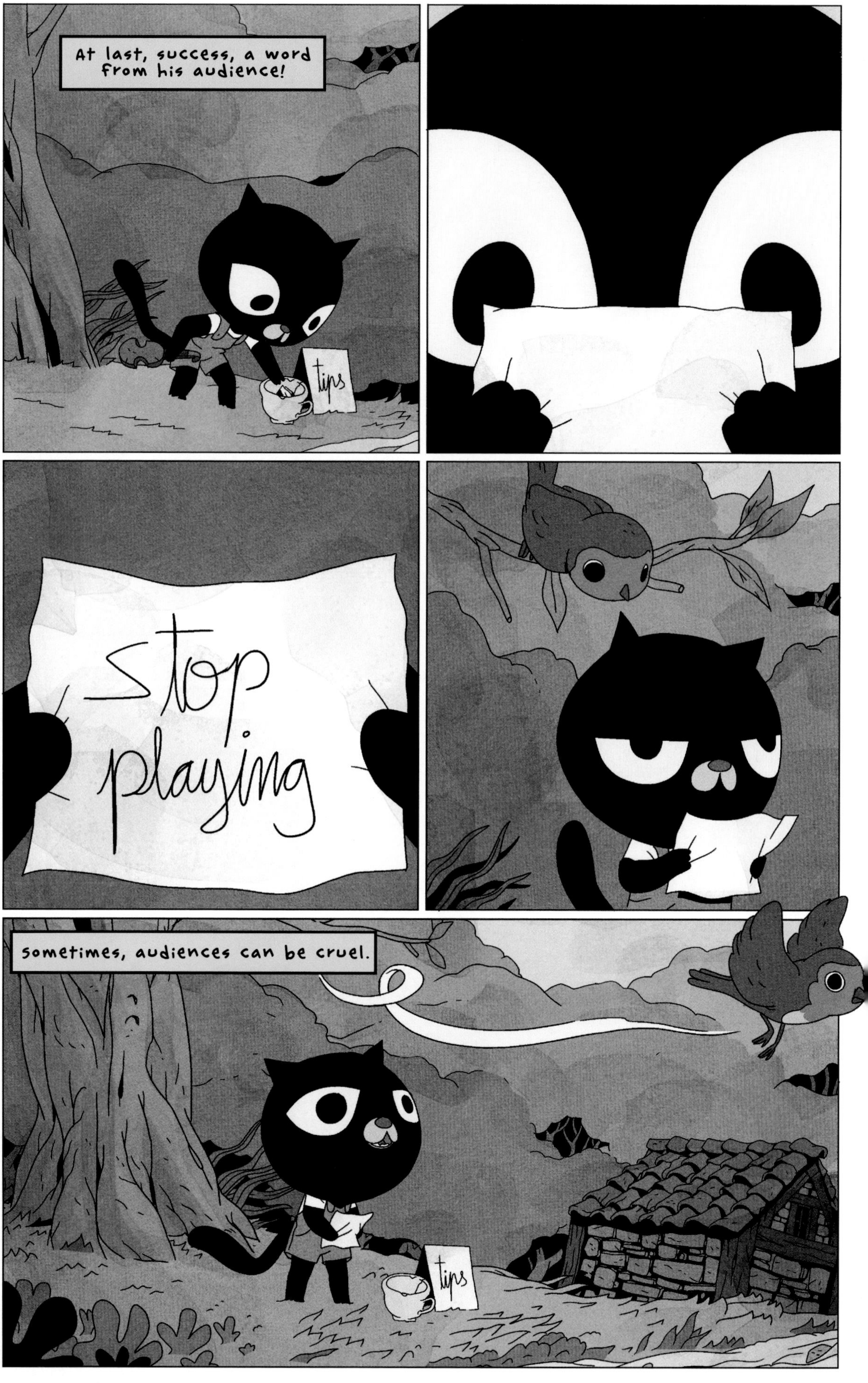
At last, success, a word from his audience!
tips
Stop playing
Sometimes, audiences can be cruel.
tips

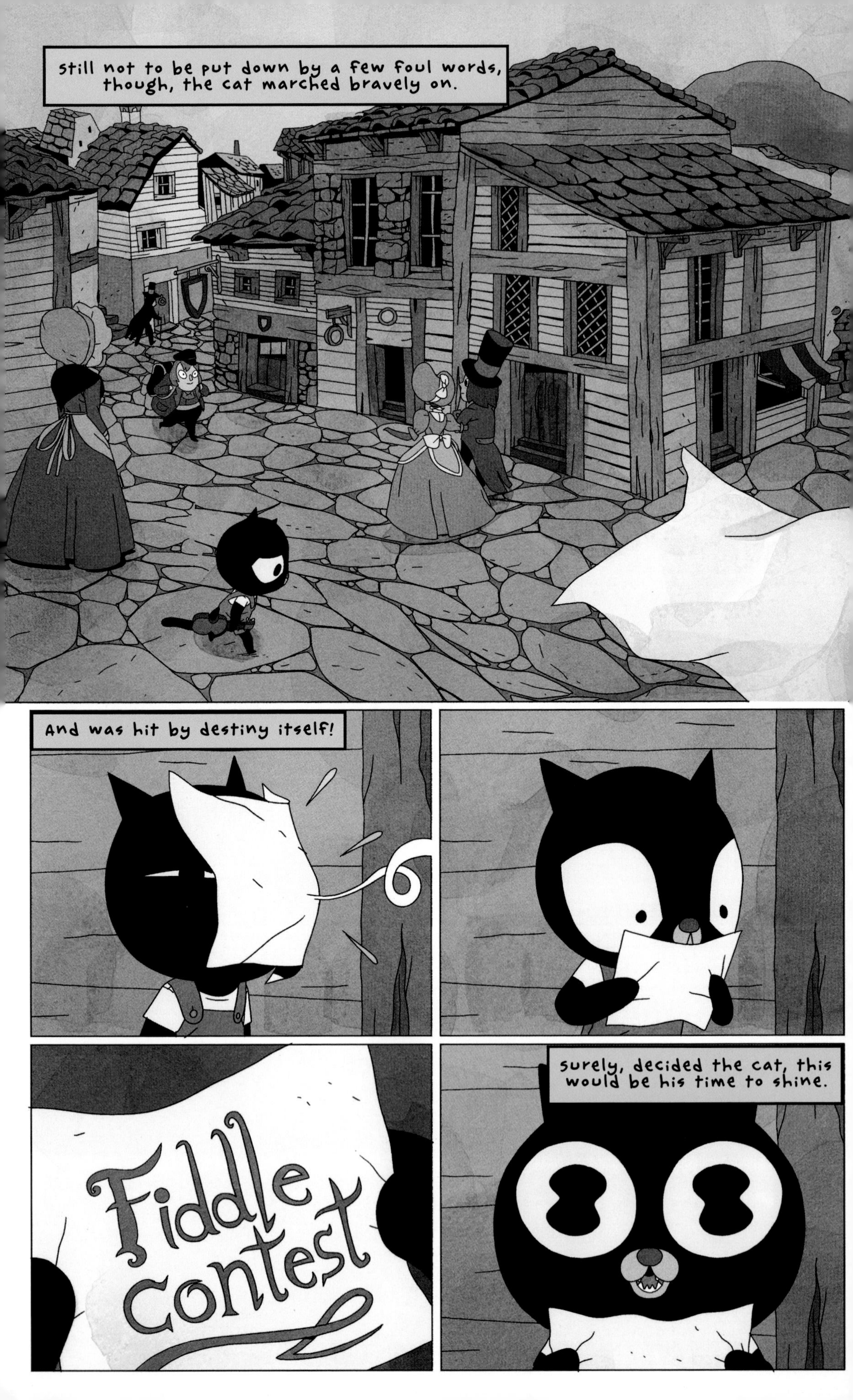
Still not to be put down by a few foul words, though, the cat marched bravely on.
And was hit by destiny itself!
Fiddle Contest
Surely, decided the cat, this would be his time to shine.

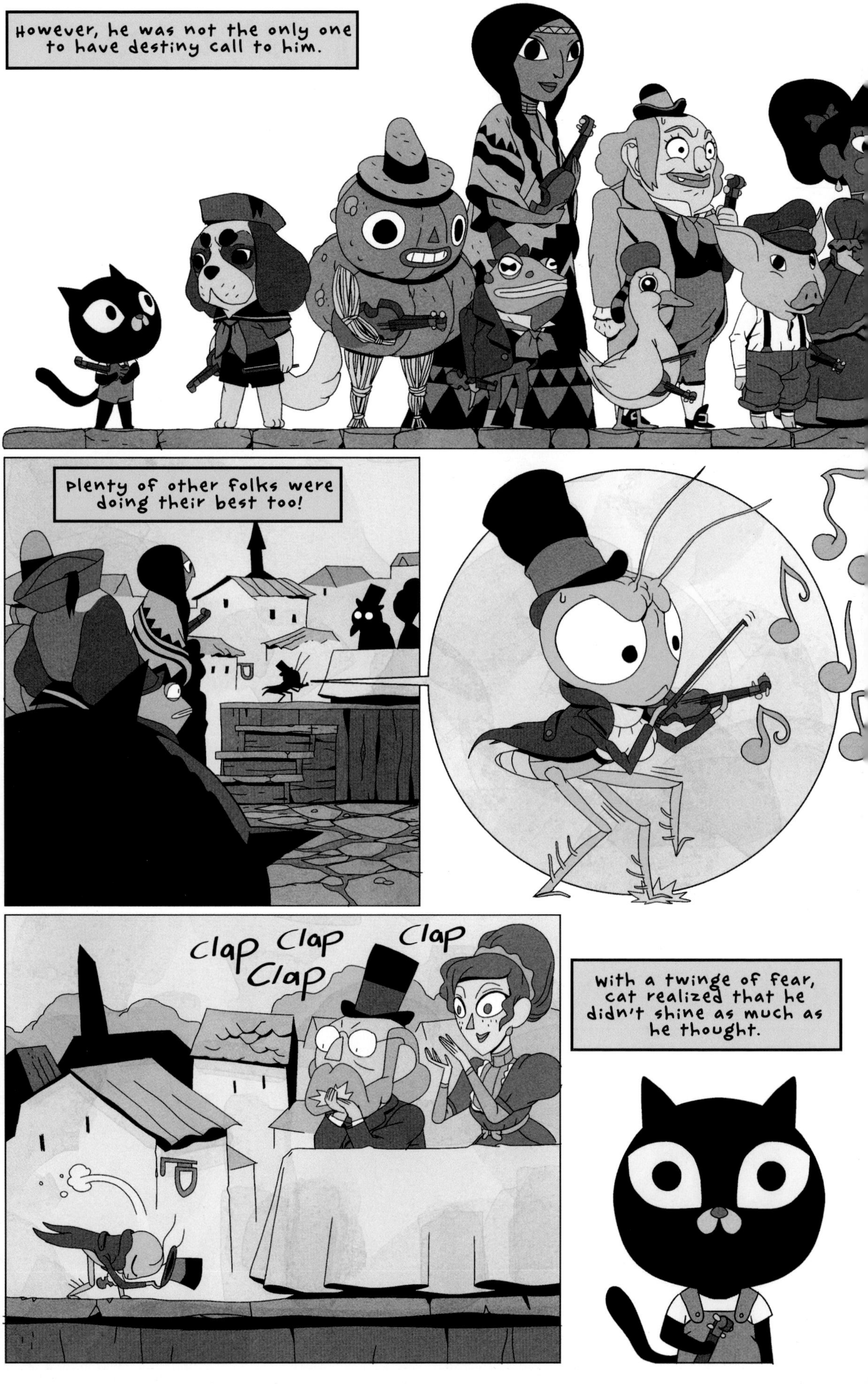
However, he was not the only one to have destiny call to him.
Plenty of other folks were doing their best too!
Clap Clap Clap Clap
With a twinge of fear, cat realized that he didn't shine as much as he thought.

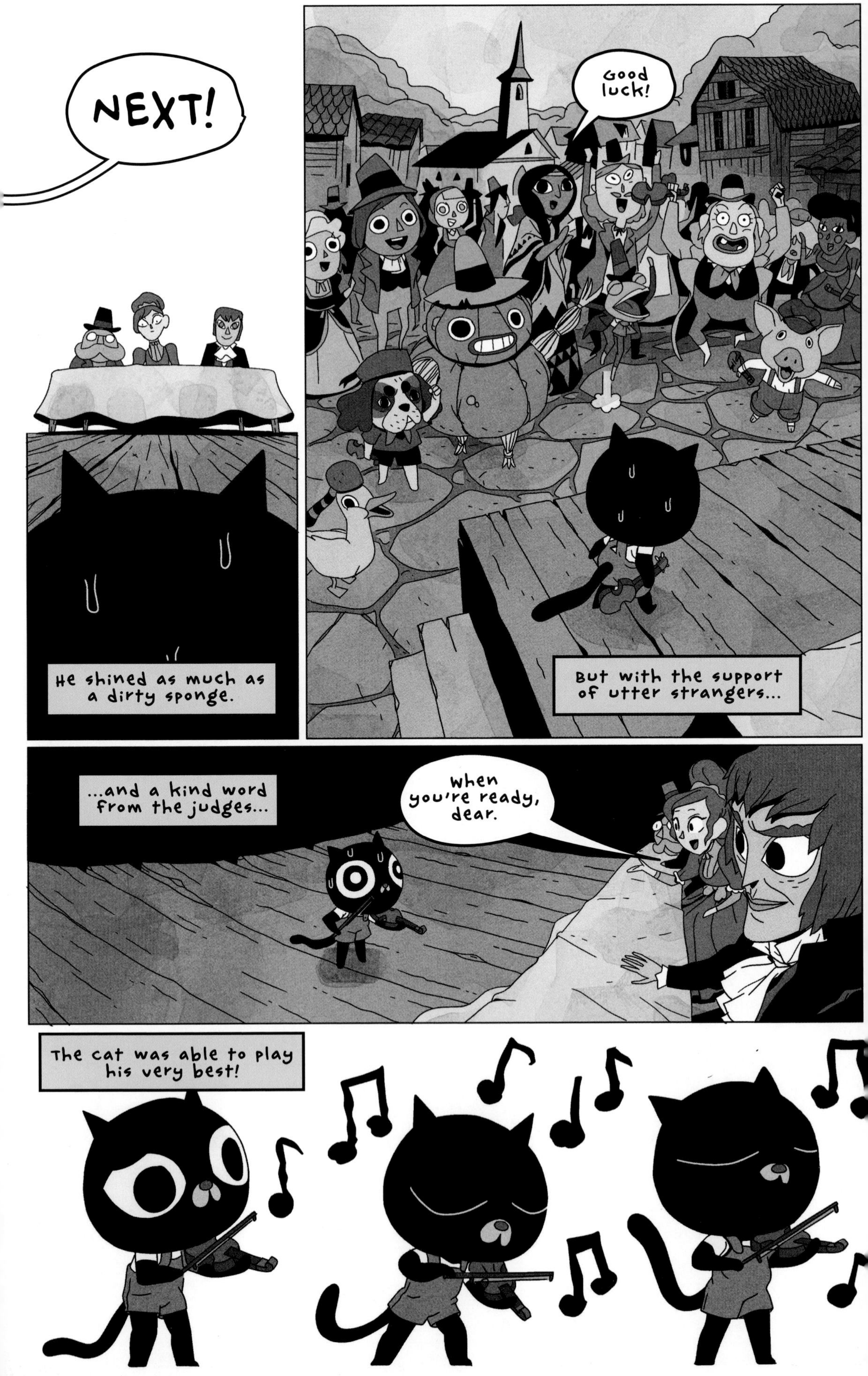
NEXT!
Good luck!
He shined as much as a dirty sponge.
But with the support of utter strangers...
...and a kind word from the judges...
When you're ready, dear.
The cat was able to play his very best!

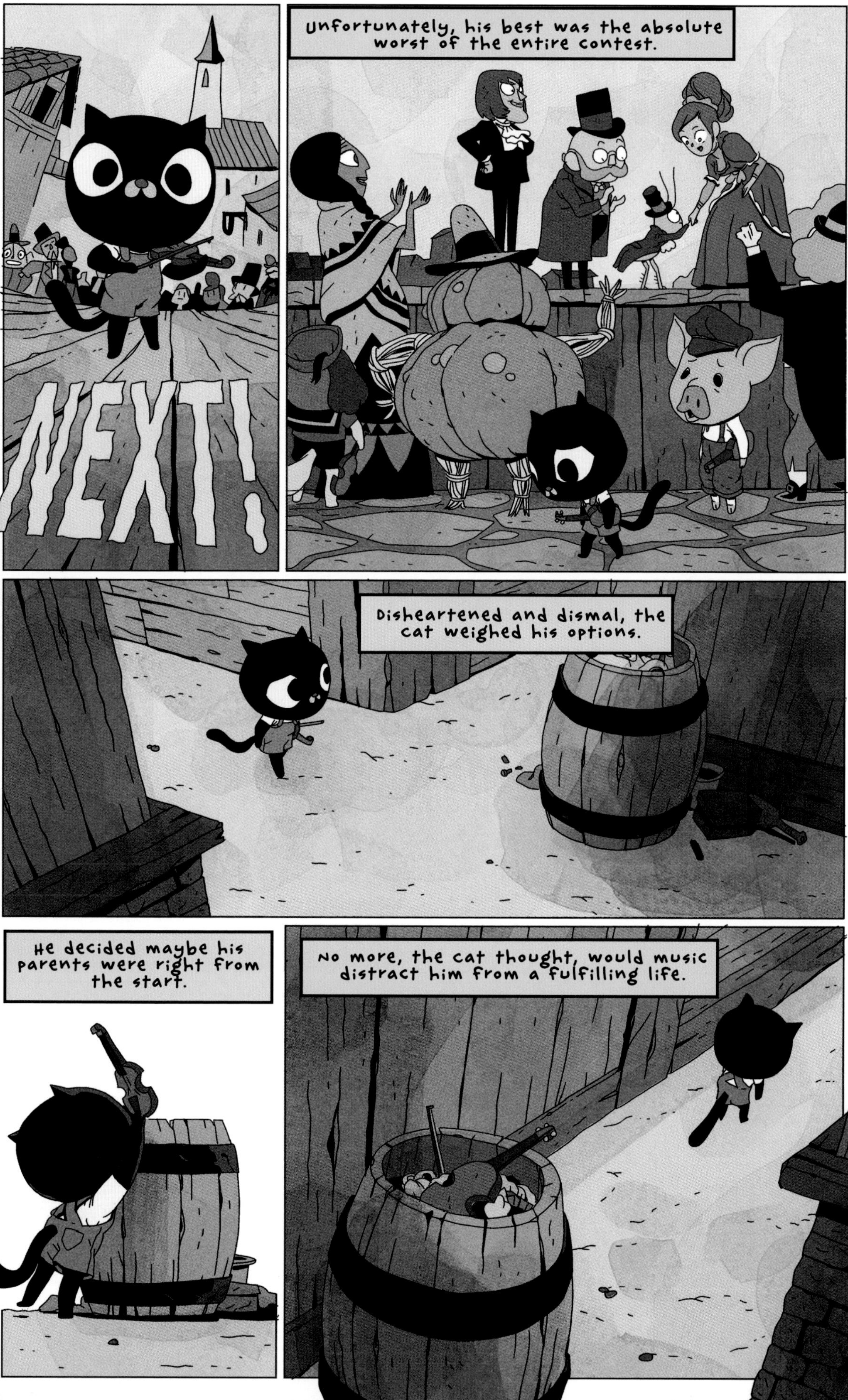
NEXT!
Unfortunately, his best was the absolute worst of the entire contest.
Disheartened and dismal, the cat weighed his options.
He decided maybe his parents were right from the start.
No more, the cat thought, would music distract him from a fulfilling life.

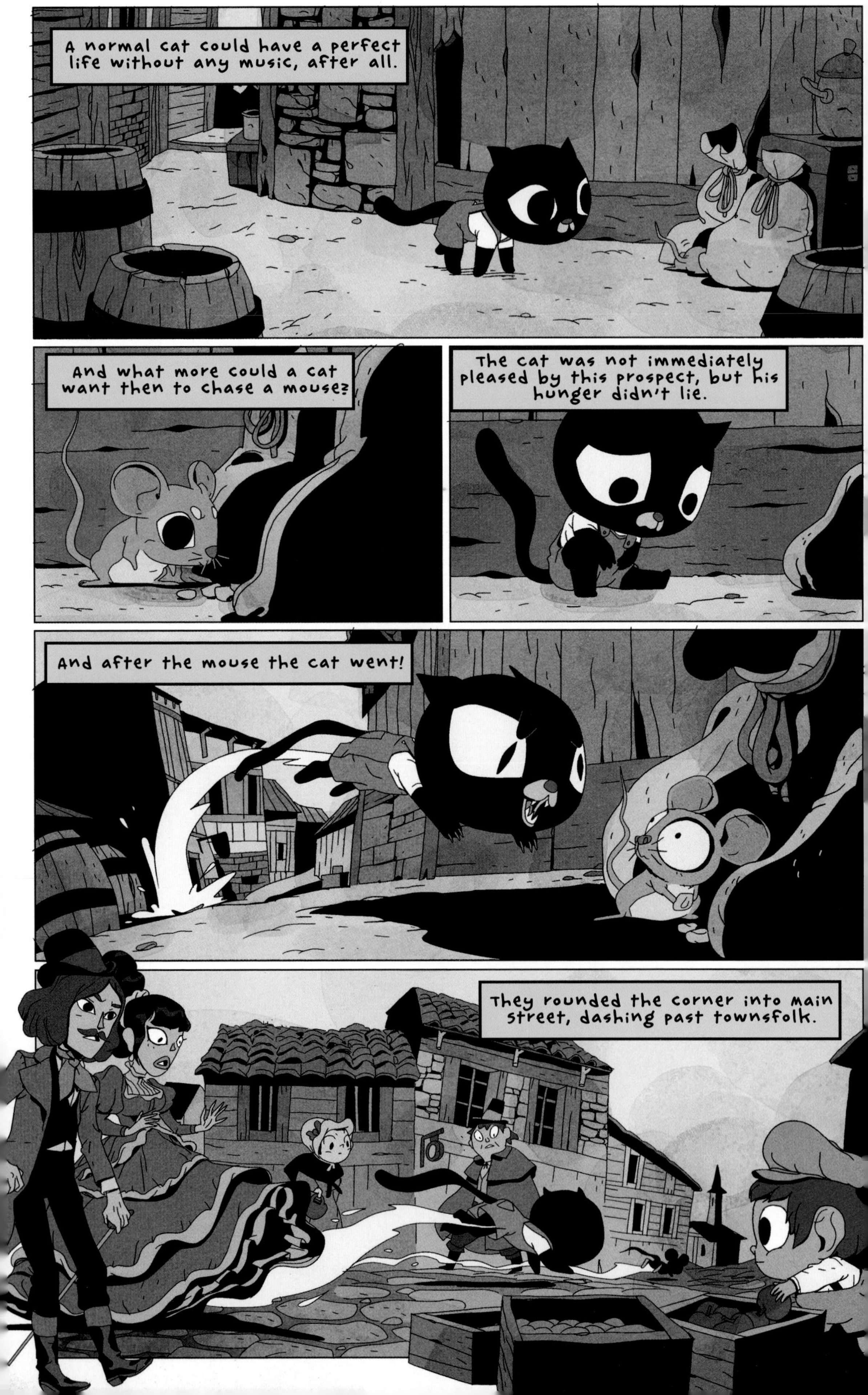
A normal cat could have a perfect life without any music, after all.
And what more could a cat want then to chase a mouse?
The cat was not immediately pleased by this prospect, but his hunger didn't lie.
And after the mouse the cat went!
They rounded the corner into main street, dashing past townsfolk.

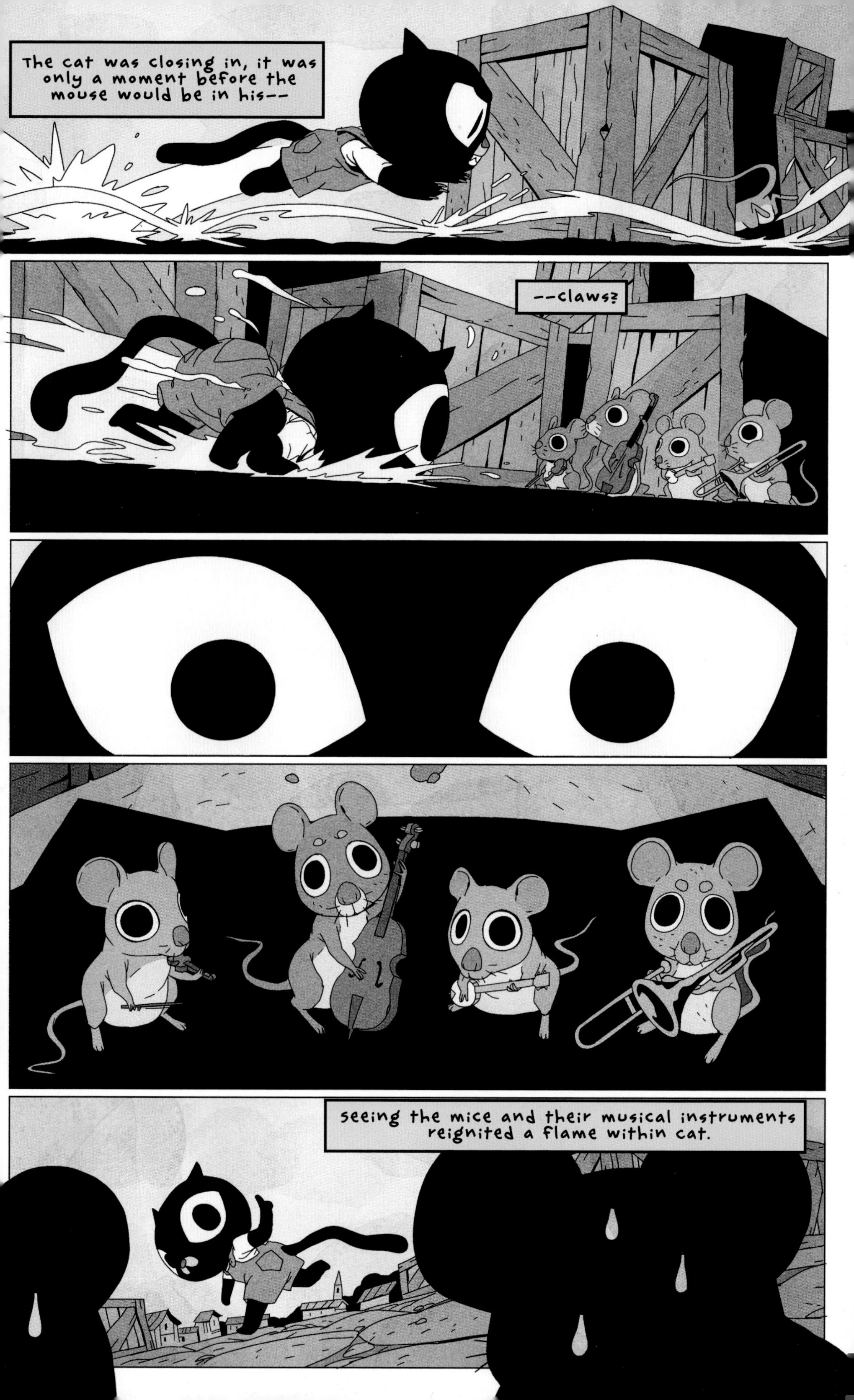
The cat was closing in, it was only a moment before the mouse would be in his--
--claws?
seeing the mice and their musical instruments reignited a flame within cat.

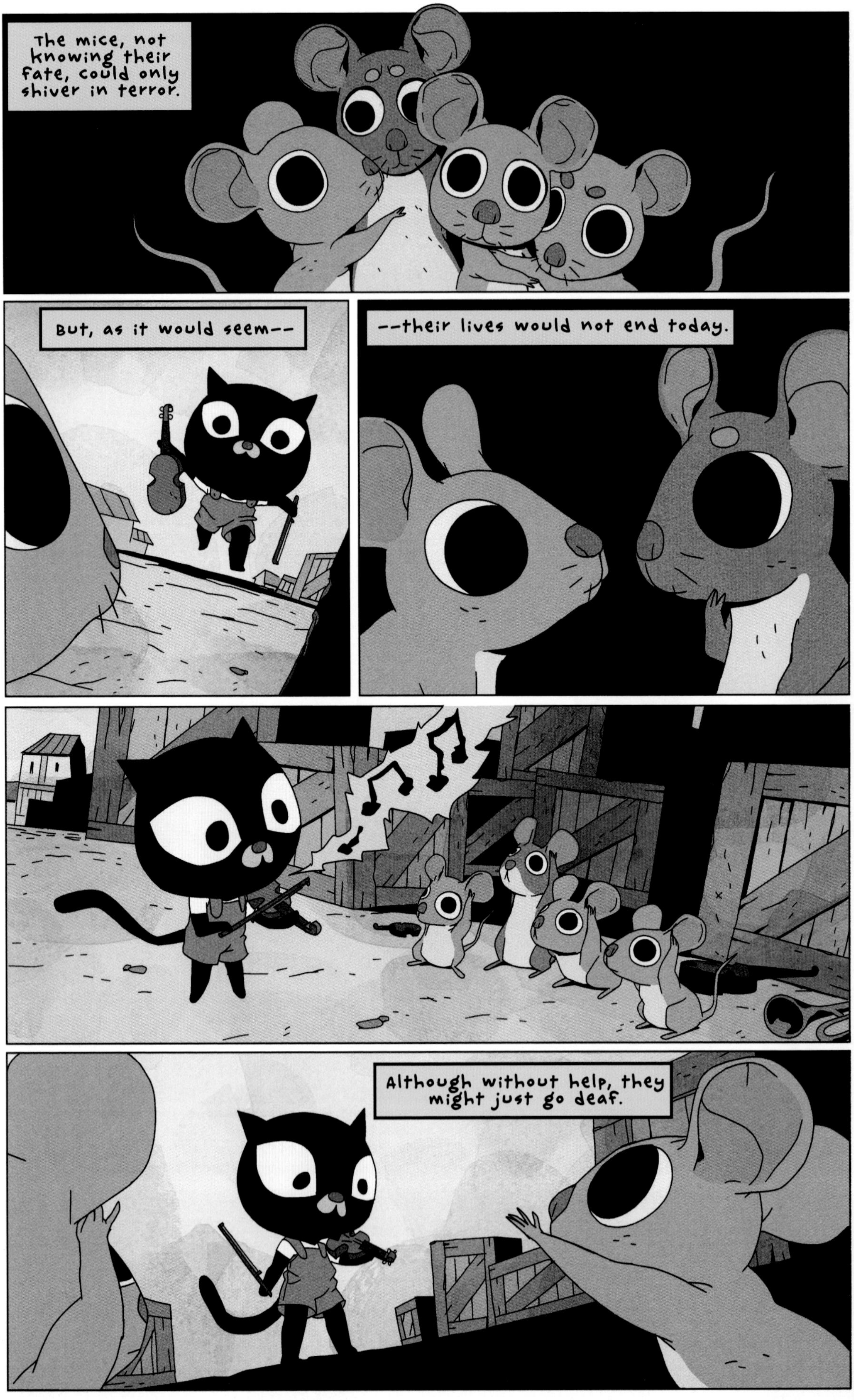
The mice, not knowing their fate, could only shiver in terror.
But, as it would seem--
--their lives would not end today.
Although without help, they might just go deaf.

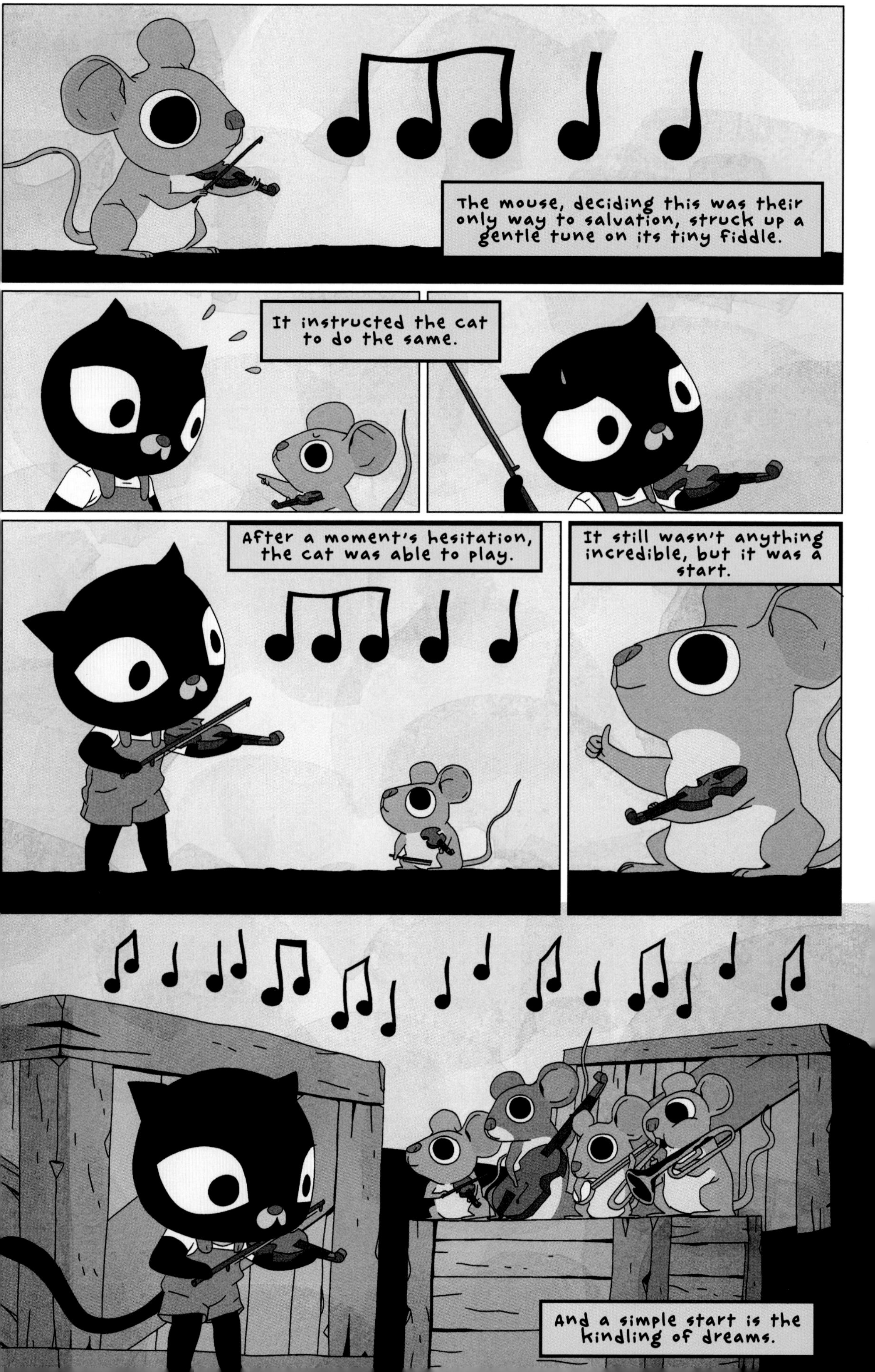

The mouse, deciding this was their only way to salvation, struck up a gentle tune on its tiny fiddle.
It instructed the cat to do the same.
After a moment's hesitation, the cat was able to play.
It still wasn't anything incredible, but it was a start.
And a simple start is the kindling of dreams.

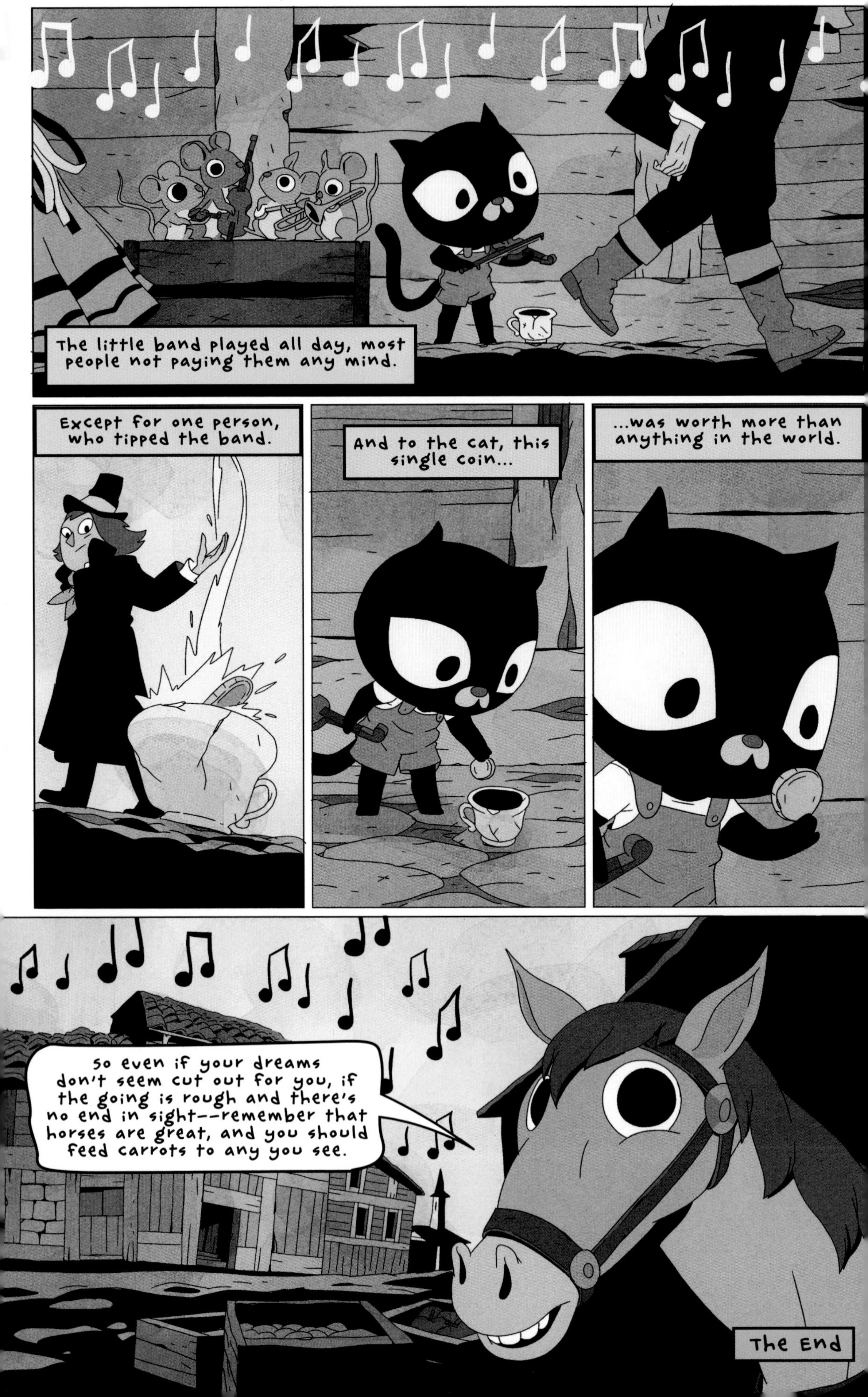
The little band played all day, most people not paying them any mind.
Except for one person, who tipped the band.
And to the cat, this single coin...
...was worth more than anything in the world.
So even if your dreams don't seem cut out for you, if the going is rough and there's no end in sight--remember that horses are great, and you should feed carrots to any you see.
The End

Turkeys and Turnkeys

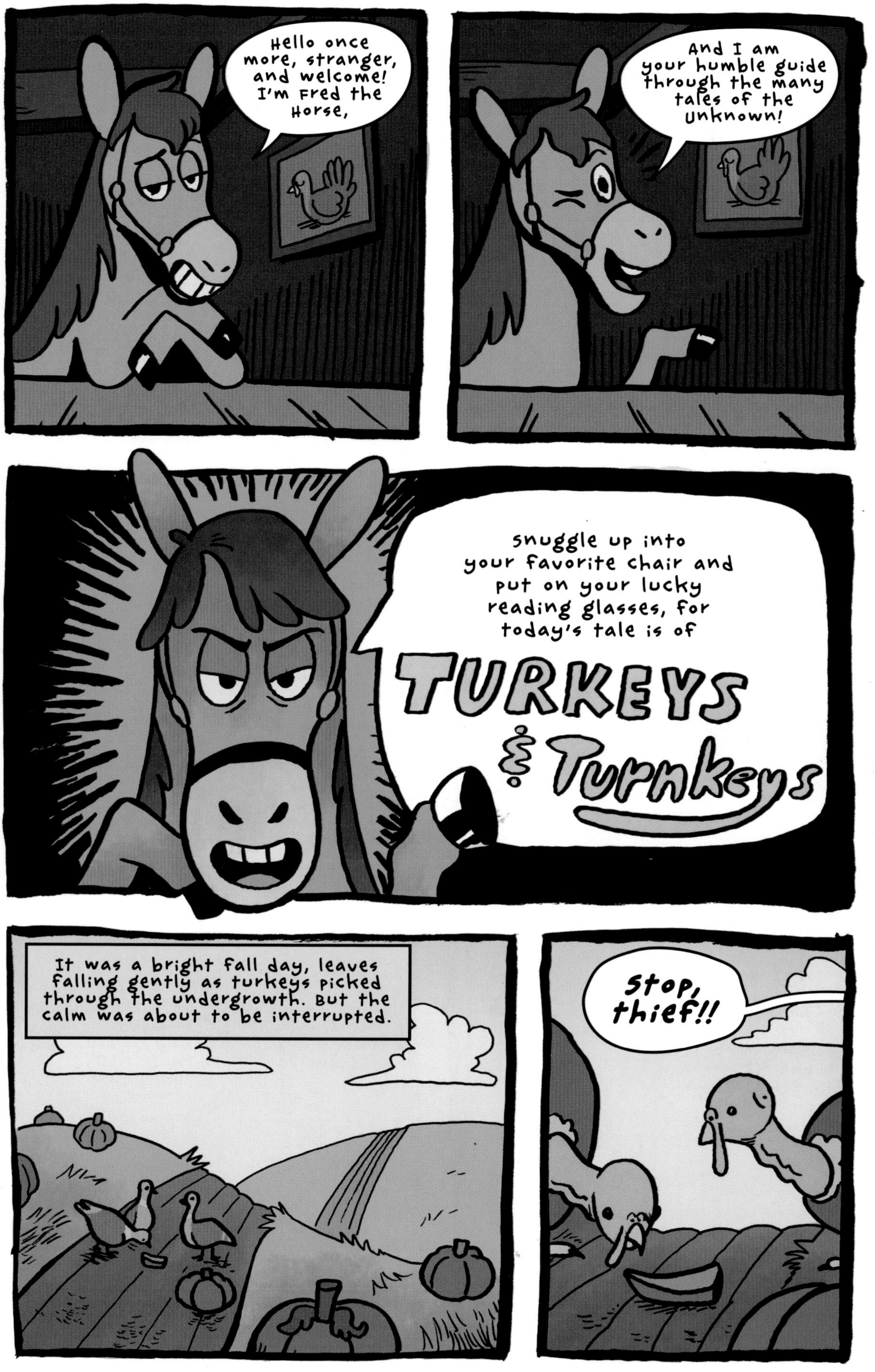
Hello once more, stranger, and welcome! I'm Fred the Horse,
And I am your humble guide through the many tales of the unknown!
Snuggle up into your favorite chair and put on your lucky reading glasses, for today's tale is of
TURKEYS & Turnkeys
It was a bright fall day, leaves falling gently as turkeys picked through the undergrowth. But the calm was about to be interrupted.
Stop, thief!!

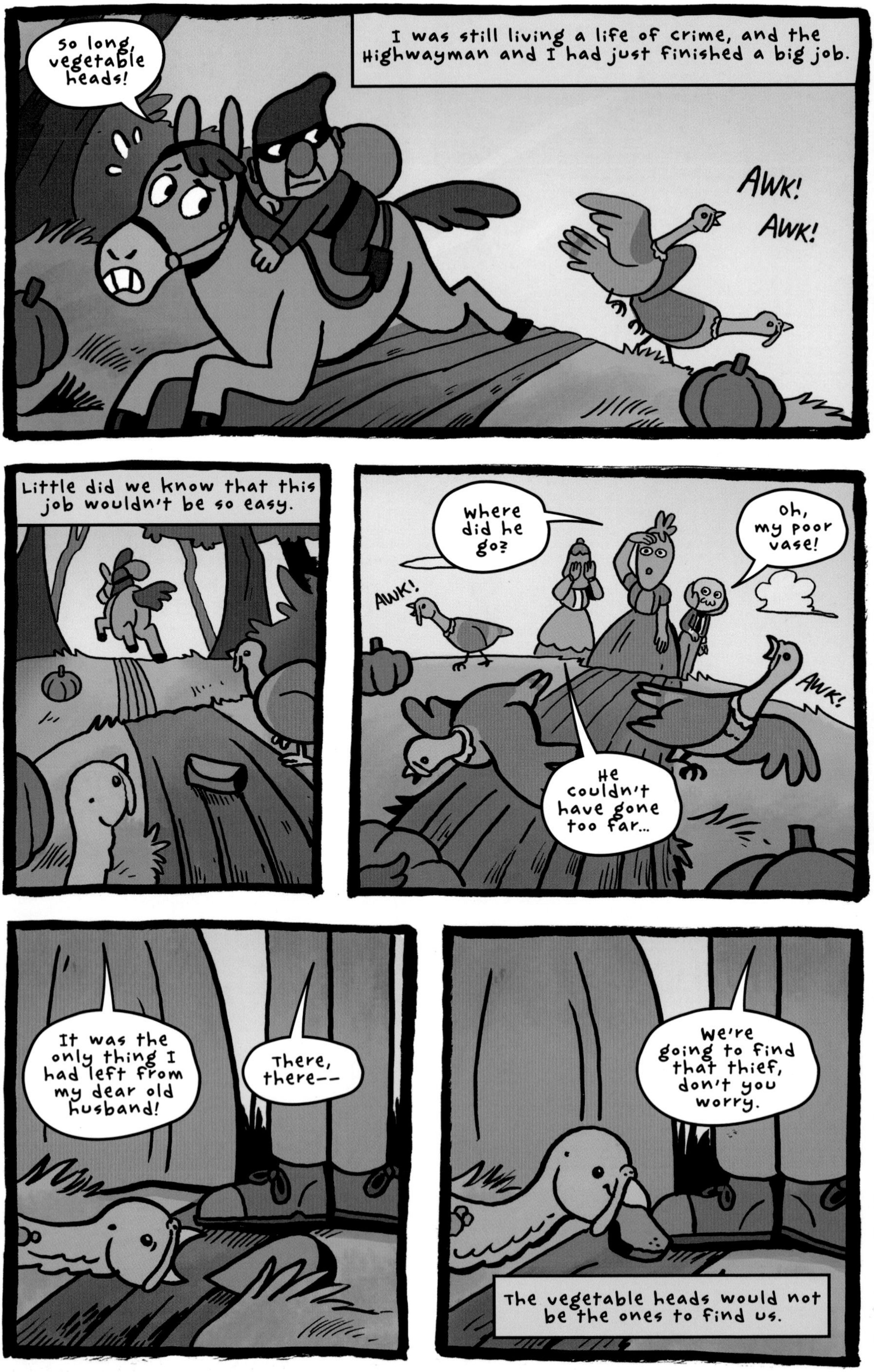

I was still living a life of crime, and the Highwayman and I had just finished a big job.
So long, vegetable heads!
AWK!
AWK!
Little did we know that this job wouldn't be so easy.
Where did he go?
Oh, my poor vase!
AWK!
AWK!
He couldn't have gone too far...
It was the only thing I had left from my dear old husband!
There, there--
We're going to find that thief, don't you worry.
The vegetable heads would not be the ones to find us.

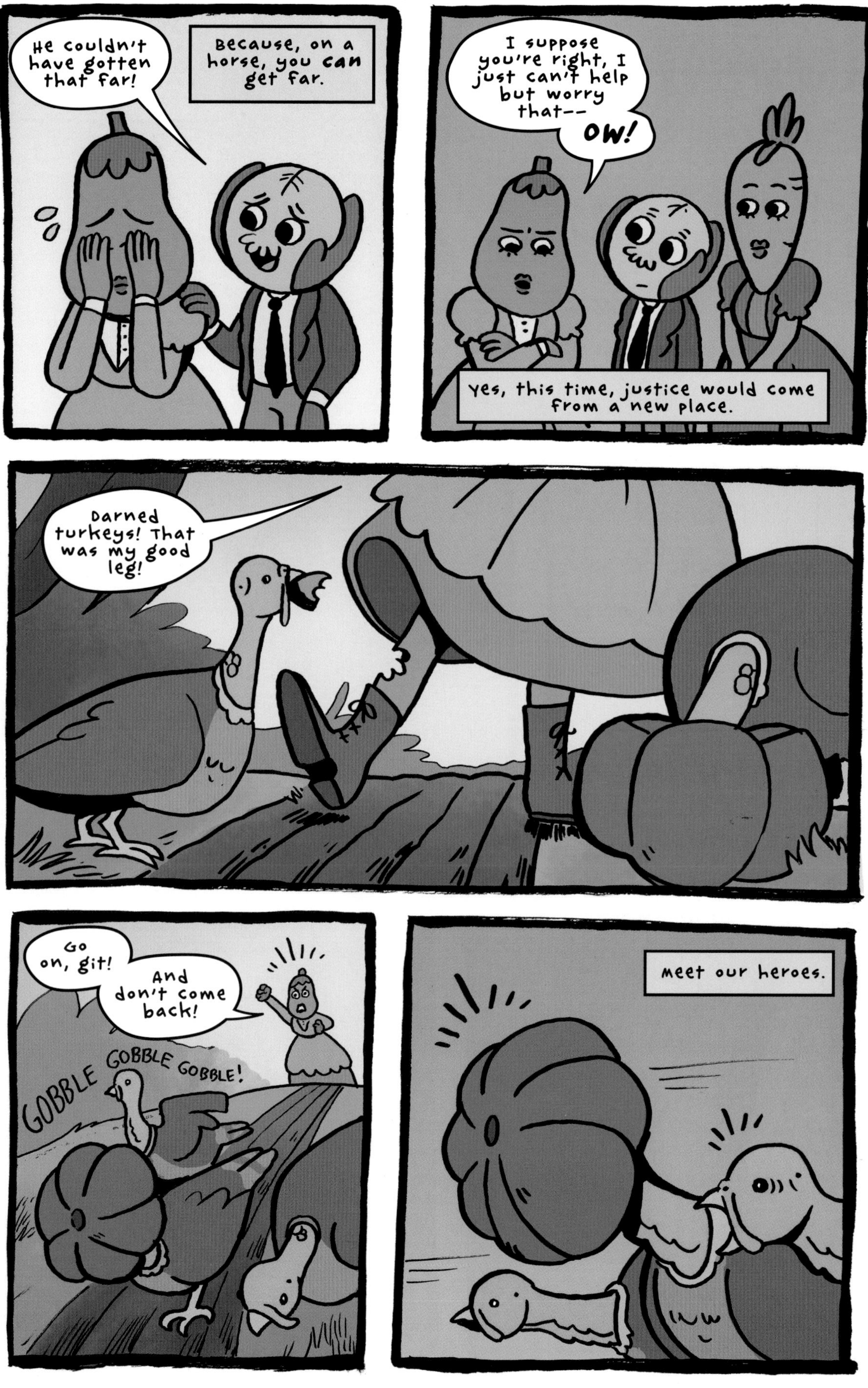

He couldn't have gotten that far!
Because, on a horse, you can get far.
I suppose you're right, I just can't help but worry that--
OW!
Yes, this time, justice would come from a new place.
Darned turkeys! That was my good leg!
Go on, git!
And don't come back!
GOBBLE GOBBLE GOBBLE!
Meet our heroes.

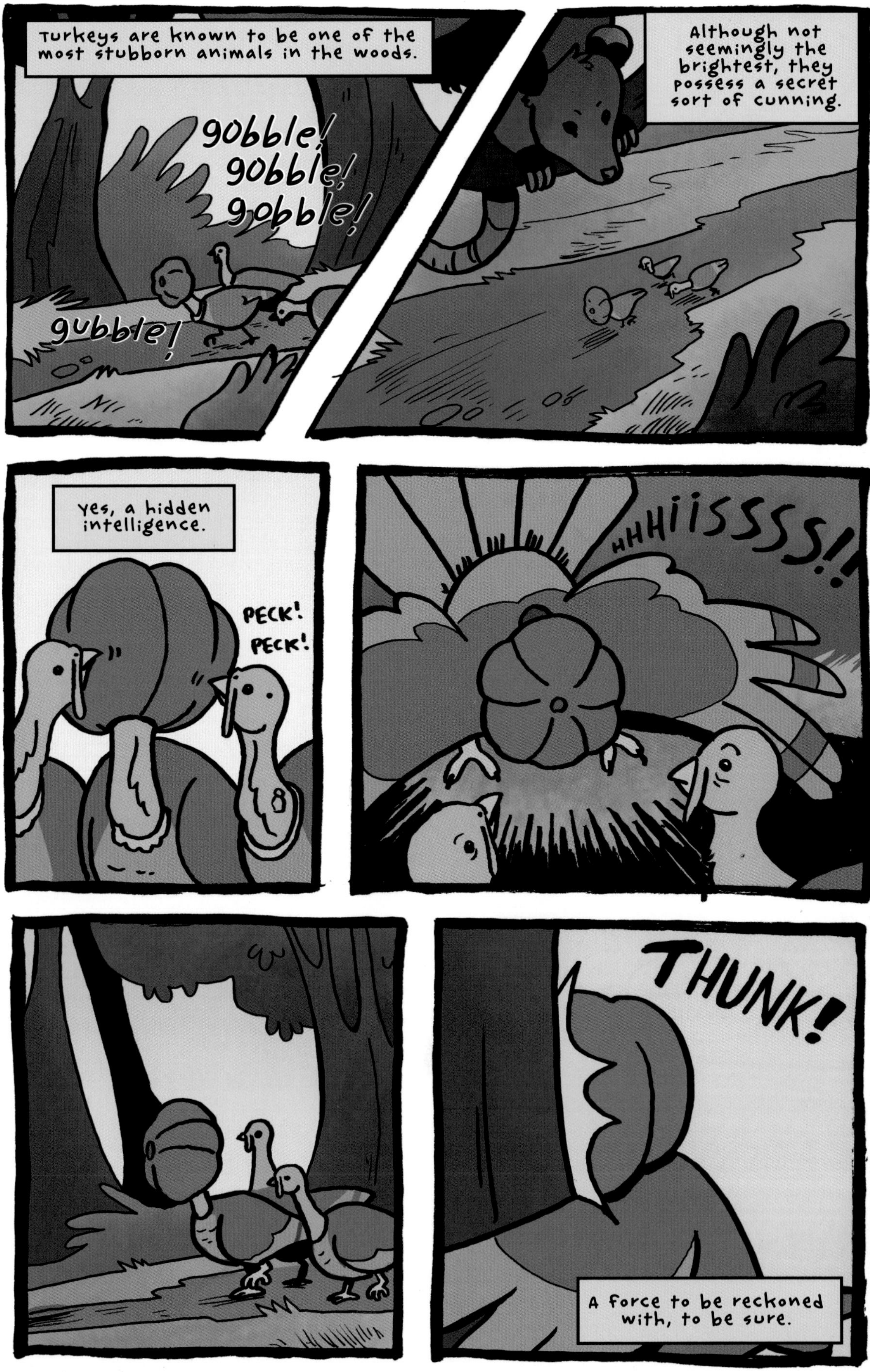
Turkeys are known to be one of the most stubborn animals in the woods.
gobble! gobble! gobble!
gubble!
Although not seemingly the brightest, they possess a secret sort of cunning.
Yes, a hidden intelligence.
PECK! PECK!
HHHIISSSSS!!
THUNK!
A force to be reckoned with, to be sure.

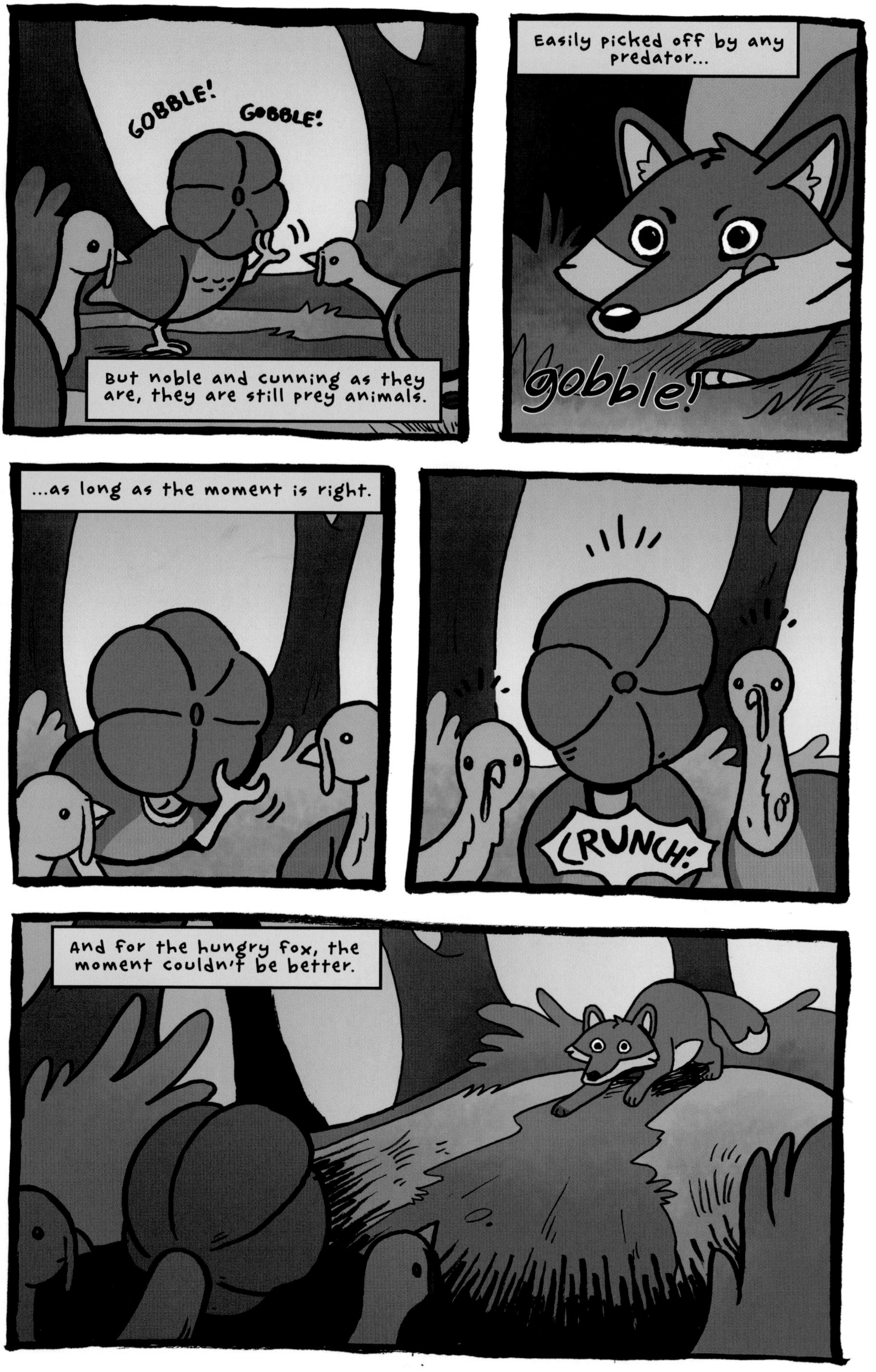
GOBBLE!
GOBBLE!
But noble and cunning as they are, they are still prey animals.
Easily picked off by any predator...
gobble!
...as long as the moment is right.
CRUNCH!
And for the hungry fox, the moment couldn't be better.

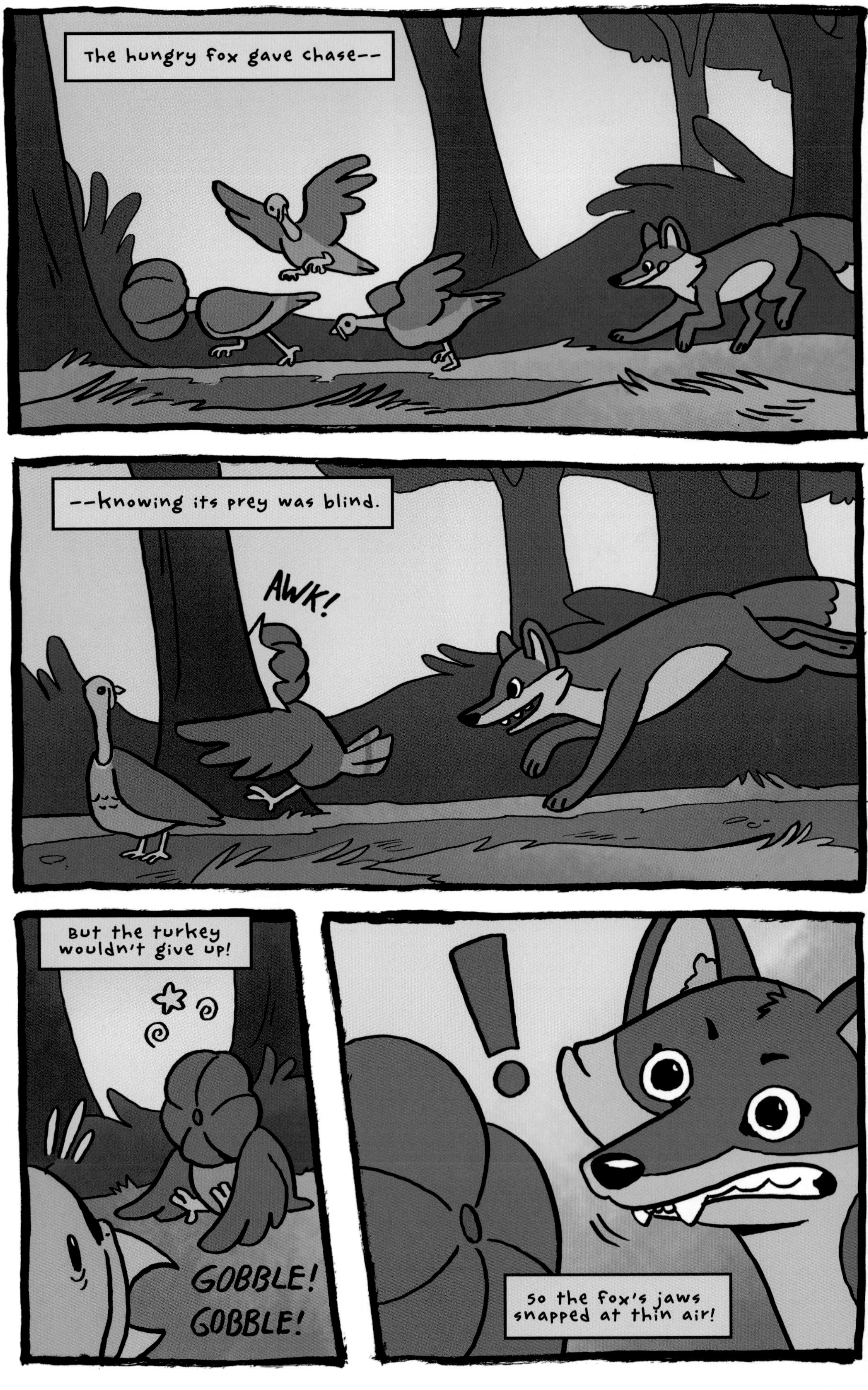
The hungry fox gave chase--
--knowing its prey was blind.
AWK!
But the turkey wouldn't give up!
GOBBLE! GOBBLE!
So the fox's jaws snapped at thin air!

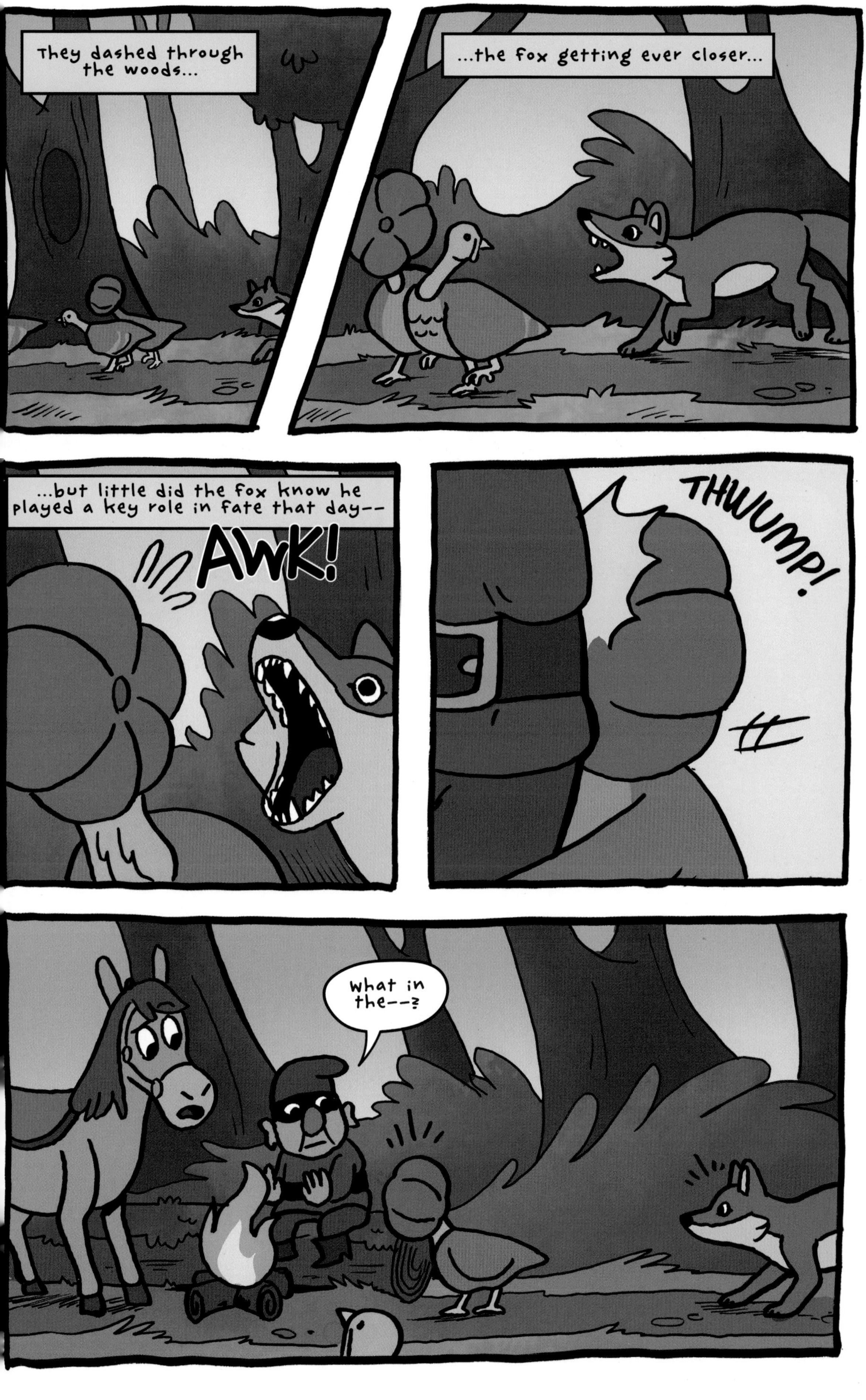
They dashed through the woods...
...the fox getting ever closer...
...but little did the fox know he played a key role in fate that day--
AWK!
THWUMP!
What in the--?

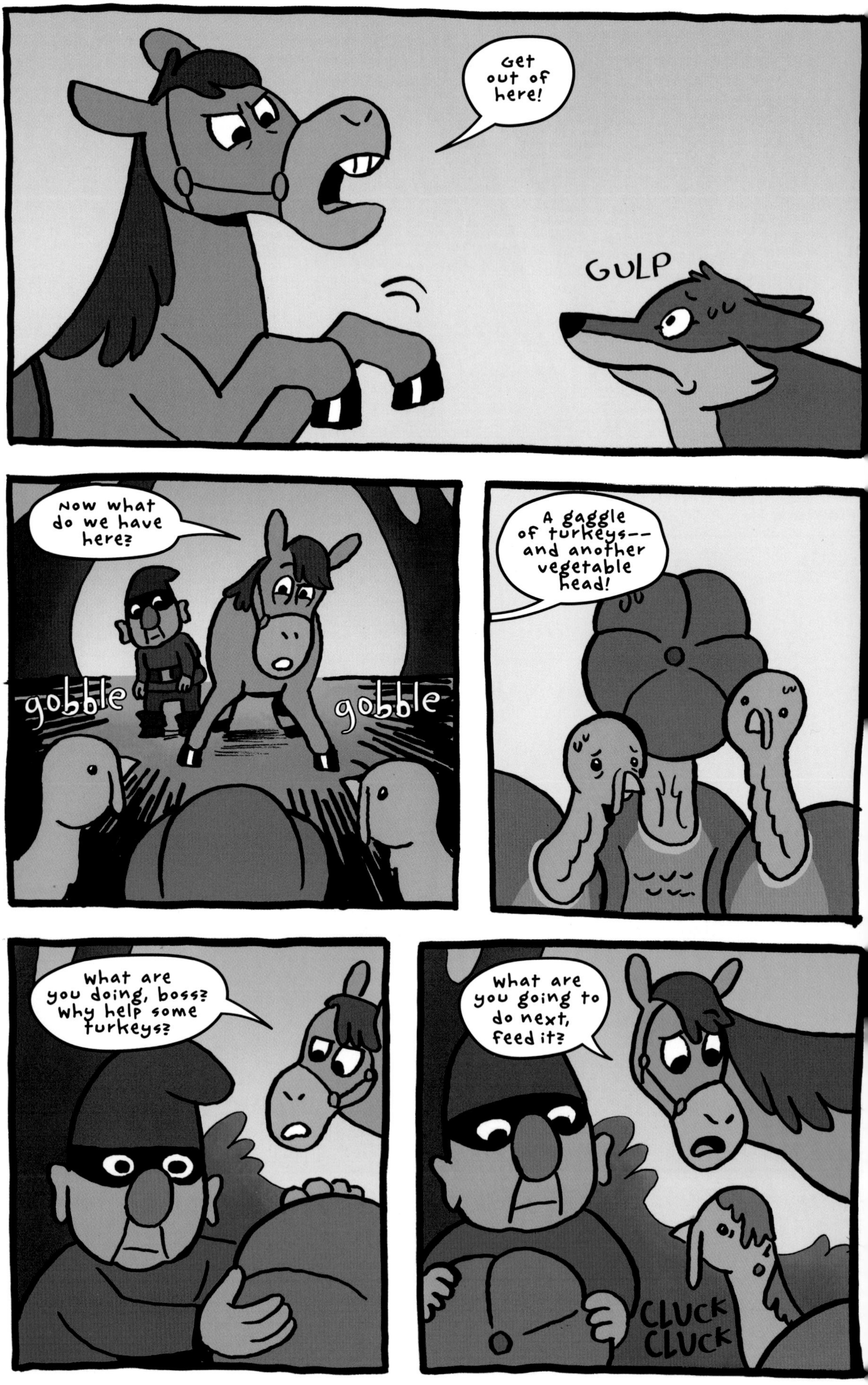
Get out of here!
GULP
Now what do we have here?
gobble
gobble
A gaggle of turkeys-- and another vegetable head!
What are you doing, boss? Why help some turkeys?
What are you going to do next, feed it?
CLUCK CLUCK

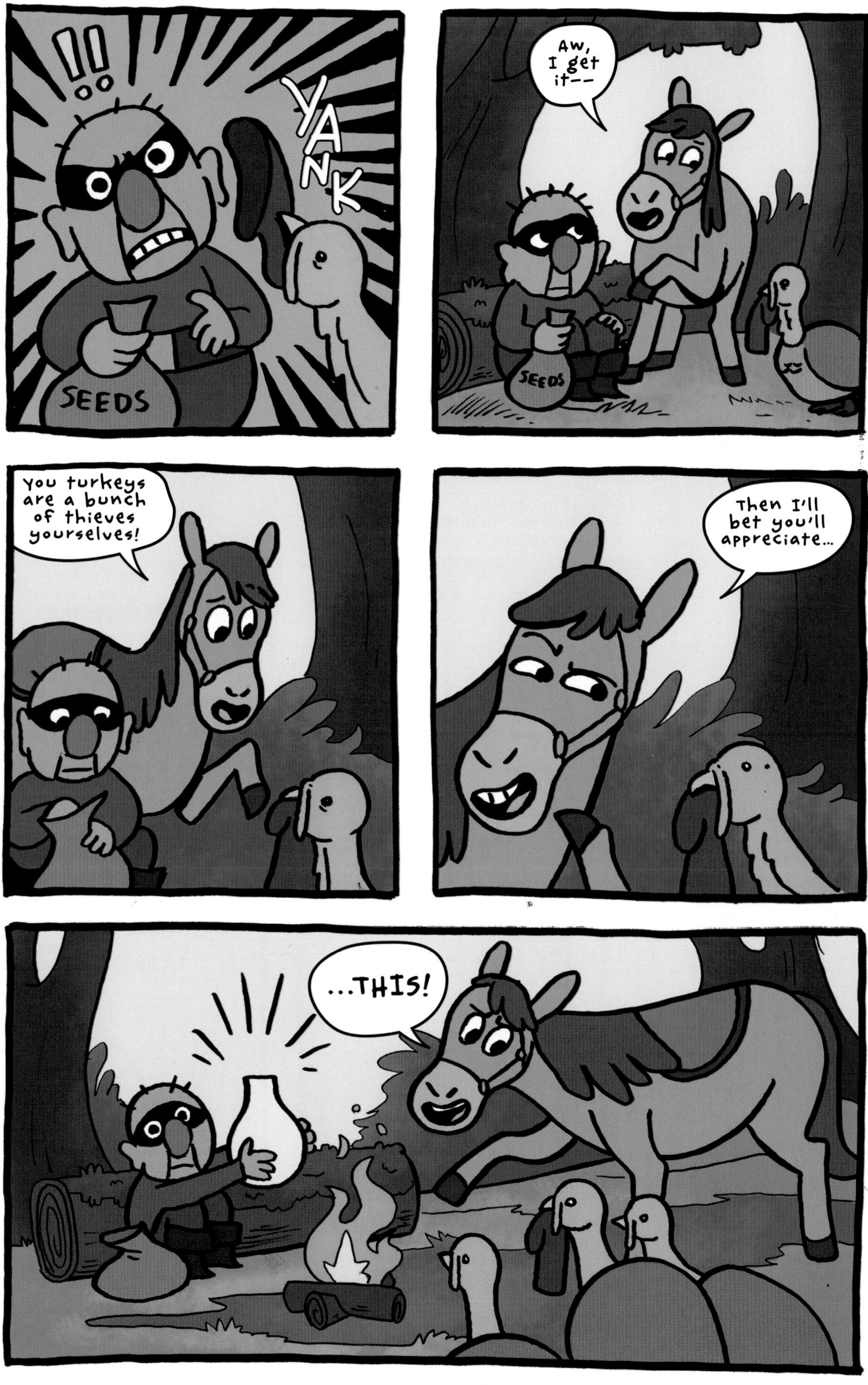
!!
YANK
SEEDS
Aw, I get it--
SEEDS
You turkeys are a bunch of thieves yourselves!
Then I'll bet you'll appreciate...
...THIS!

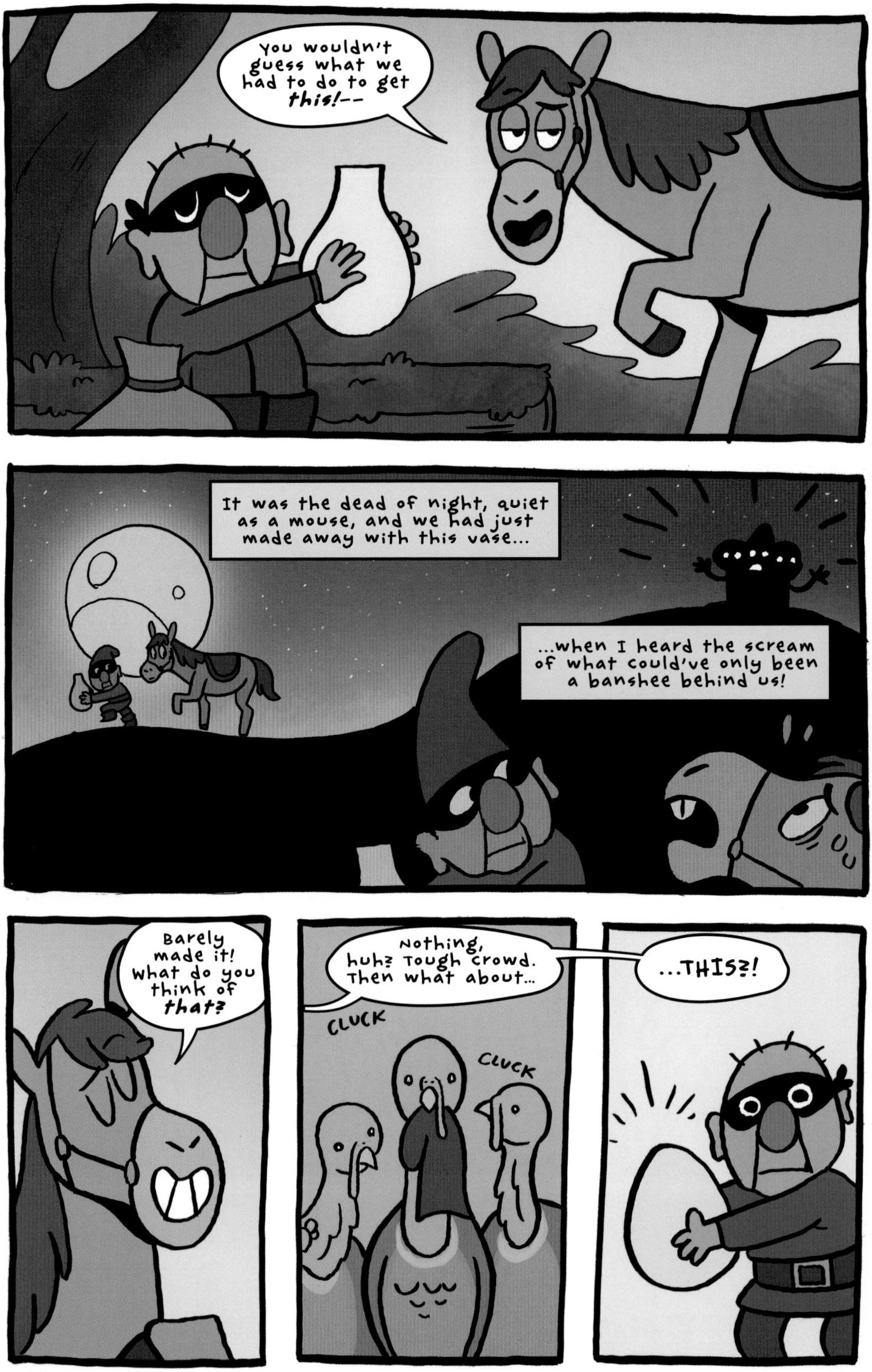
You wouldn't guess what we had to do to get *this!*--
It was the dead of night, quiet as a mouse, and we had just made away with this vase...
...when I heard the scream of what could've only been a banshee behind us!
Barely made it! What do you think of *that?*
Nothing, huh? Tough crowd. Then what about...
CLUCK
CLUCK
...THIS?!

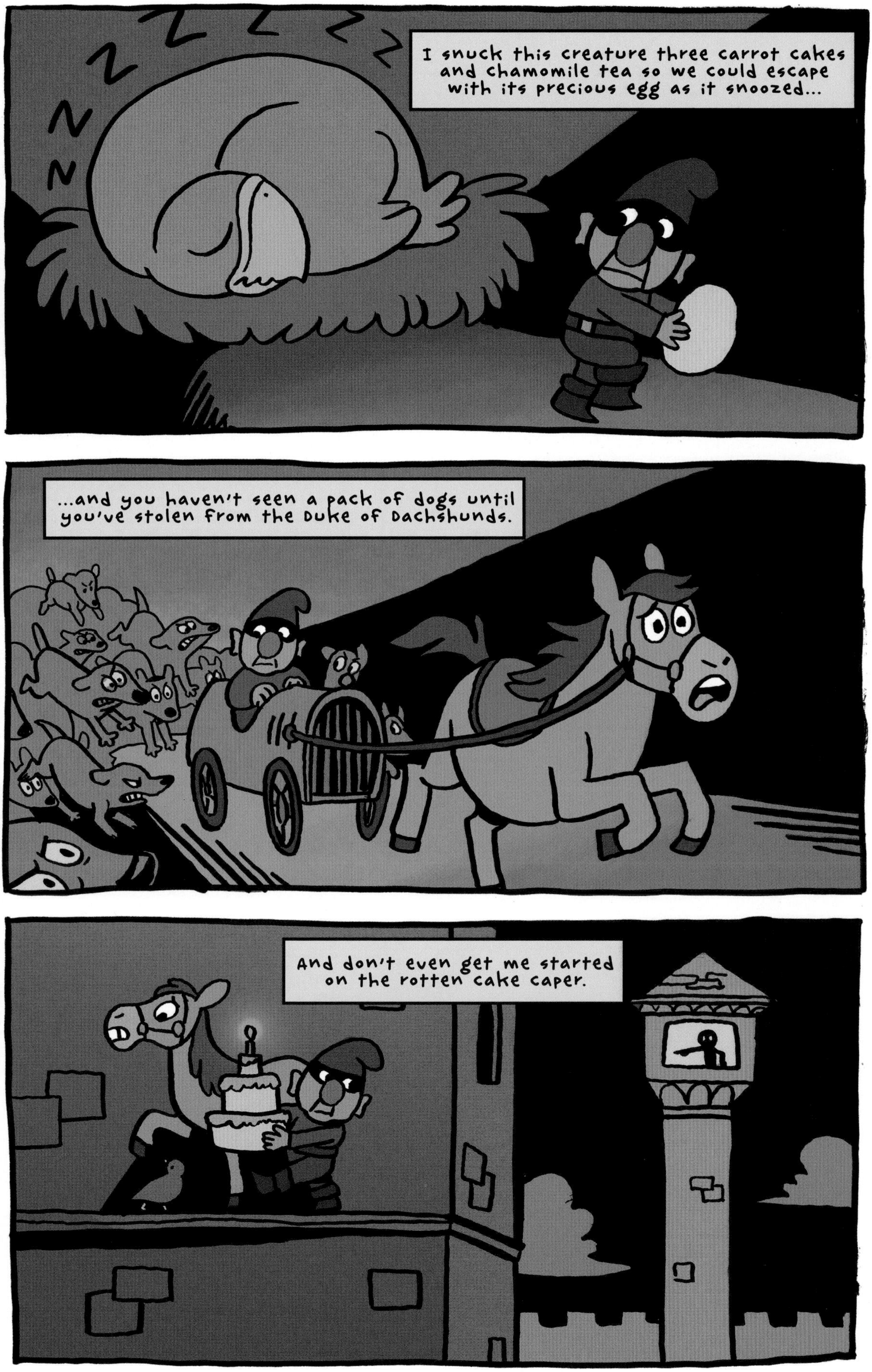
I snuck this creature three carrot cakes and chamomile tea so we could escape with its precious egg as it snoozed...
...and you haven't seen a pack of dogs until you've stolen from the Duke of Dachshunds.
And don't even get me started on the rotten cake caper.

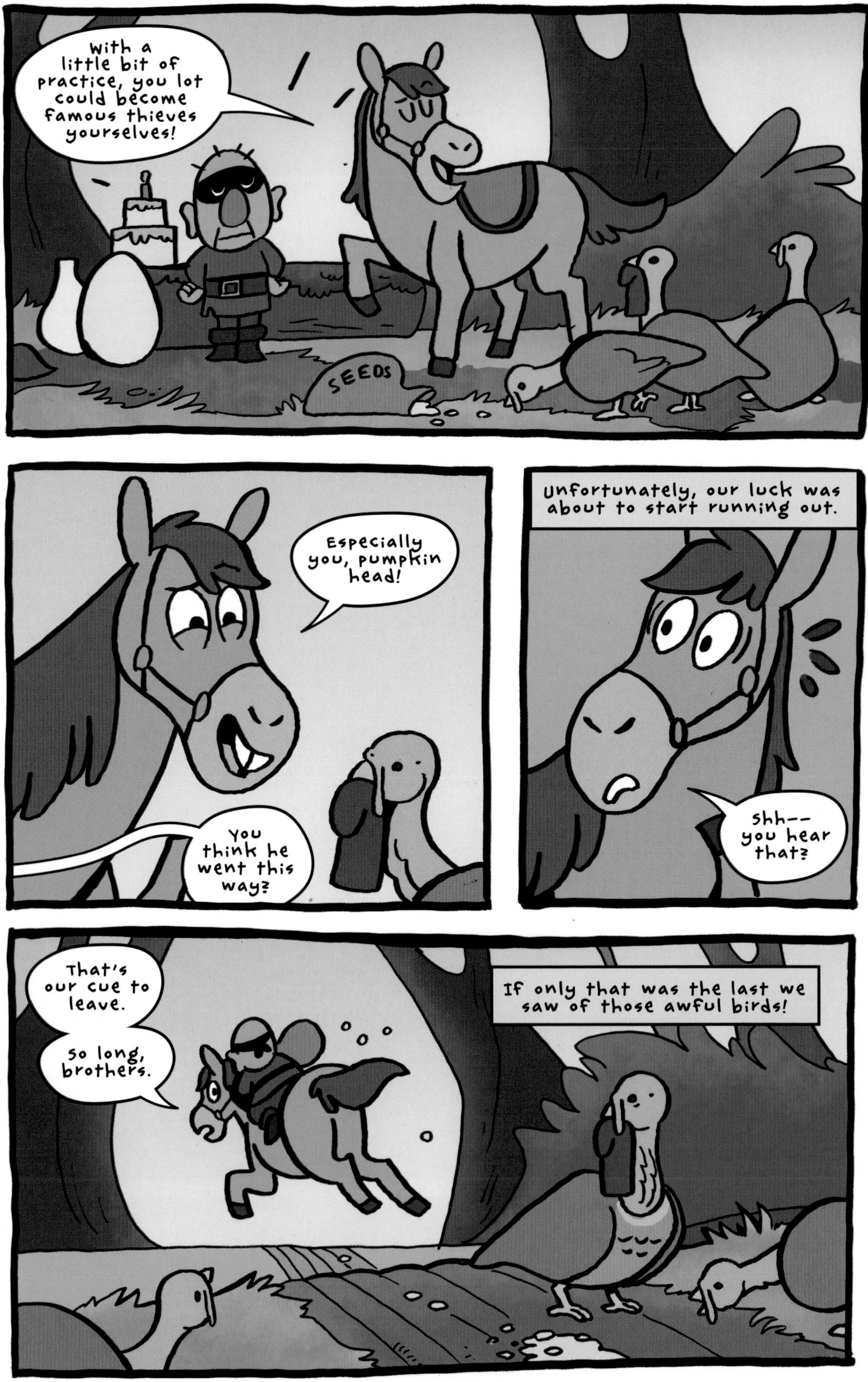
With a little bit of practice, you lot could become famous thieves yourselves!
SEEDS
Especially you, pumpkin head!
You think he went this way?
Unfortunately, our luck was about to start running out.
Shh-- you hear that?
That's our cue to leave.
So long, brothers.
If only that was the last we saw of those awful birds!

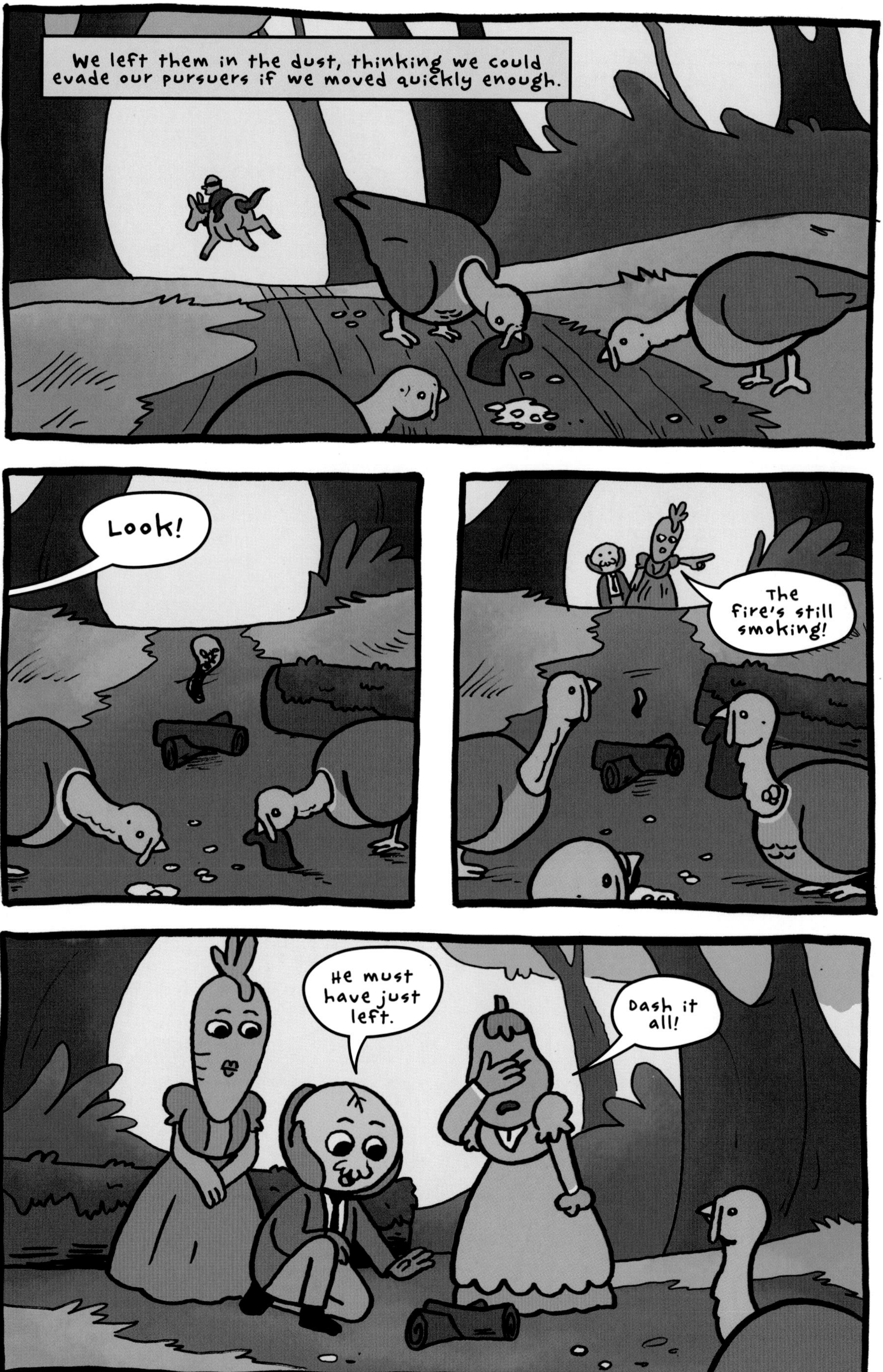
We left them in the dust, thinking we could evade our pursuers if we moved quickly enough.
Look!
The fire's still smoking!
He must have just left.
Dash it all!

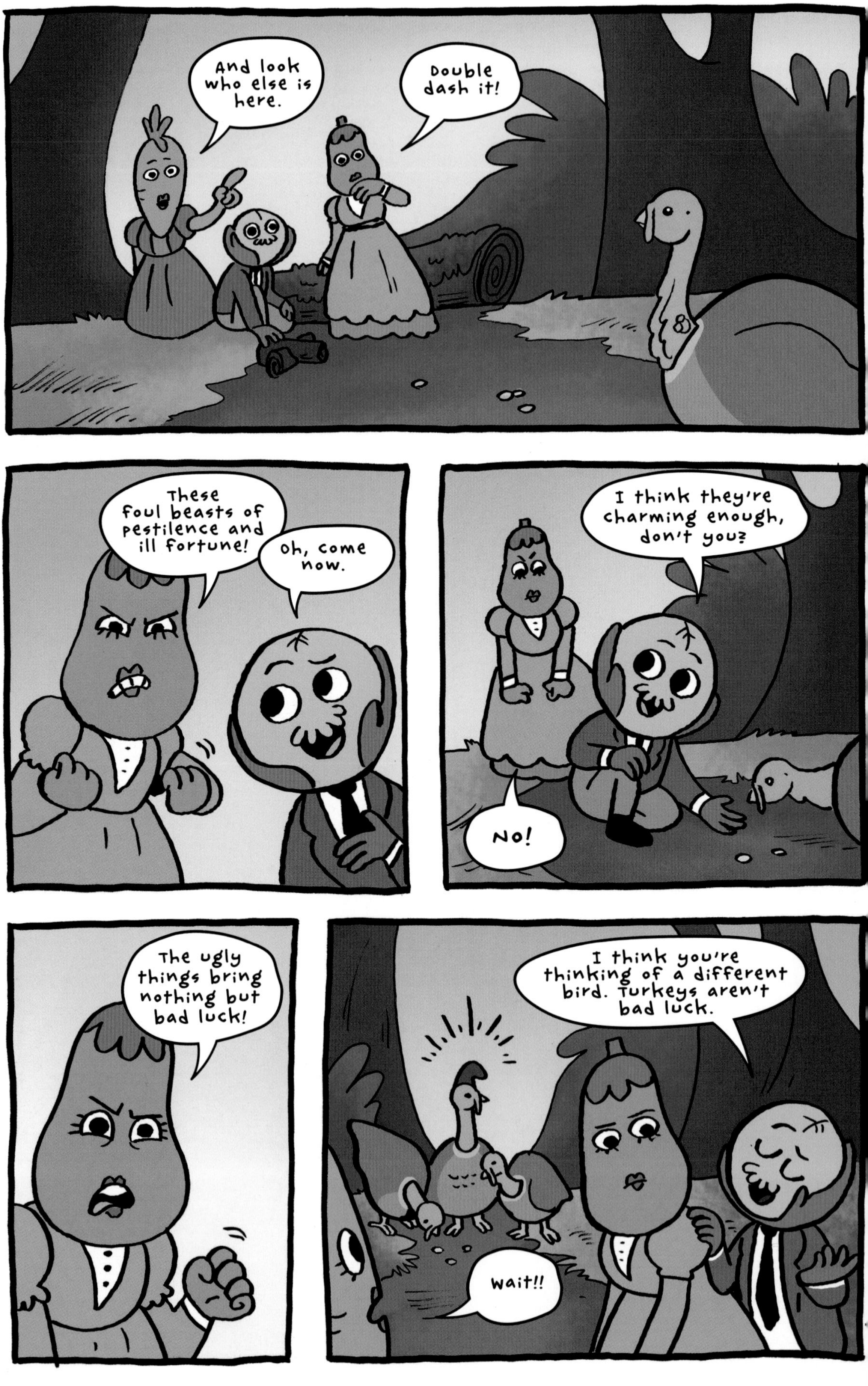
And look who else is here.
Double dash it!
These foul beasts of pestilence and ill fortune!
Oh, come now.
I think they're charming enough, don't you?
No!
The ugly things bring nothing but bad luck!
I think you're thinking of a different bird. Turkeys aren't bad luck.
Wait!!

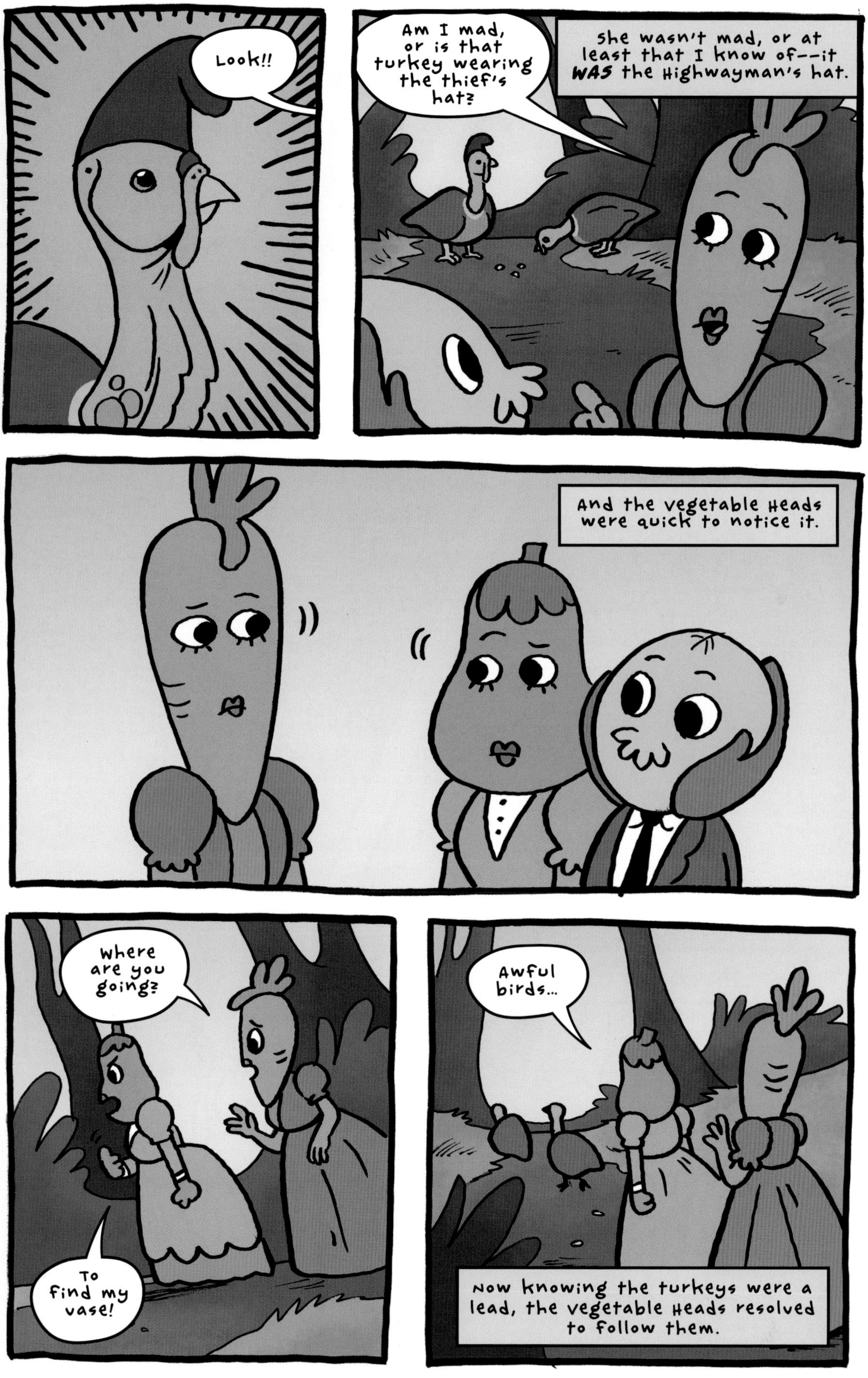
Look!!
Am I mad, or is that turkey wearing the thief's hat?
She wasn't mad, or at least that I know of--it WAS the Highwayman's hat.
And the vegetable Heads were quick to notice it.
Where are you going?
To find my vase!
Awful birds...
Now knowing the turkeys were a lead, the vegetable Heads resolved to follow them.

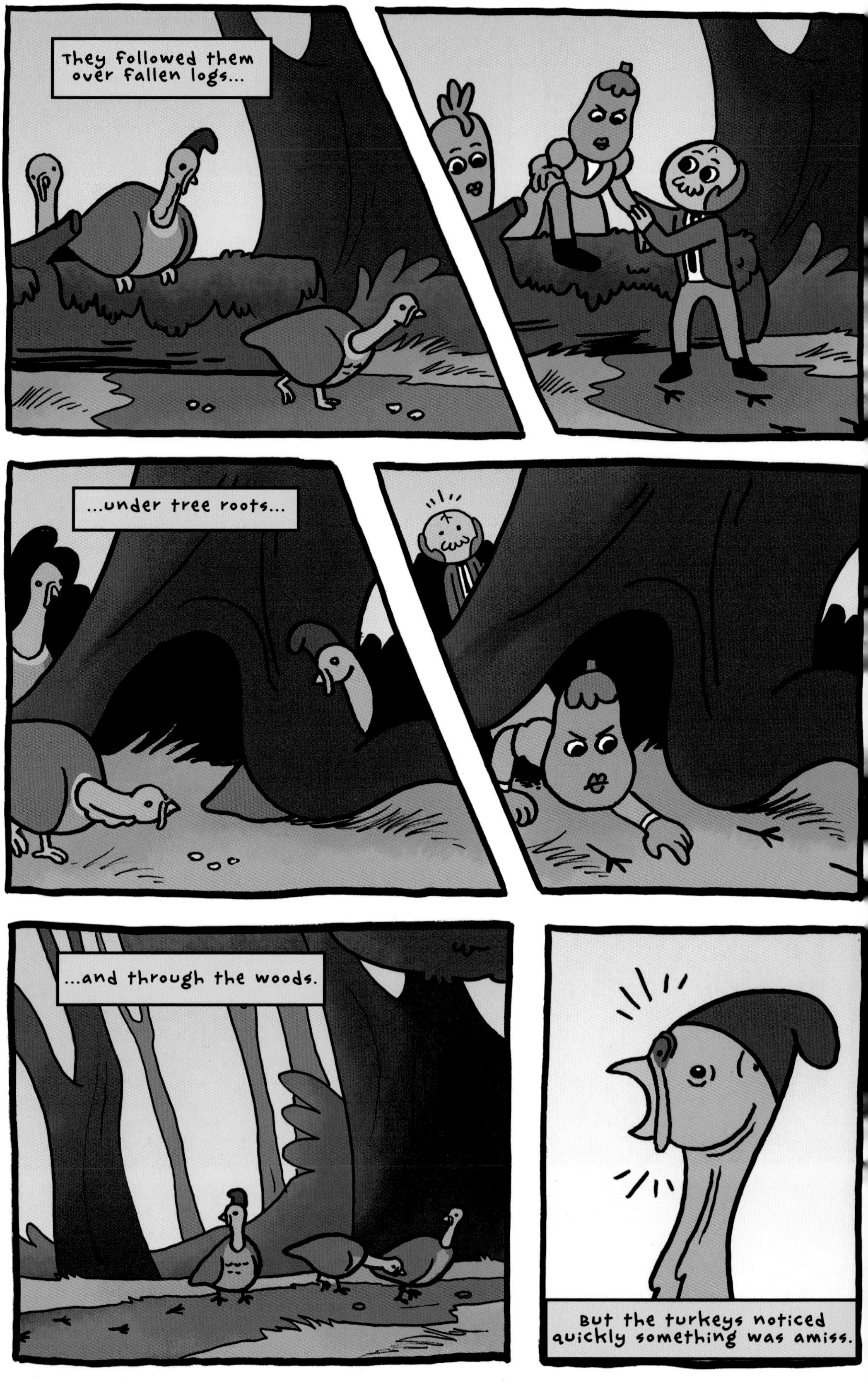
They followed them over fallen logs...
...under tree roots...
...and through the woods.
But the turkeys noticed quickly something was amiss.

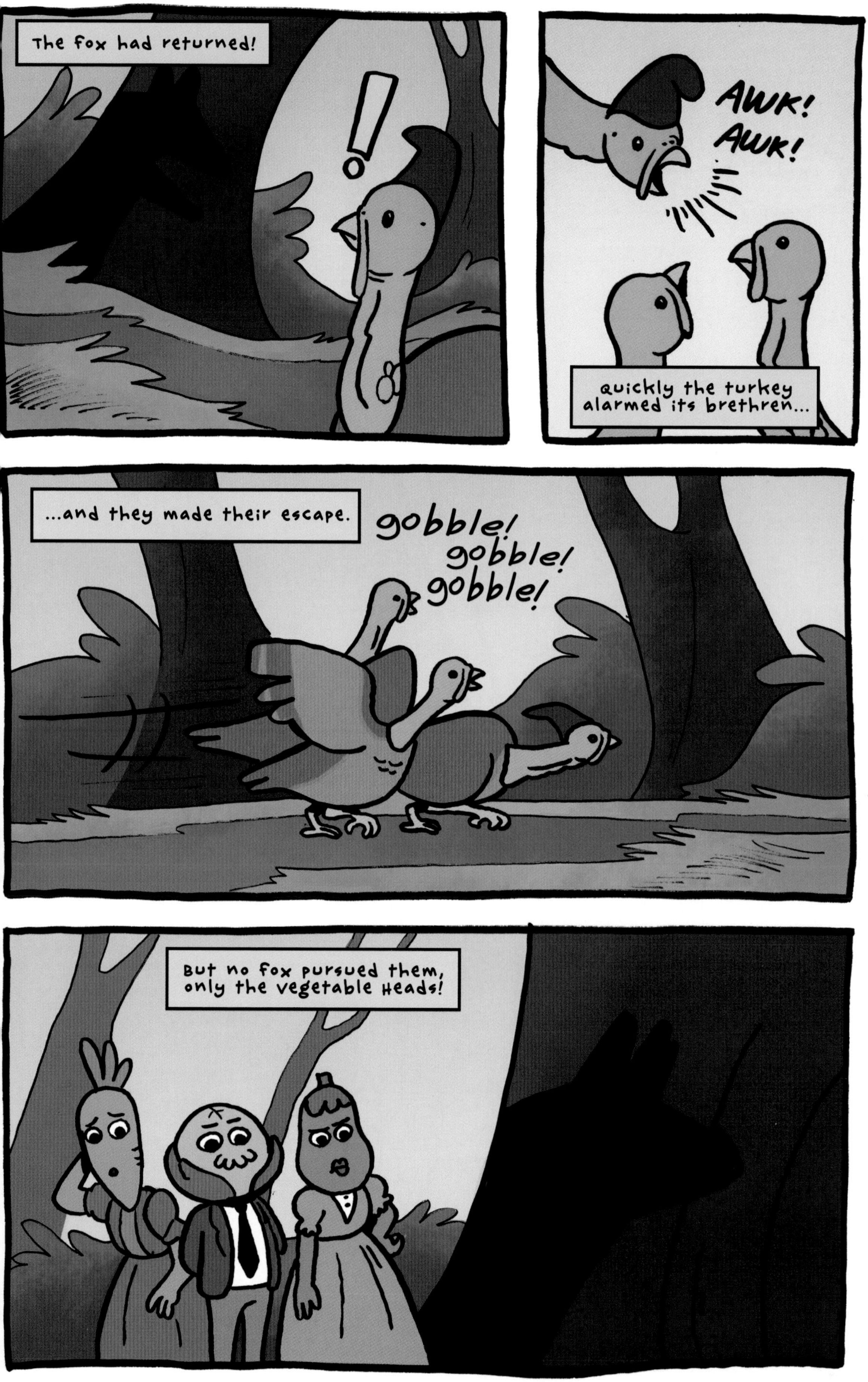
The fox had returned!
!
AWK! AWK!
quickly the turkey alarmed its brethren...
...and they made their escape.
gobble! gobble! gobble!
But no fox pursued them, only the vegetable Heads!

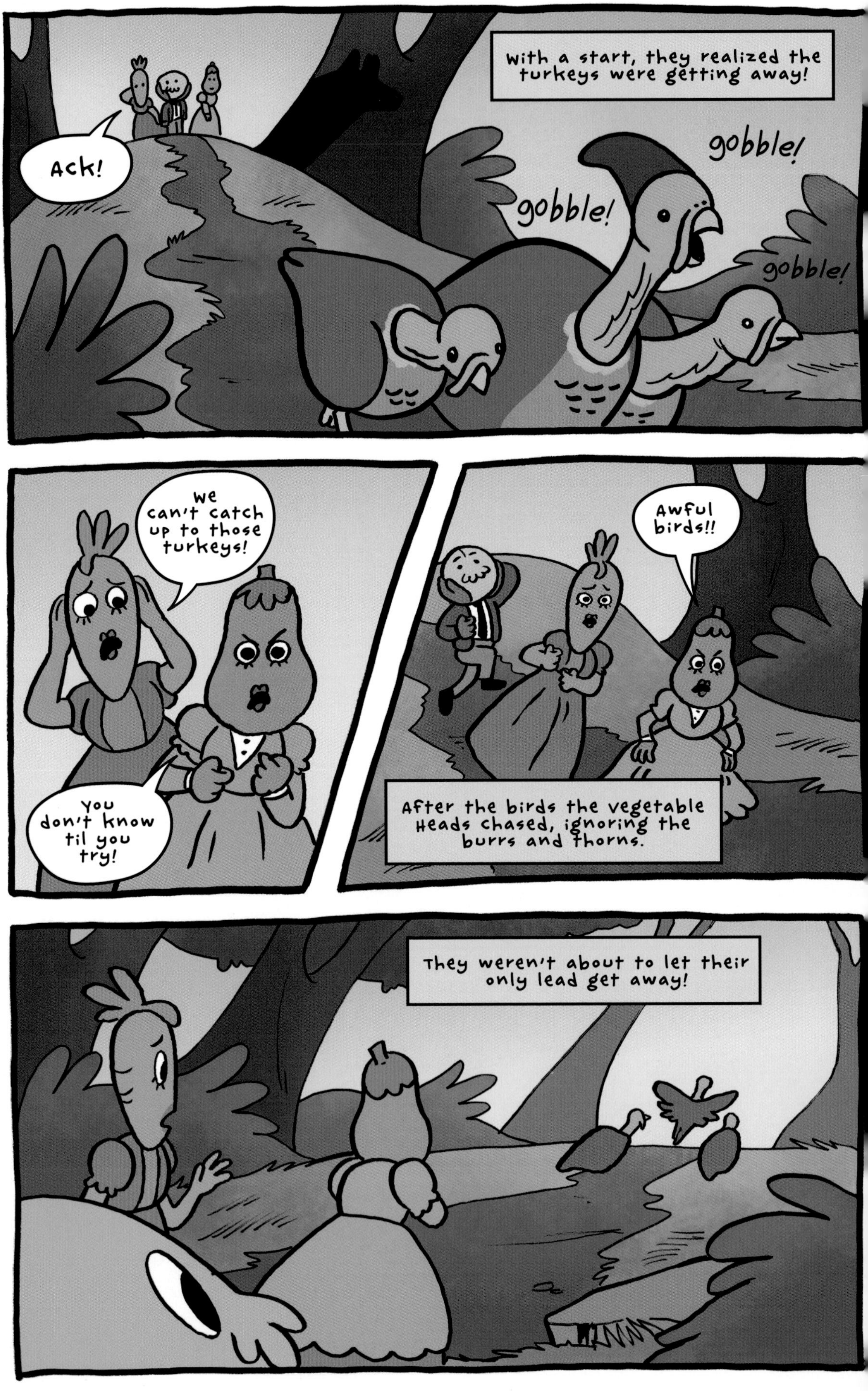
With a start, they realized the turkeys were getting away!
Ack!
gobble!
gobble!
gobble!
We can't catch up to those turkeys!
You don't know til you try!
Awful birds!!
After the birds the vegetable Heads chased, ignoring the burrs and thorns.
They weren't about to let their only lead get away!

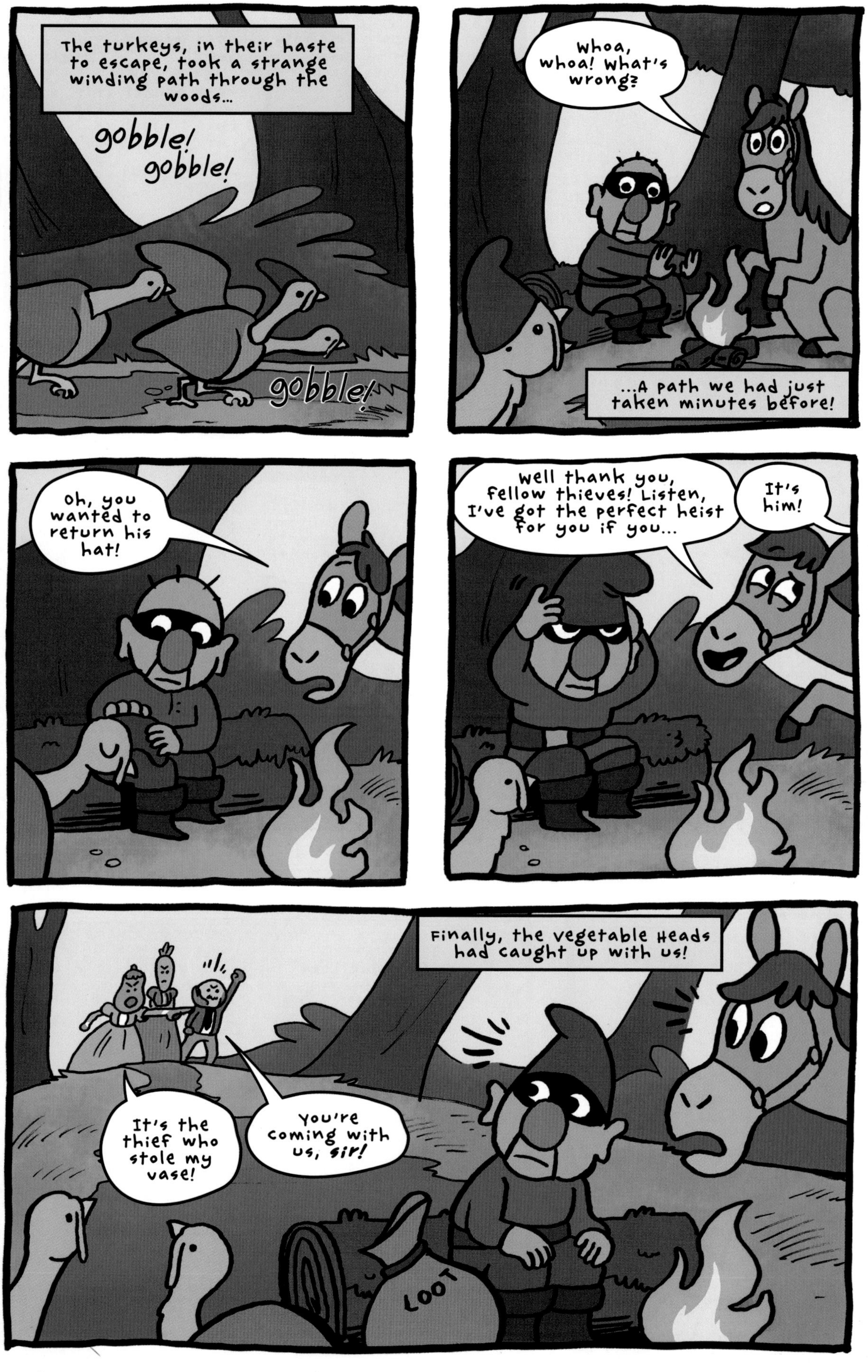
The turkeys, in their haste to escape, took a strange winding path through the woods...
gobble! gobble!
gobble!
Whoa, whoa! What's wrong?
...A path we had just taken minutes before!
Oh, you wanted to return his hat!
Well thank you, fellow thieves! Listen, I've got the perfect heist for you if you...
It's him!
Finally, the vegetable Heads had caught up with us!
It's the thief who stole my vase!
You're coming with us, sir!
LOOT

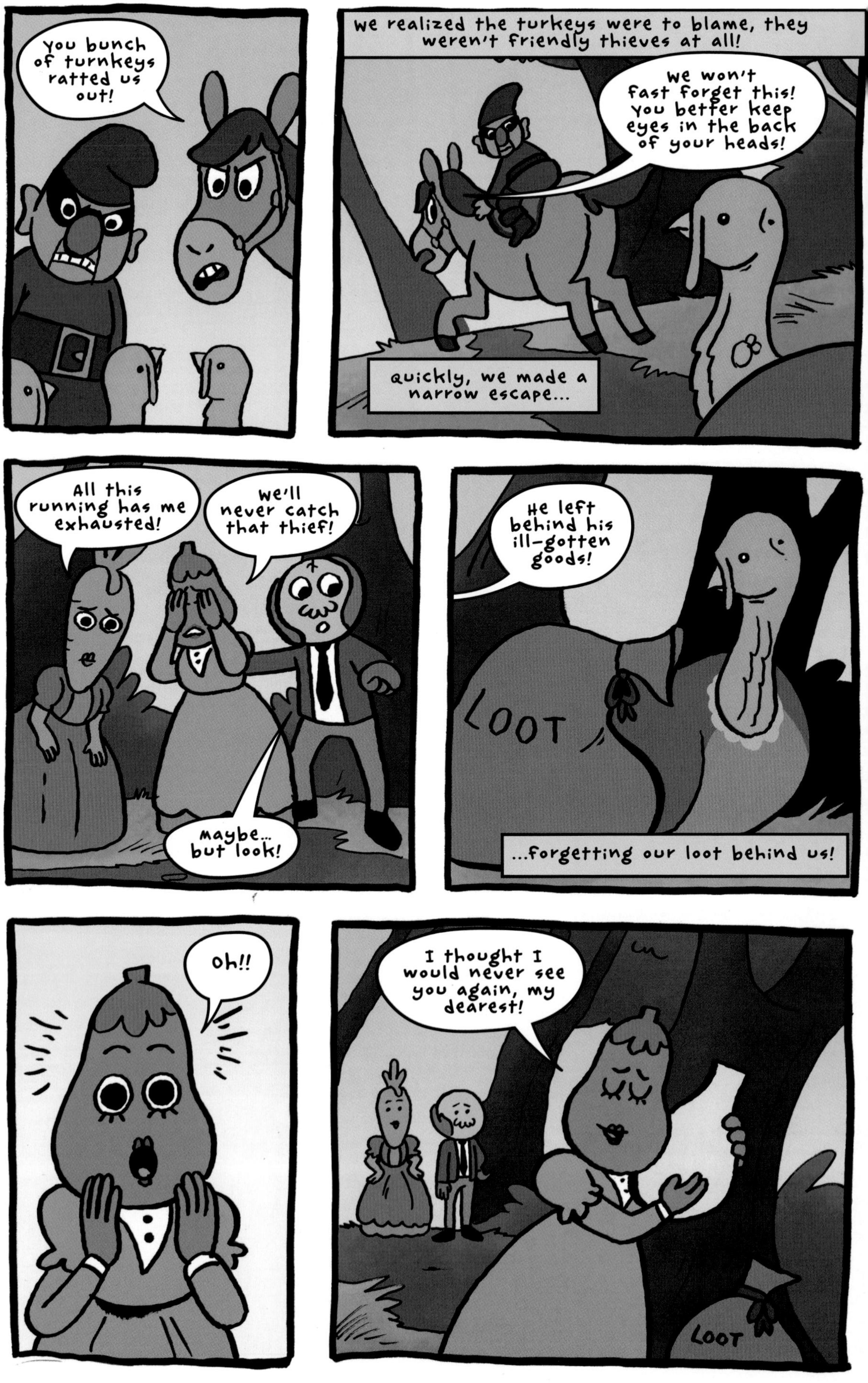
You bunch of turnkeys ratted us out!
We realized the turkeys were to blame, they weren't friendly thieves at all!
We won't fast forget this! You better keep eyes in the back of your heads!
Quickly, we made a narrow escape...
All this running has me exhausted!
We'll never catch that thief!
maybe... but look!
He left behind his ill-gotten goods!
LOOT
...forgetting our loot behind us!
Oh!!
I thought I would never see you again, my dearest!
LOOT

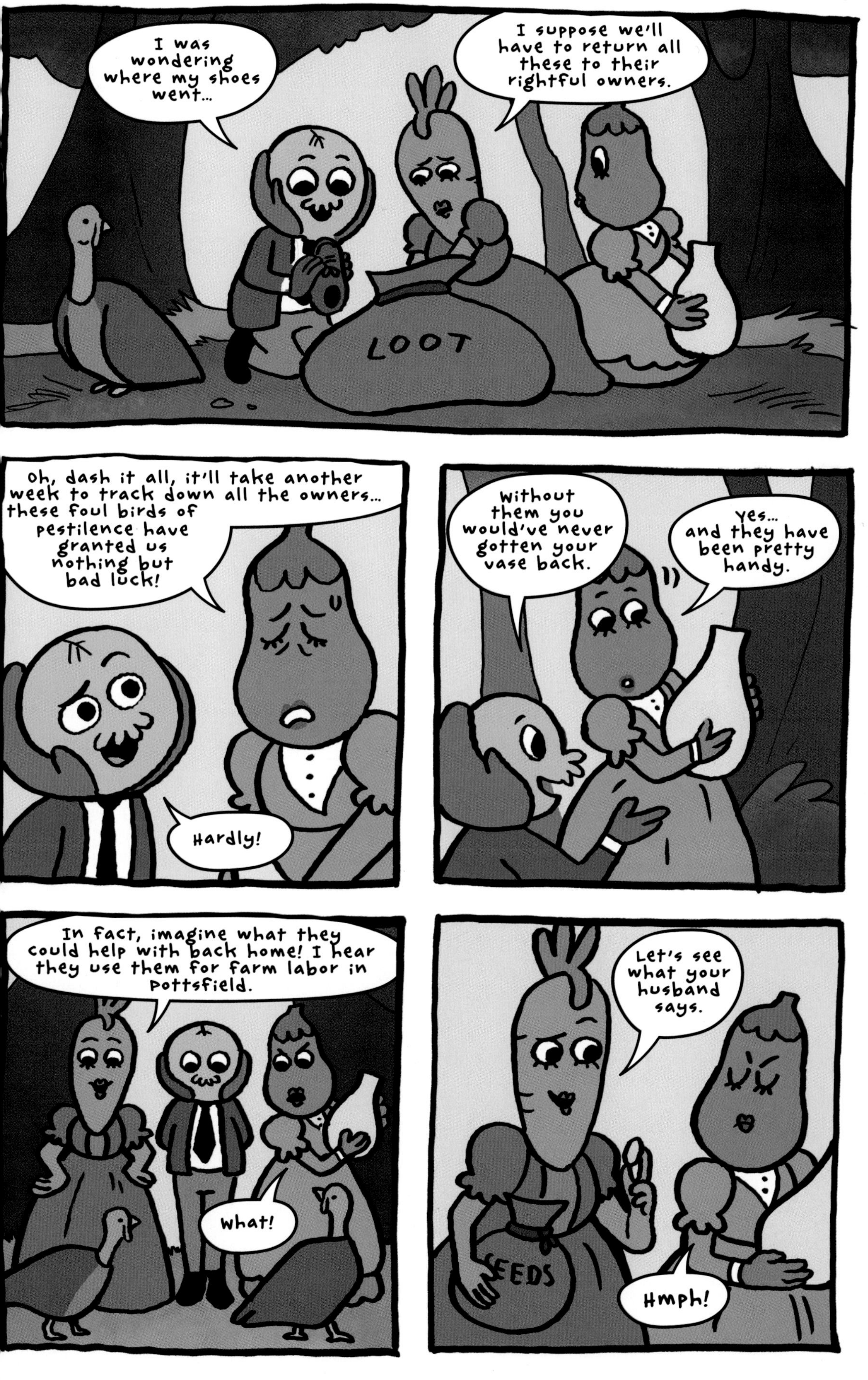
I was wondering where my shoes went...
I suppose we'll have to return all these to their rightful owners.
LOOT
Oh, dash it all, it'll take another week to track down all the owners... these foul birds of pestilence have granted us nothing but bad luck!
Hardly!
Without them you would've never gotten your vase back.
Yes... and they have been pretty handy.
In fact, imagine what they could help with back home! I hear they use them for farm labor in Pottsfield.
What!
Let's see what your husband says.
SEEDS
Hmph!

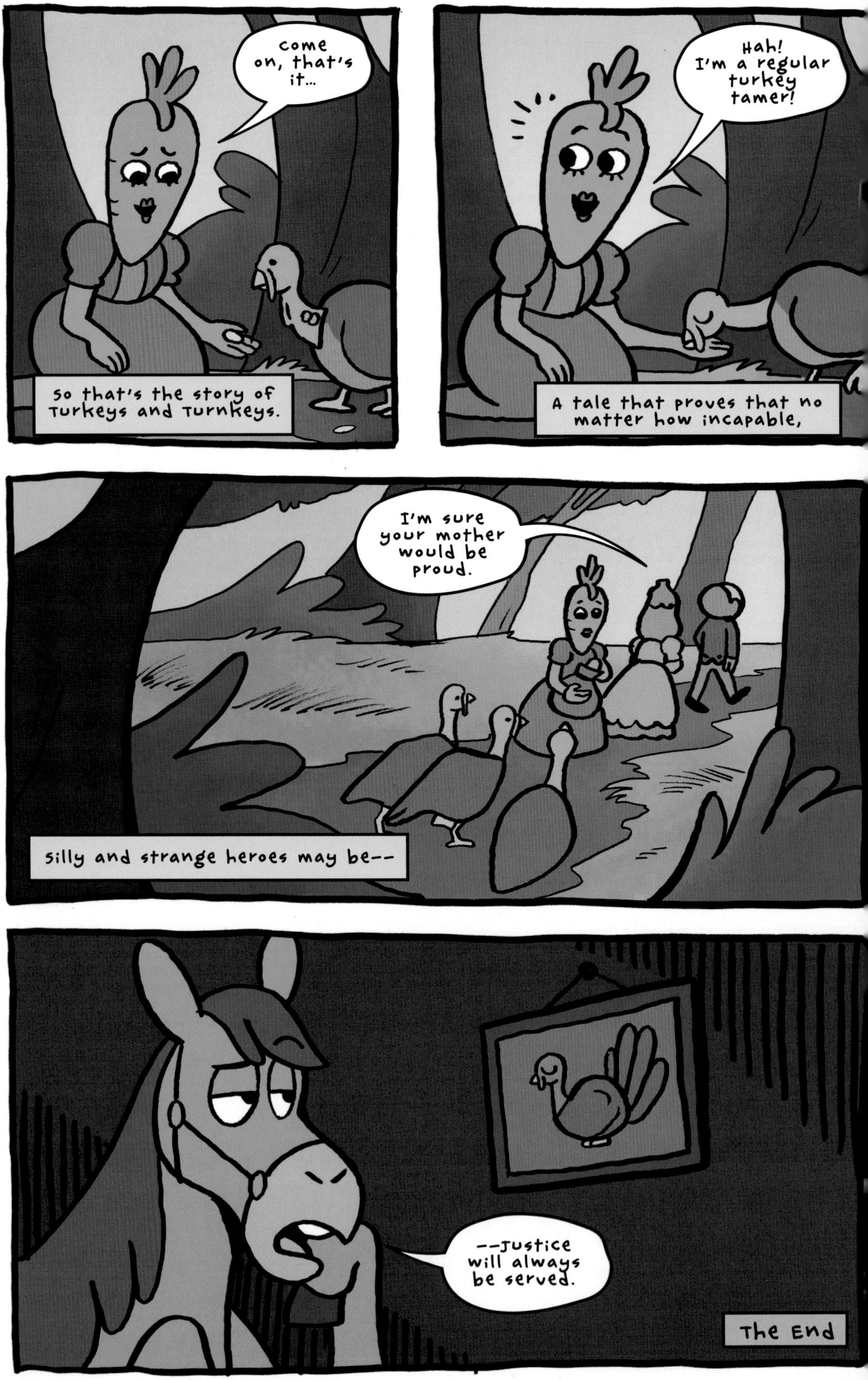
come on, that's it...
So that's the story of Turkeys and Turnkeys.
Hah! I'm a regular turkey tamer!
A tale that proves that no matter how incapable,
I'm sure your mother would be proud.
silly and strange heroes may be--
--Justice will always be served.
The End

GO FISH

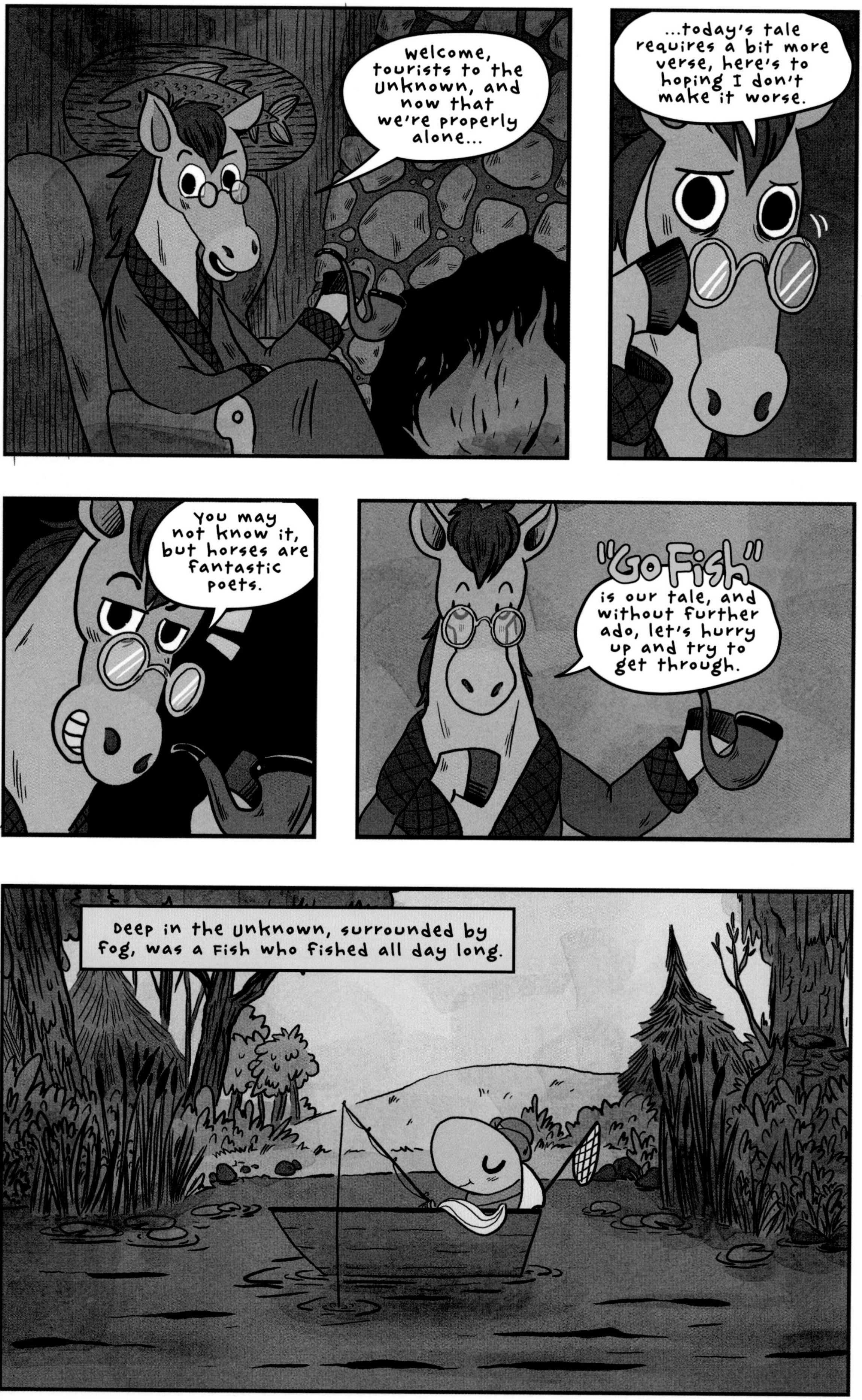
Welcome, tourists to the Unknown, and now that we're properly alone...
...today's tale requires a bit more verse, here's to hoping I don't make it worse.
You may not know it, but horses are fantastic poets.
"Go Fish"
is our tale, and without further ado, let's hurry up and try to get through.
Deep in the Unknown, surrounded by fog, was a Fish who fished all day long.

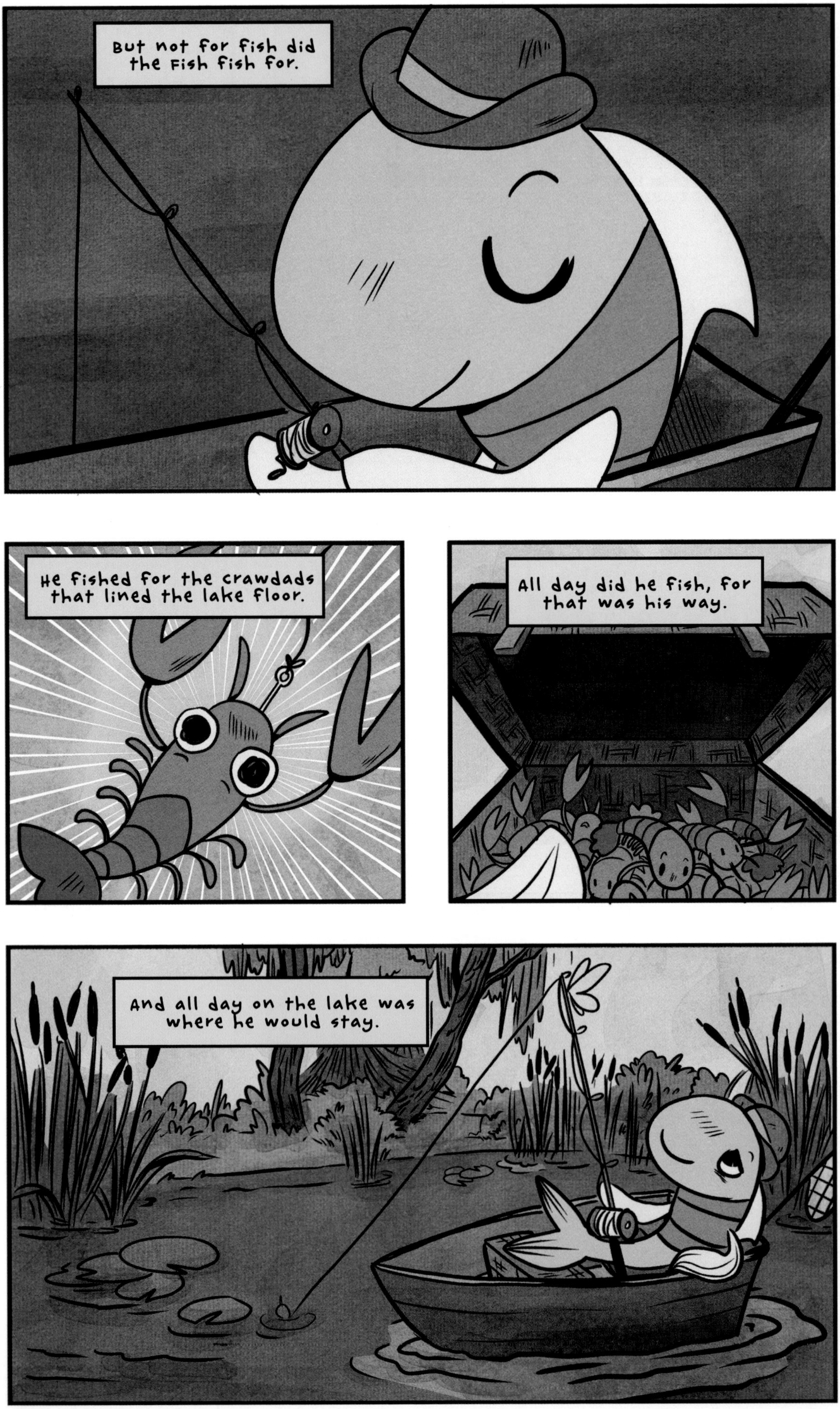

But not for fish did the Fish fish for.
He fished for the crawdads that lined the lake floor.
All day did he fish, for that was his way.
And all day on the lake was where he would stay.

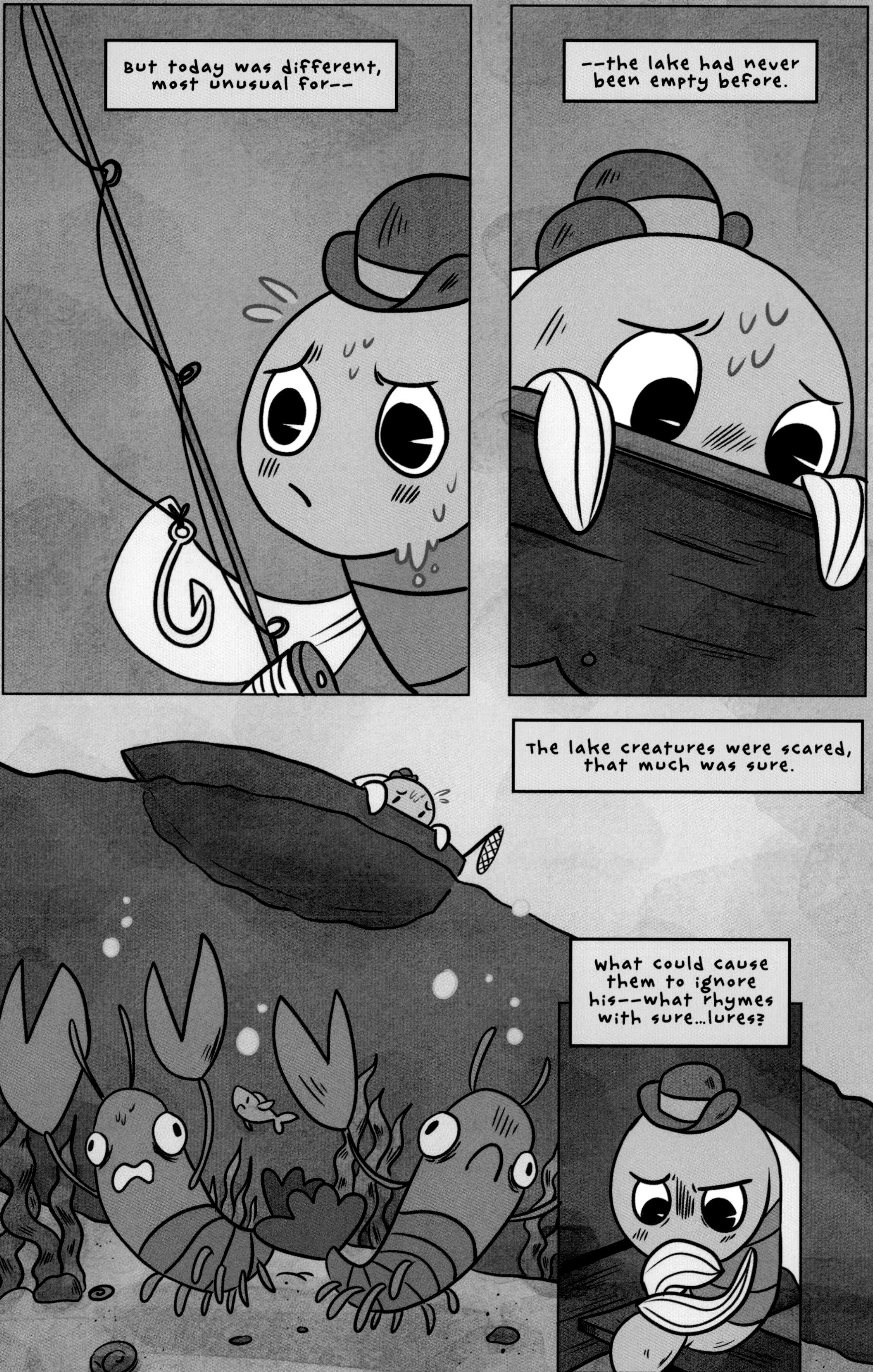
But today was different, most unusual for--
--the lake had never been empty before.
The lake creatures were scared, that much was sure.
What could cause them to ignore his--what rhymes with sure...lures?

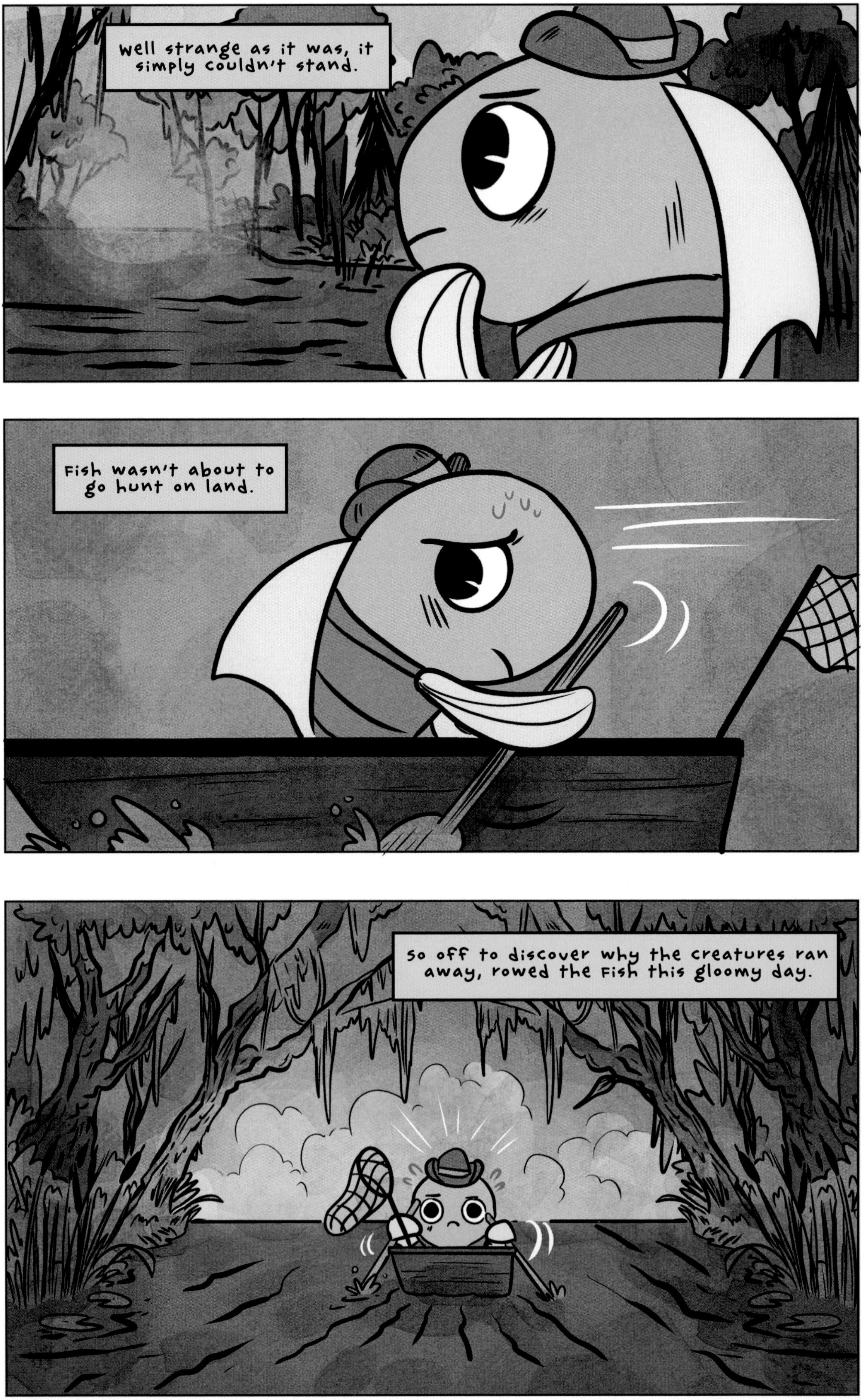
Well strange as it was, it simply couldn't stand.
Fish wasn't about to go hunt on land.
So off to discover why the creatures ran away, rowed the Fish this gloomy day.

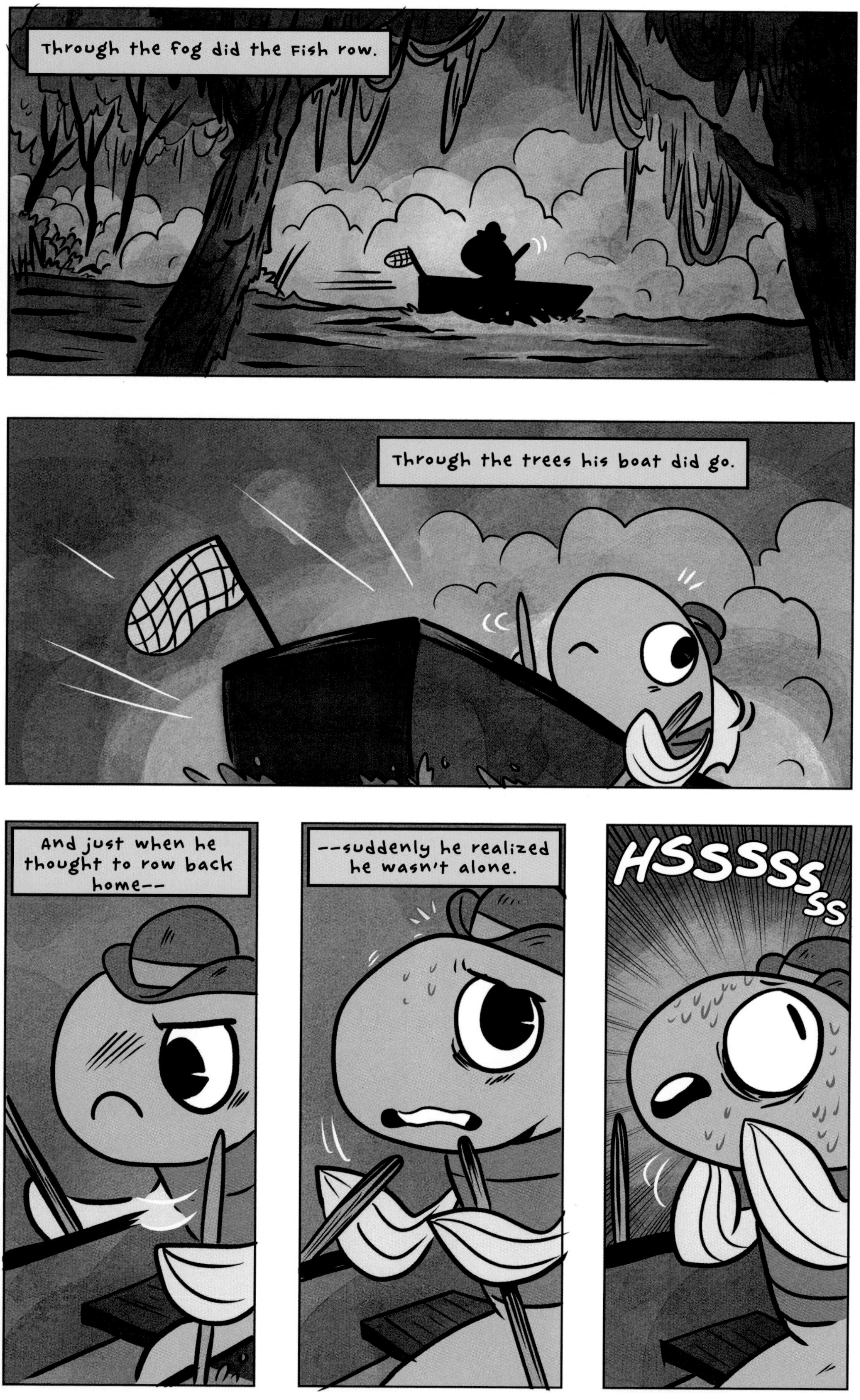
Through the fog did the Fish row.
Through the trees his boat did go.
And just when he thought to row back home--
--suddenly he realized he wasn't alone.
HSSSSSSS

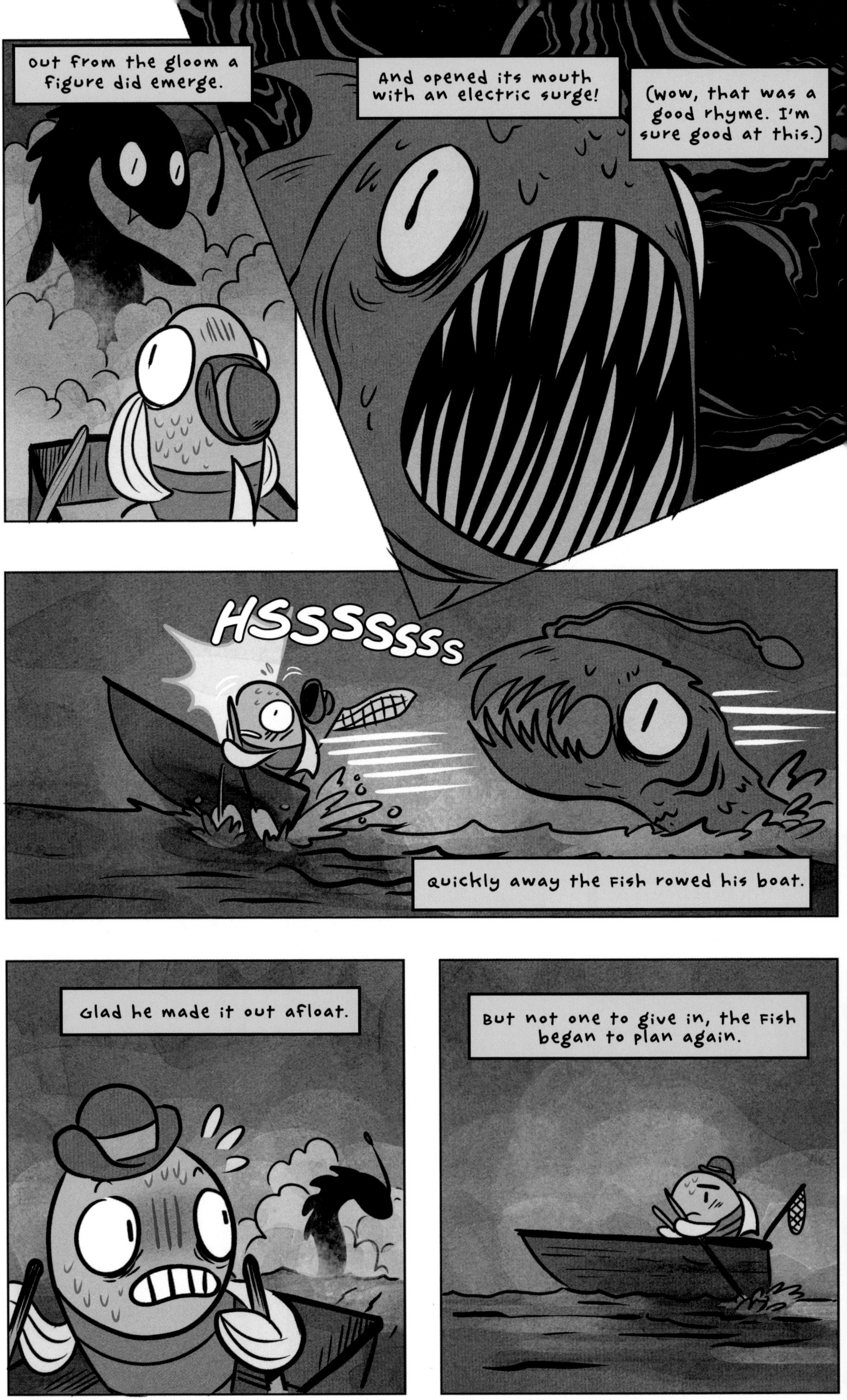
Out from the gloom a figure did emerge.
And opened its mouth with an electric surge!
(Wow, that was a good rhyme. I'm sure good at this.)
HSSSSSSS
Quickly away the Fish rowed his boat.
Glad he made it out afloat.
But not one to give in, the Fish began to plan again.

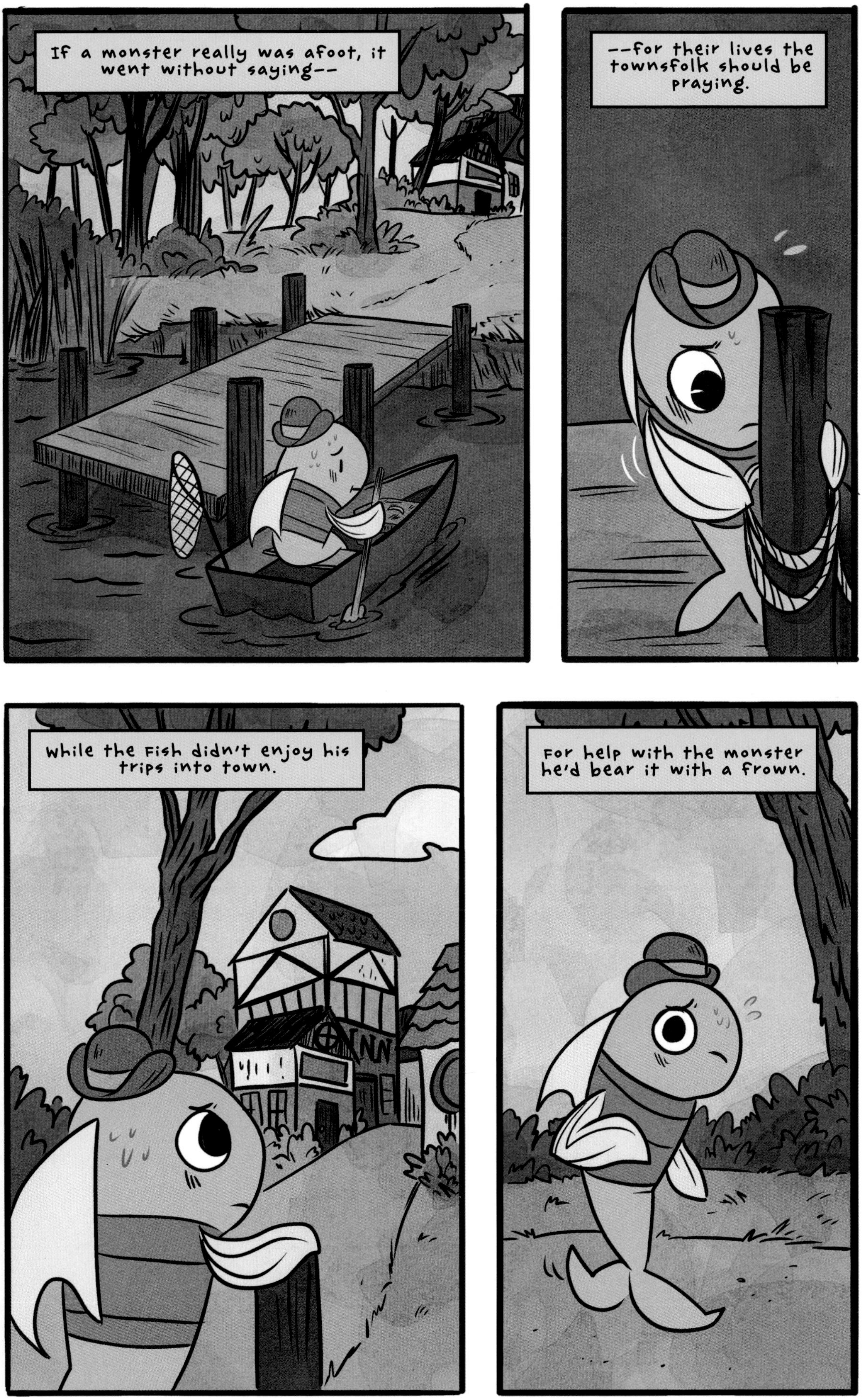
If a monster really was afoot, it went without saying--
--for their lives the townsfolk should be praying.
While the Fish didn't enjoy his trips into town.
INN
For help with the monster he'd bear it with a frown.

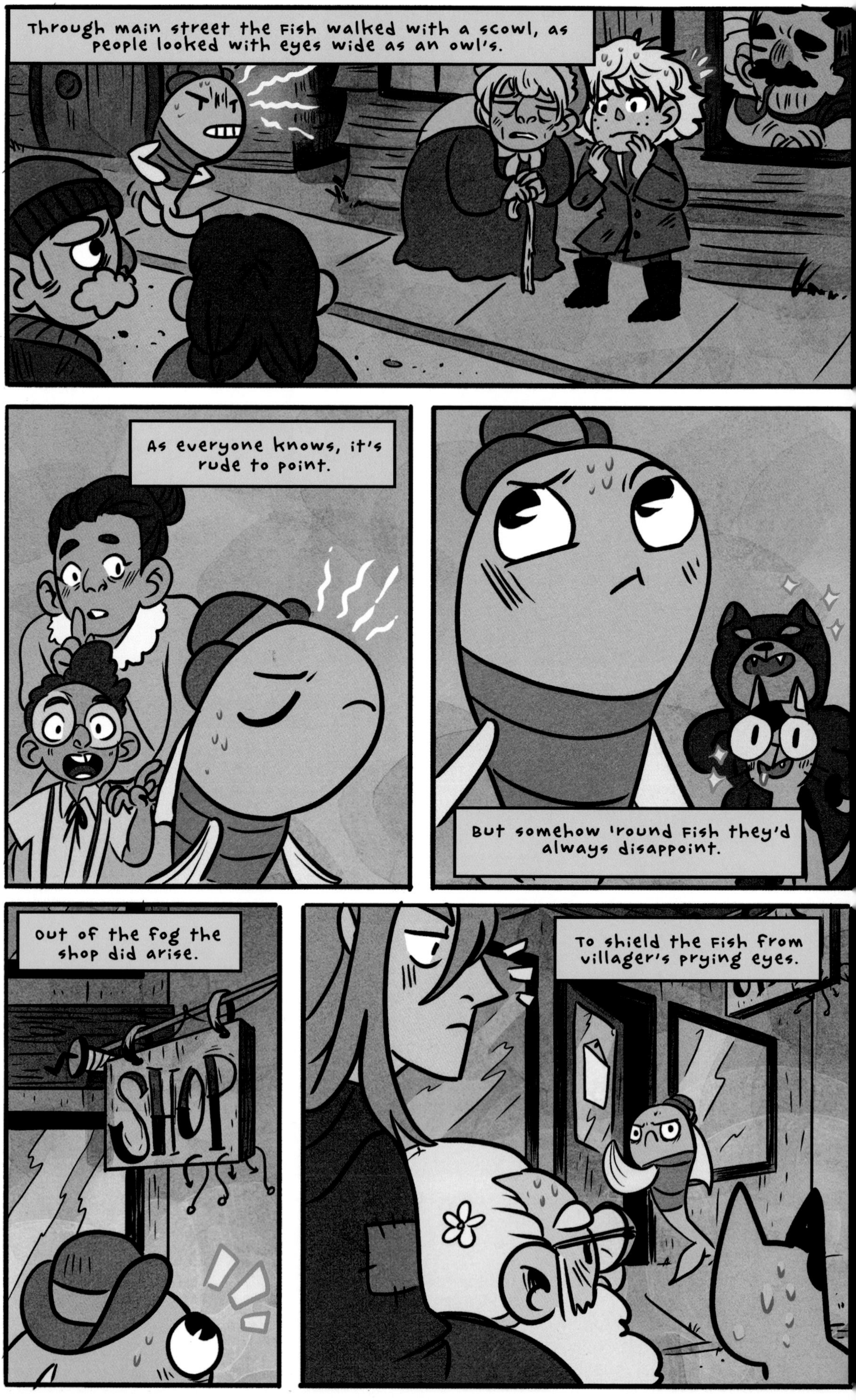
Through main street the Fish walked with a scowl, as people looked with eyes wide as an owl's.
As everyone knows, it's rude to point.
But somehow 'round Fish they'd always disappoint.
Out of the fog the shop did arise.
SHOP
To shield the Fish from villager's prying eyes.

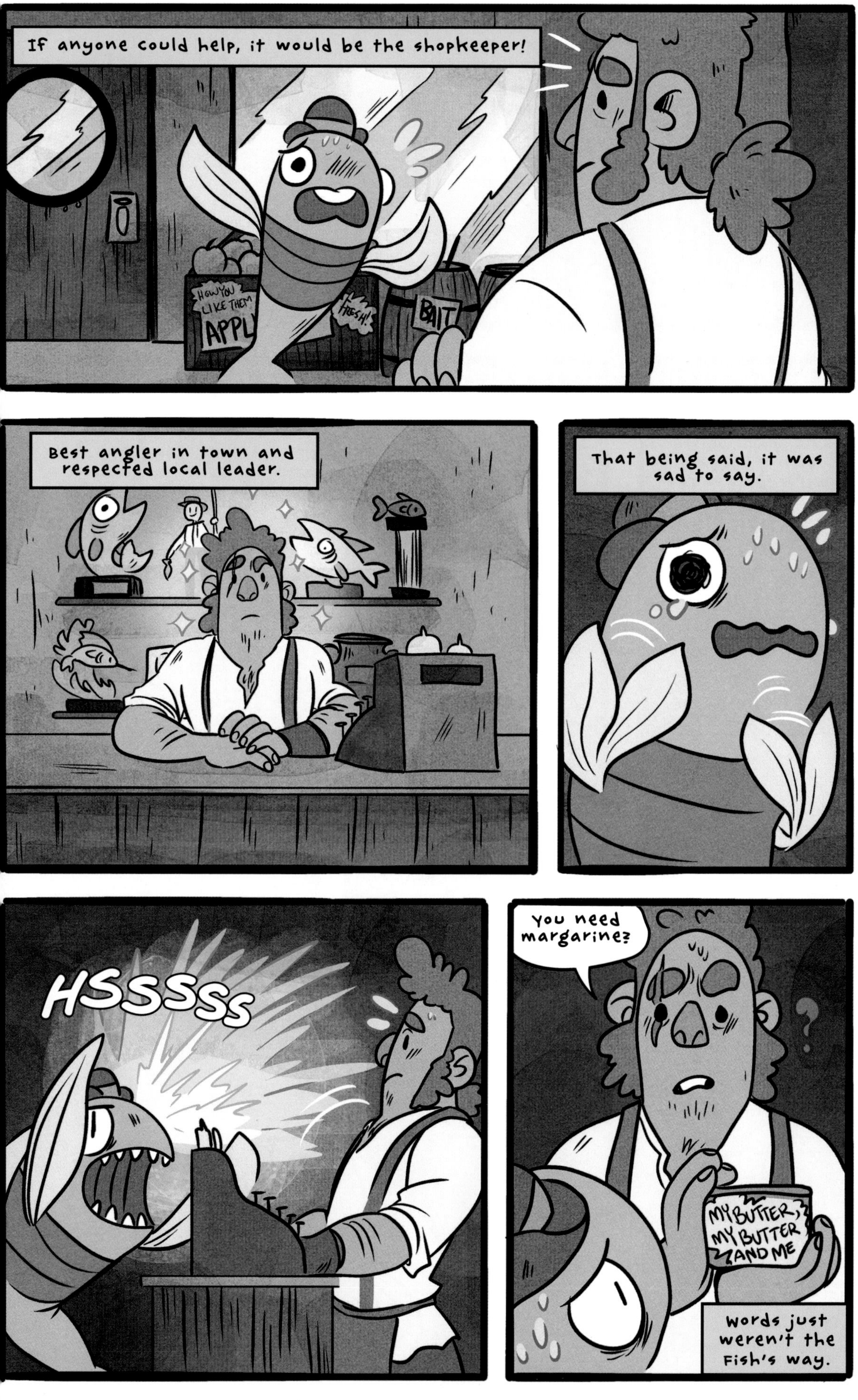
If anyone could help, it would be the shopkeeper!
HOW YOU LIKE THEM APPL
FRESH!
BAIT
Best angler in town and respected local leader.
That being said, it was sad to say.
HSSSSS
You need margarine?
MY BUTTER, MY BUTTER AND ME
Words just weren't the Fish's way.

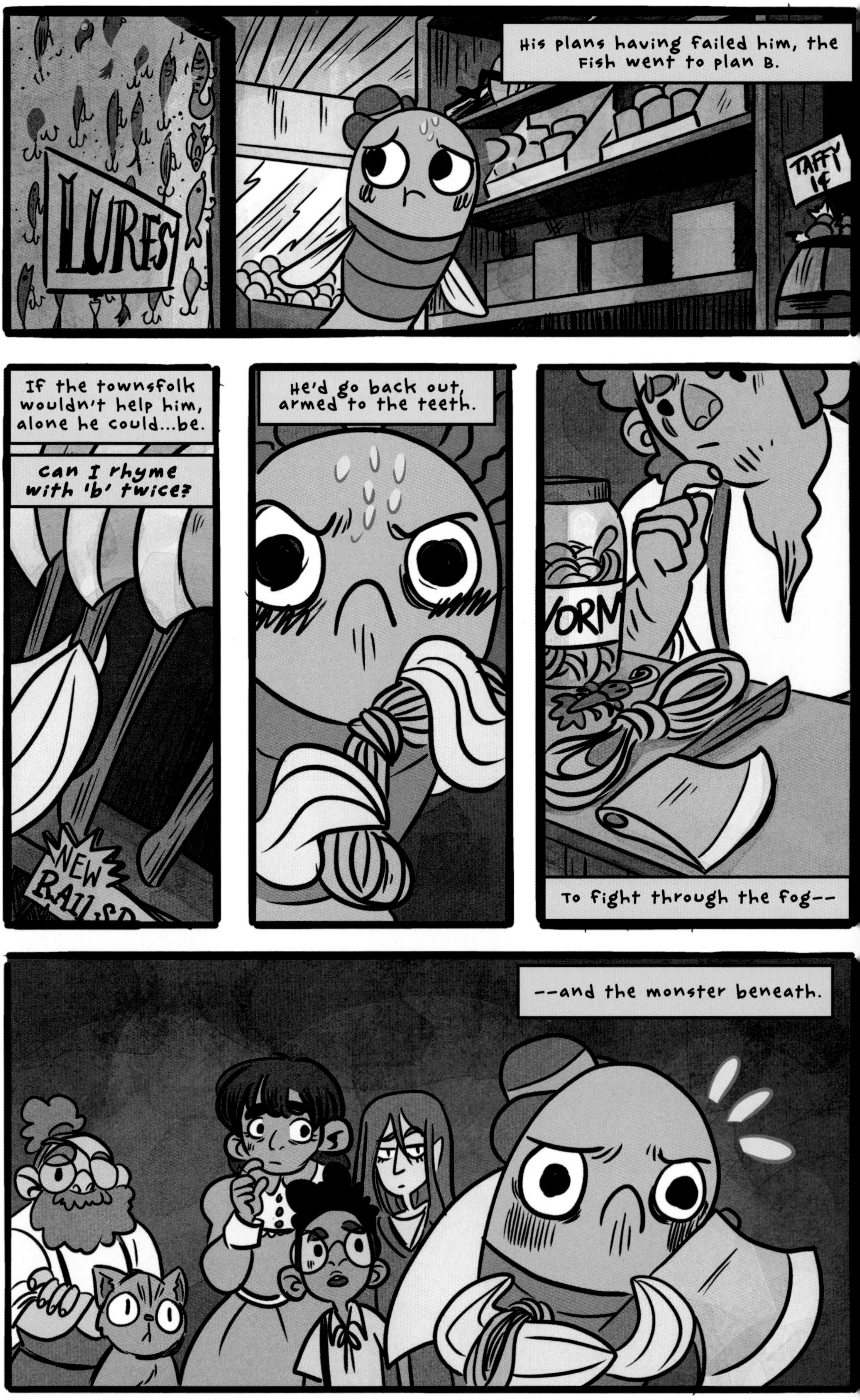

His plans having failed him, the Fish went to plan B.
LURES
TAFFY 1¢
If the townsfolk wouldn't help him, alone he could...be.
can I rhyme with 'b' twice?
NEW
He'd go back out, armed to the teeth.
WORM
To fight through the fog--
--and the monster beneath.

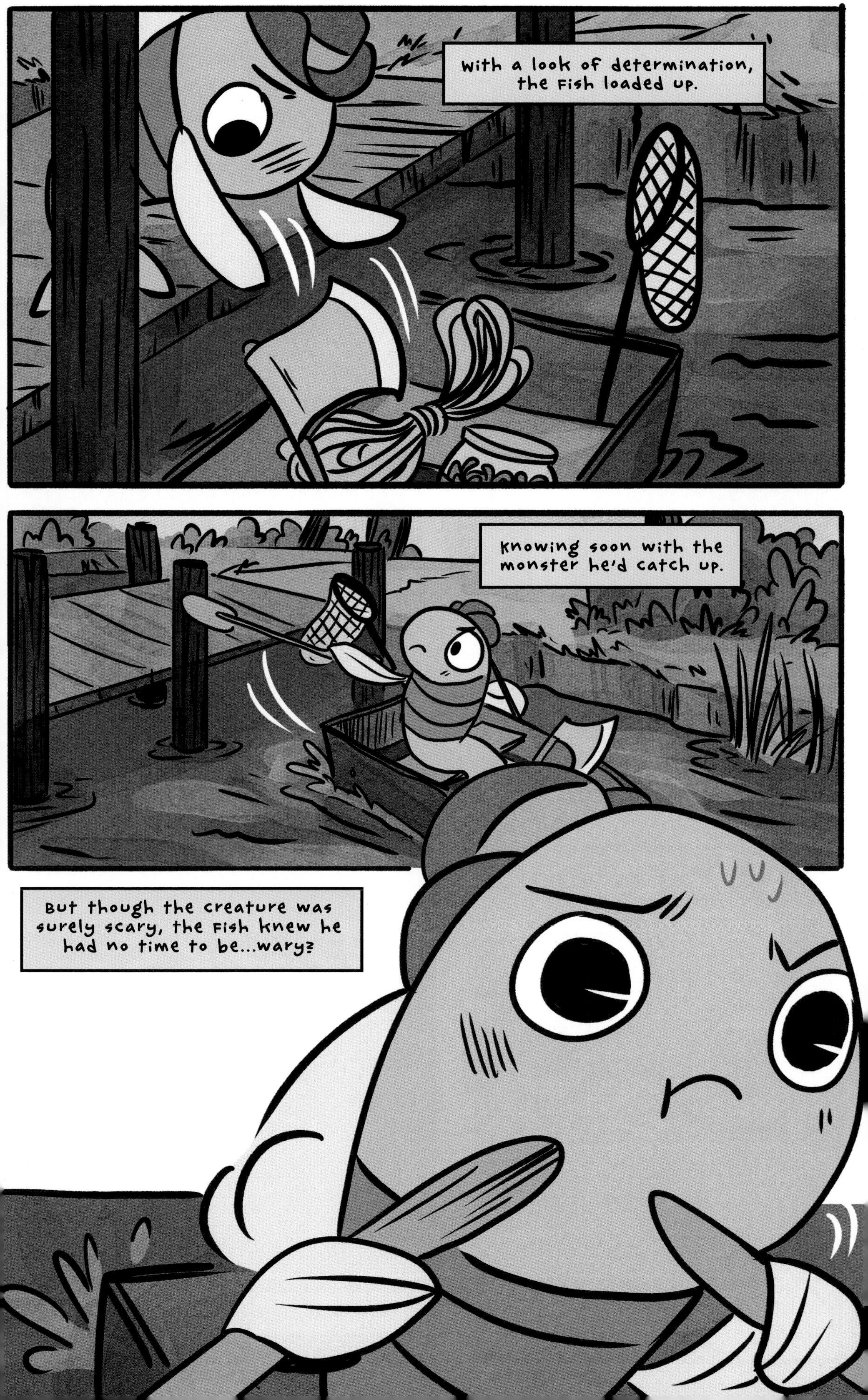
With a look of determination, the Fish loaded up.
Knowing soon with the monster he'd catch up.
But though the creature was surely scary, the Fish knew he had no time to be...wary?

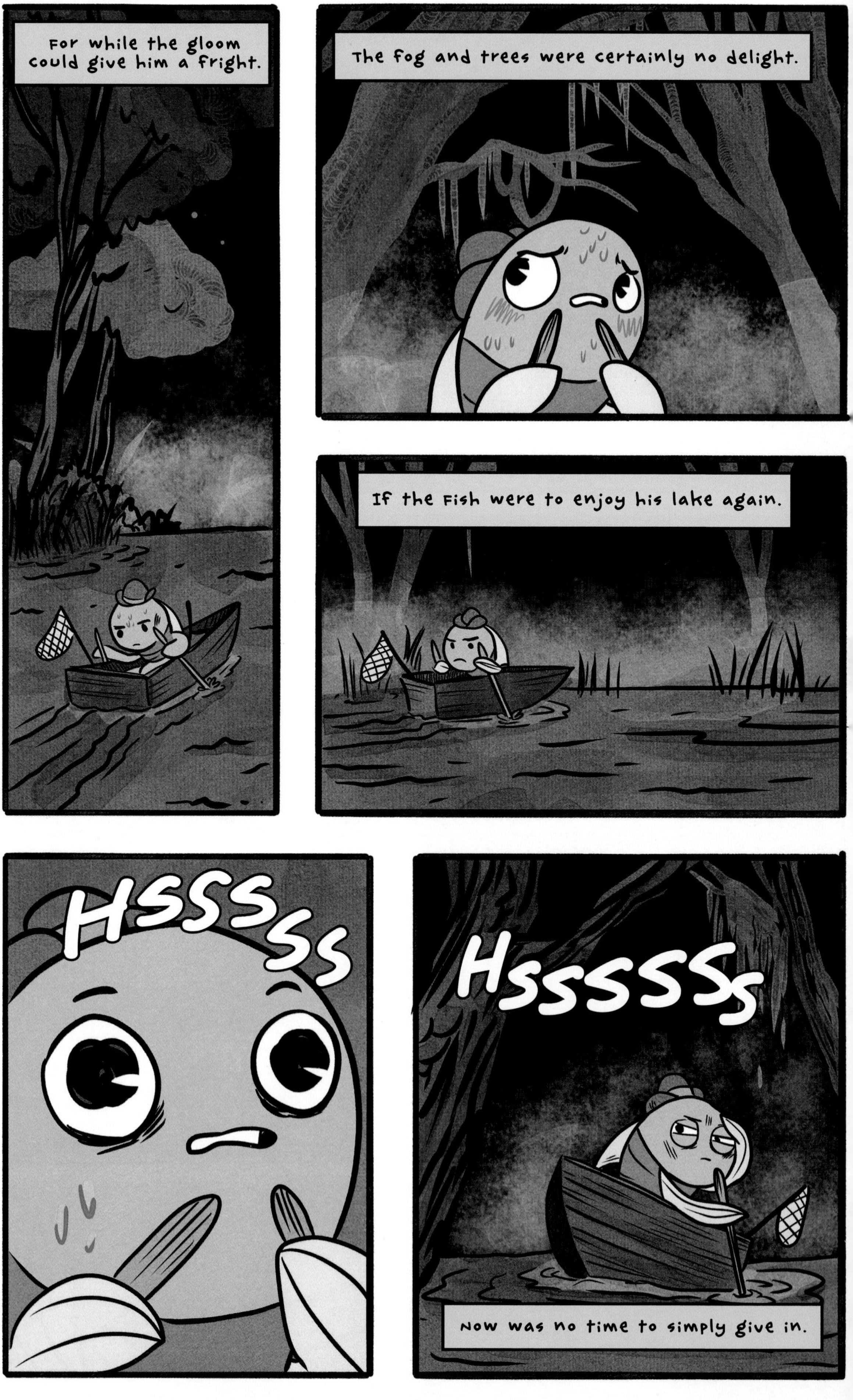
For while the gloom could give him a fright.
The fog and trees were certainly no delight.
If the Fish were to enjoy his lake again.
HSSSSS
HSSSSSS
Now was no time to simply give in.

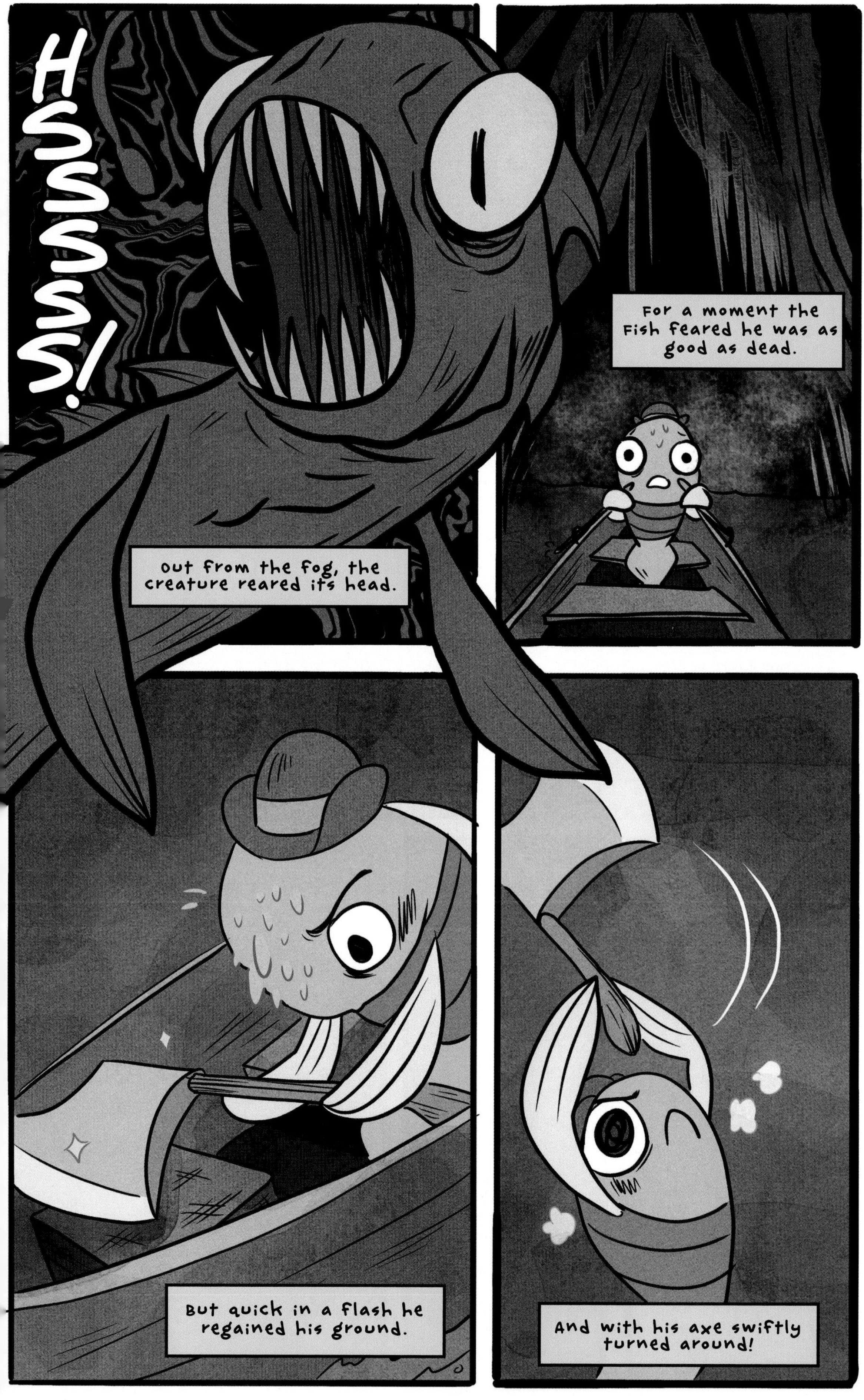
HSSSSS!
Out from the fog, the creature reared its head.
For a moment the Fish feared he was as good as dead.
But quick in a flash he regained his ground.
And with his axe swiftly turned around!

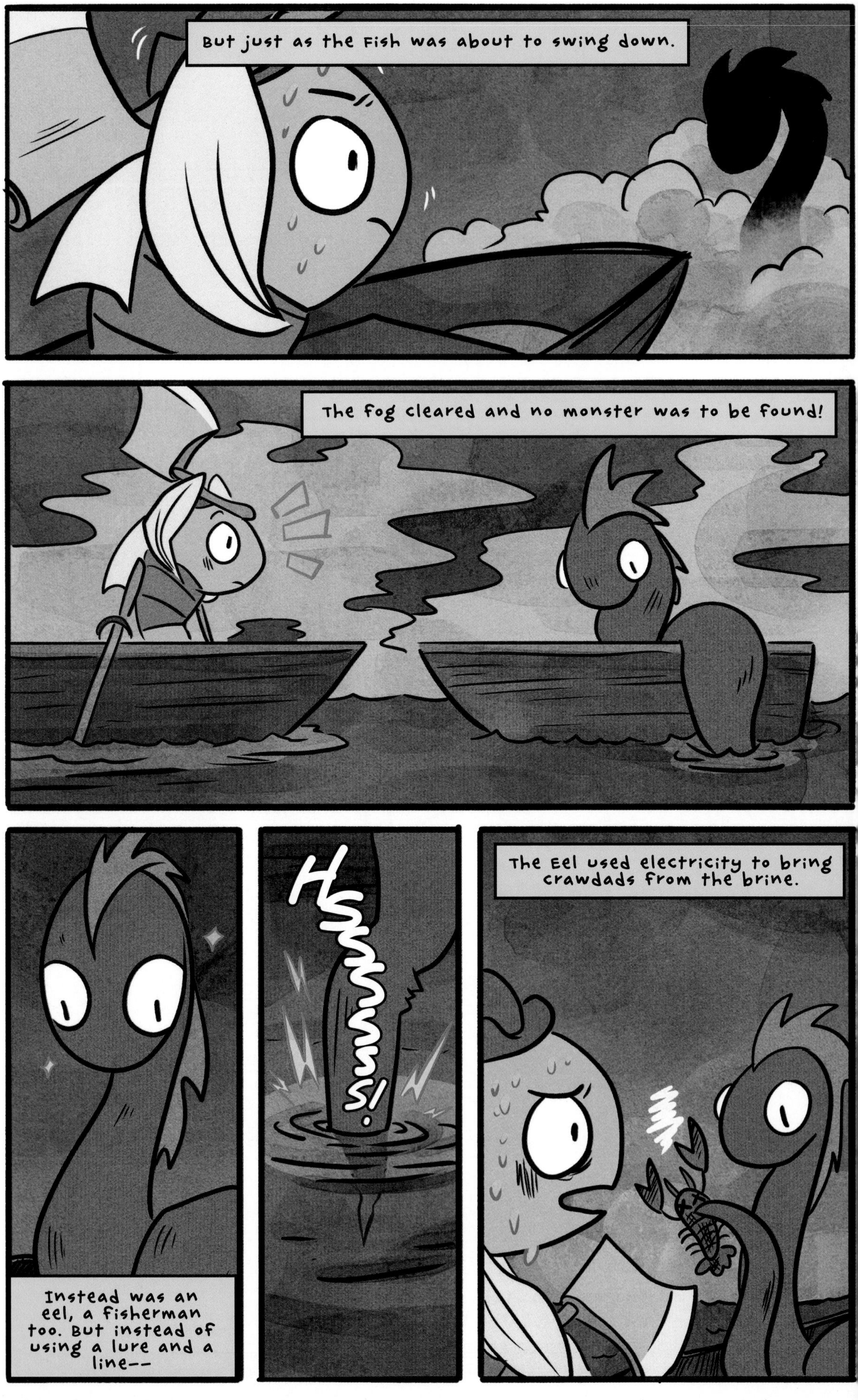
But just as the Fish was about to swing down.
The fog cleared and no monster was to be found!
Instead was an eel, a fisherman too. But instead of using a lure and a line--
Hmmmms!
The Eel used electricity to bring crawdads from the brine.

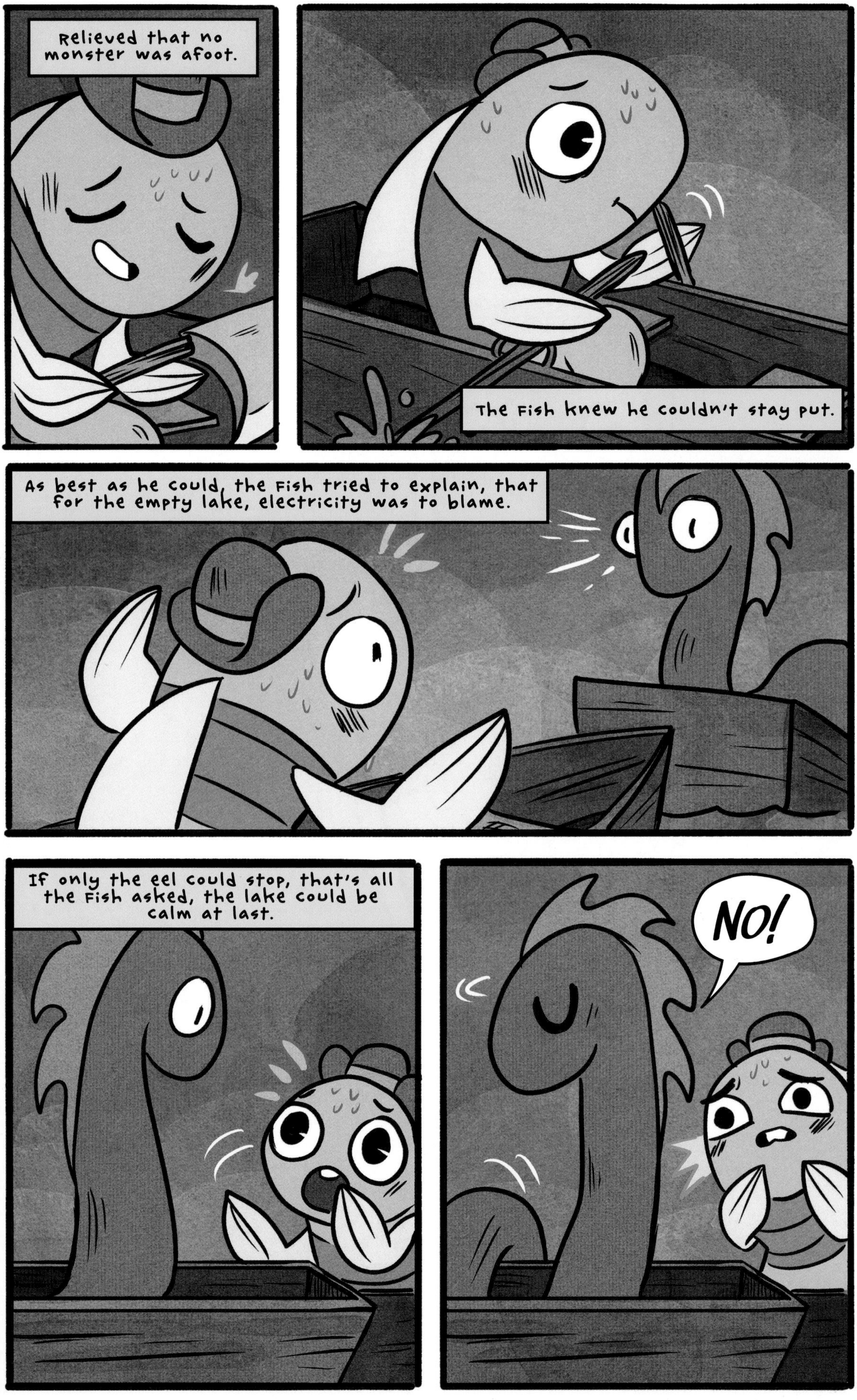
Relieved that no monster was afoot.
The Fish knew he couldn't stay put.
As best as he could, the Fish tried to explain, that for the empty lake, electricity was to blame.
If only the eel could stop, that's all the Fish asked, the lake could be calm at last.
NO!

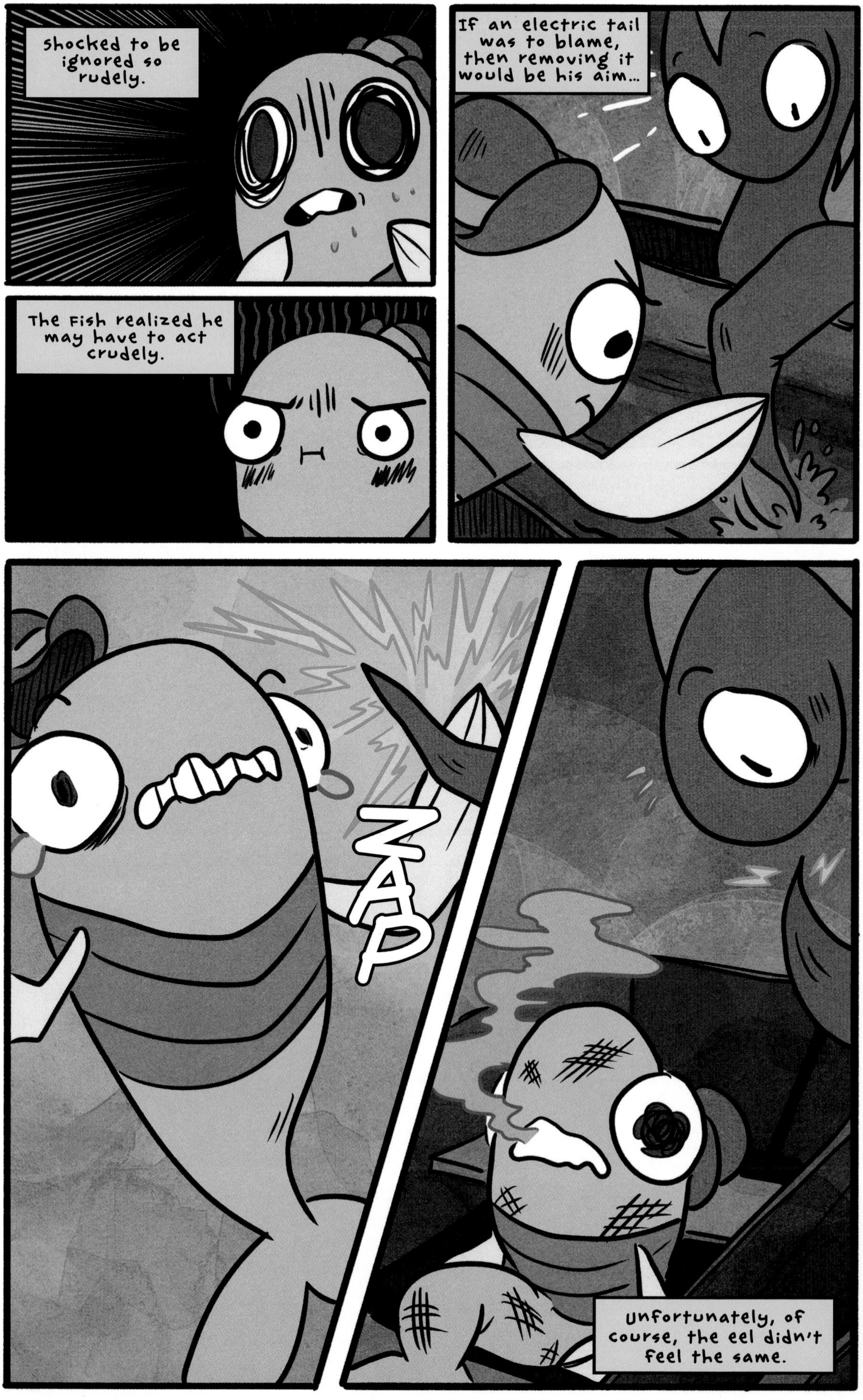
Shocked to be ignored so rudely.
If an electric tail was to blame, then removing it would be his aim...
The Fish realized he may have to act crudely.
ZAP
Unfortunately, of course, the eel didn't feel the same.

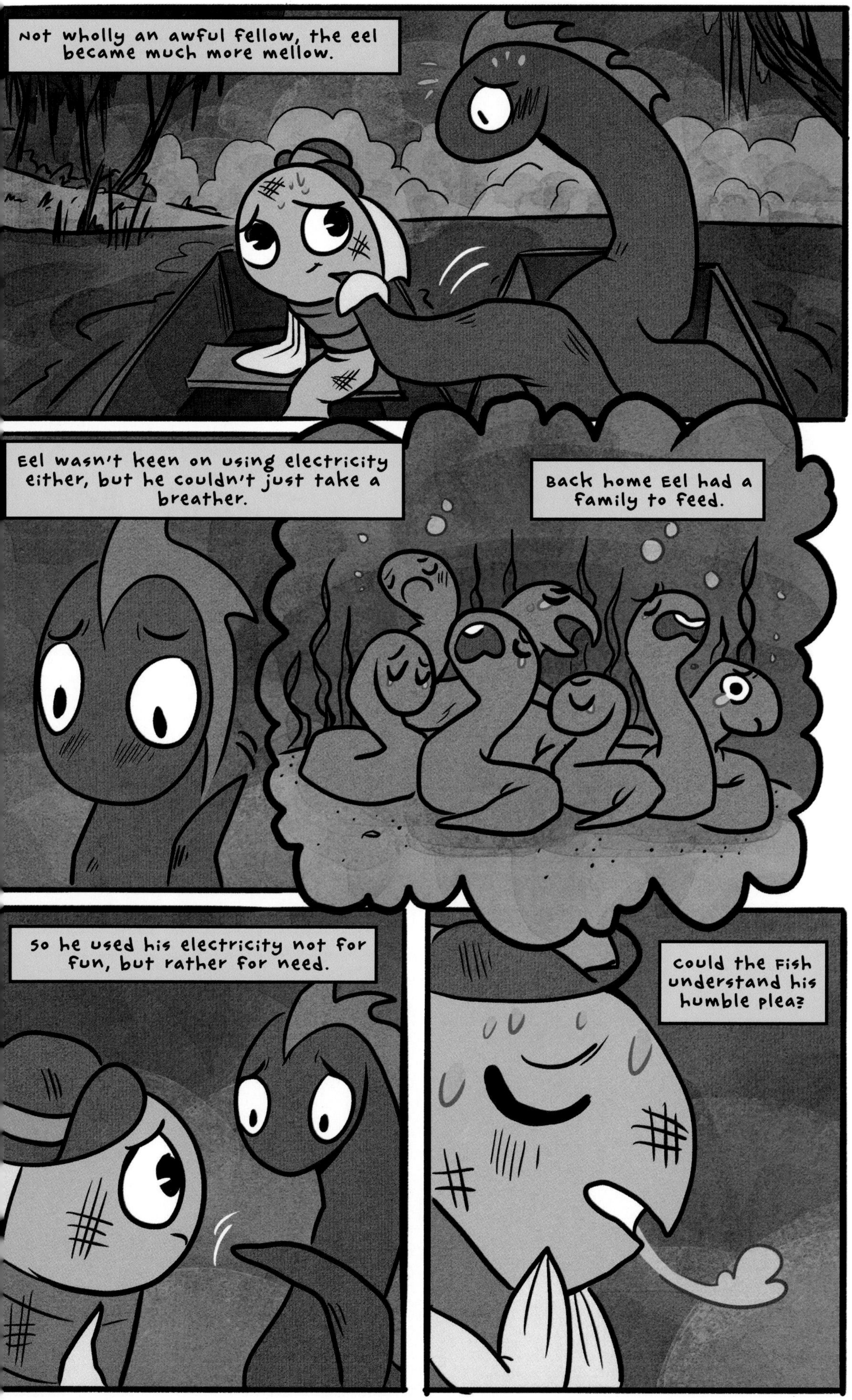
Not wholly an awful fellow, the eel became much more mellow.
Eel wasn't keen on using electricity either, but he couldn't just take a breather.
Back home Eel had a family to feed.
So he used his electricity not for fun, but rather for need.
Could the Fish understand his humble plea?

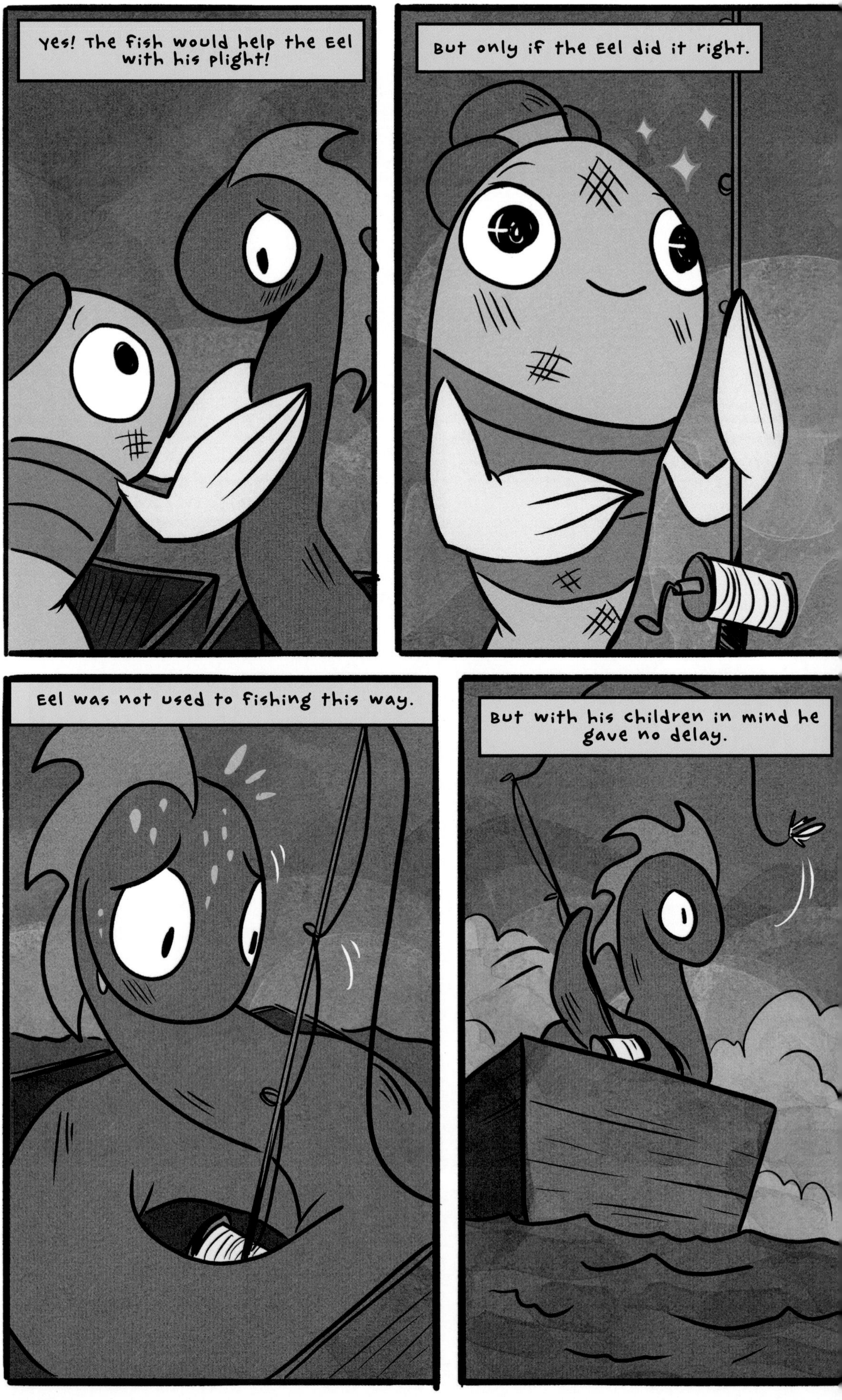
Yes! The fish would help the Eel with his plight!
But only if the Eel did it right.
Eel was not used to fishing this way.
But with his children in mind he gave no delay.

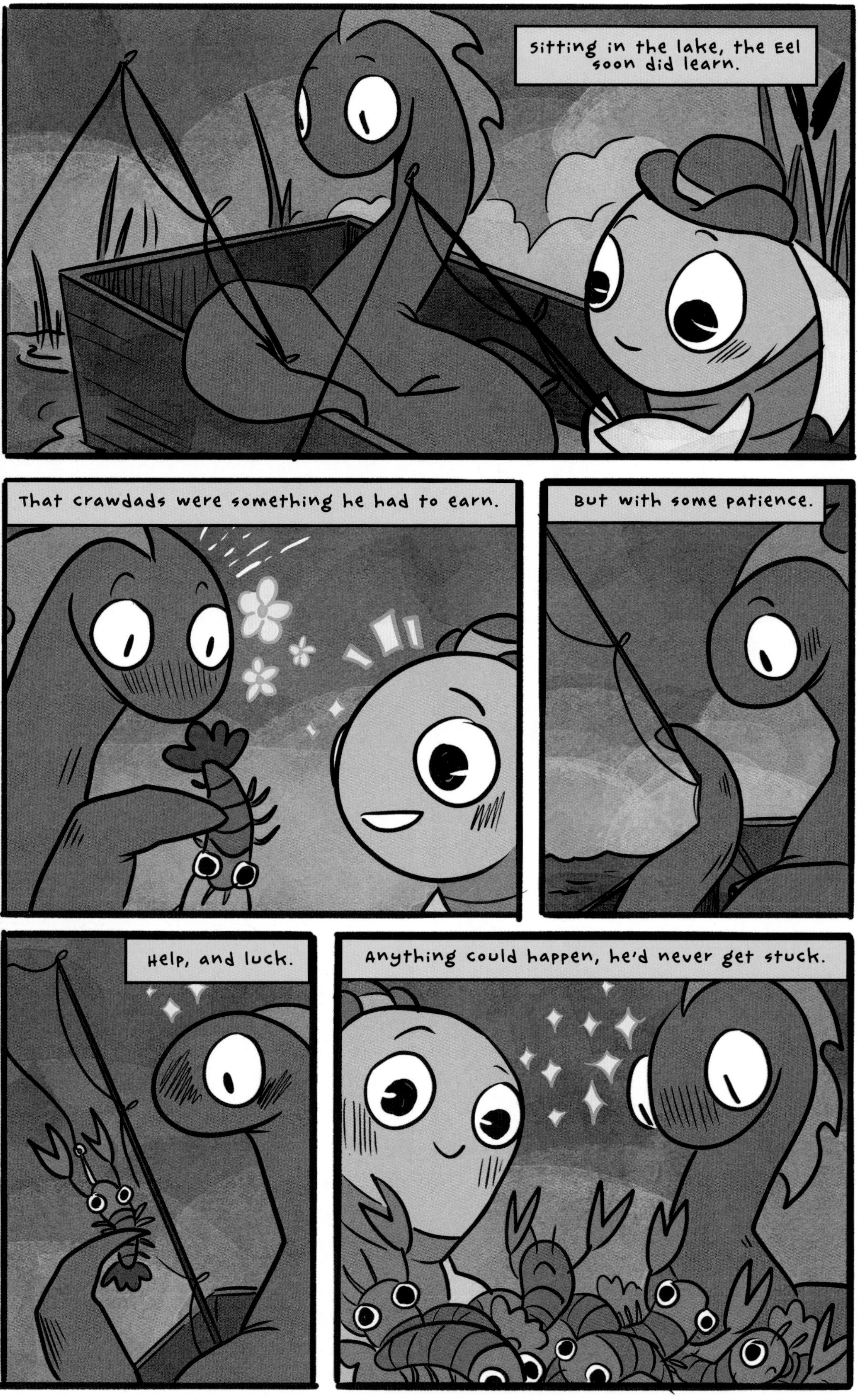
Sitting in the lake, the Eel soon did learn.
That crawdads were something he had to earn.
But with some patience.
Help, and luck.
Anything could happen, he'd never get stuck.

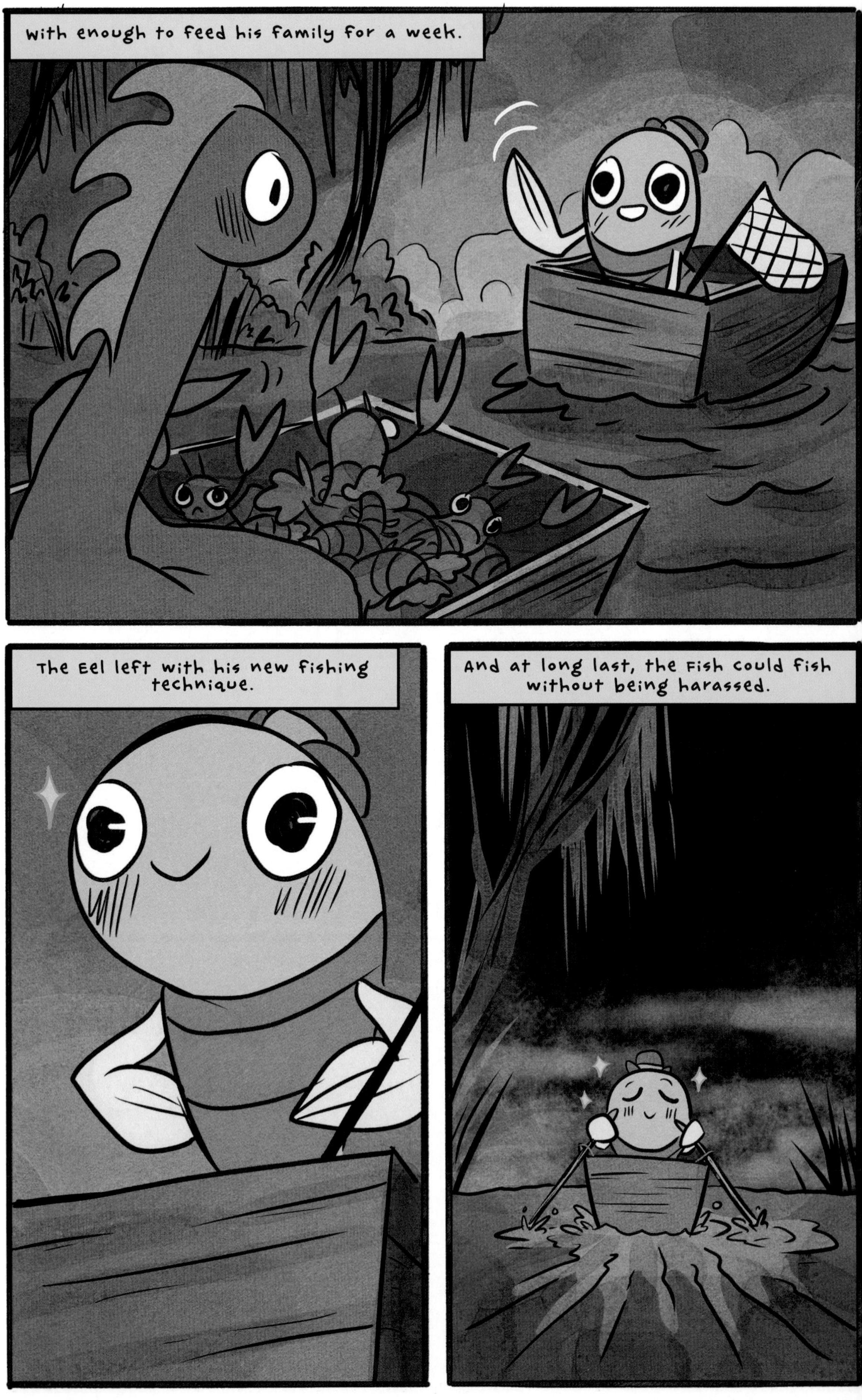
With enough to feed his family for a week.
The Eel left with his new fishing technique.
And at long last, the Fish could fish without being harassed.

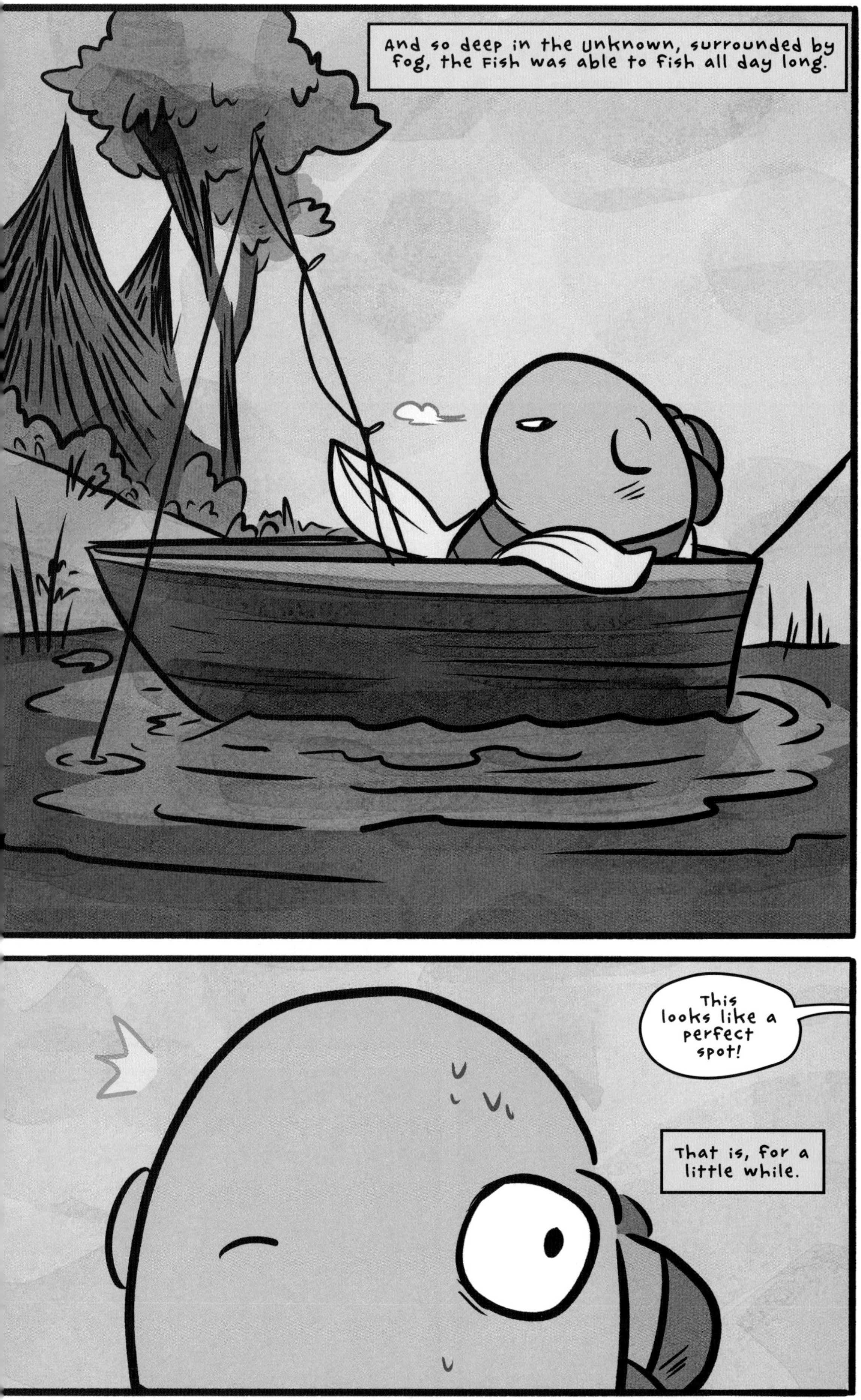
And so deep in the unknown, surrounded by fog, the Fish was able to fish all day long.
This looks like a perfect spot!
That is, for a little while.

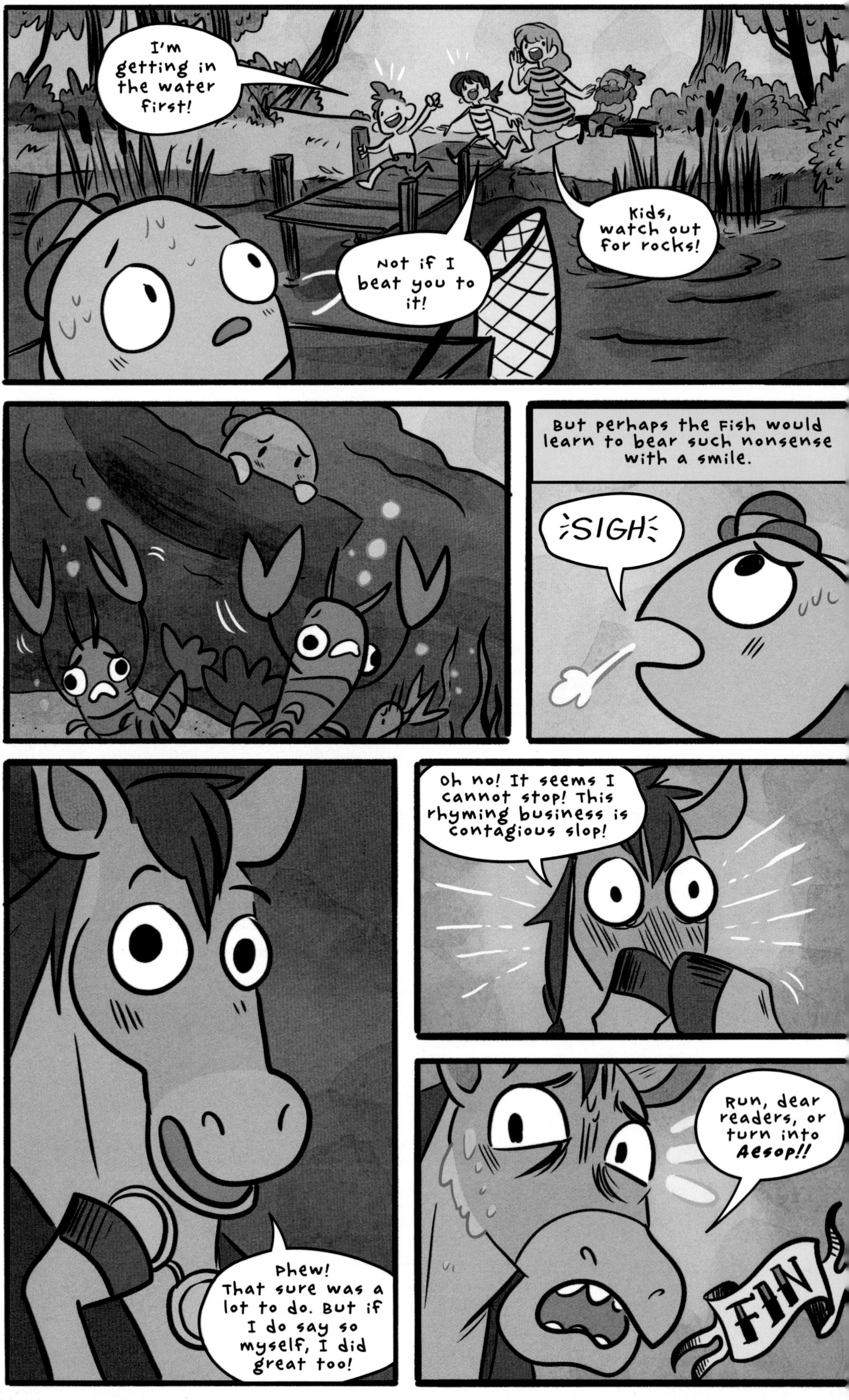
I'm getting in the water first!
Not if I beat you to it!
Kids, watch out for rocks!
But perhaps the Fish would learn to bear such nonsense with a smile.
SIGH
Phew! That sure was a lot to do. But if I do say so myself, I did great too!
Oh no! It seems I cannot stop! This rhyming business is contagious slop!
Run, dear readers, or turn into Aesop!!
FIN

TEA'D OFF

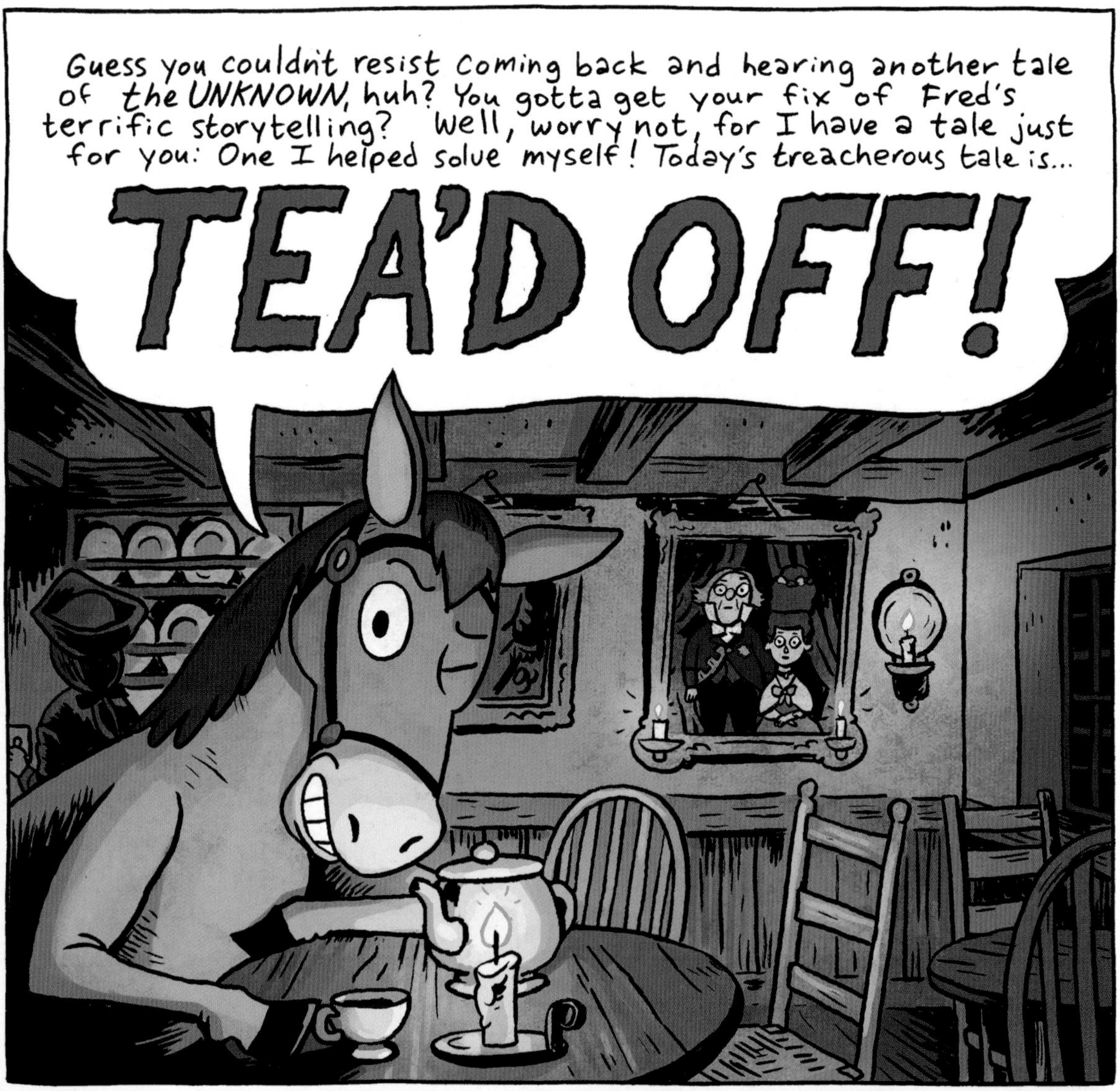
Guess you couldn't resist coming back and hearing another tale of the UNKNOWN, huh? You gotta get your fix of Fred's terrific storytelling? Well, worry not, for I have a tale just for you: One I helped solve myself! Today's treacherous tale is...
TEA'D OFF!

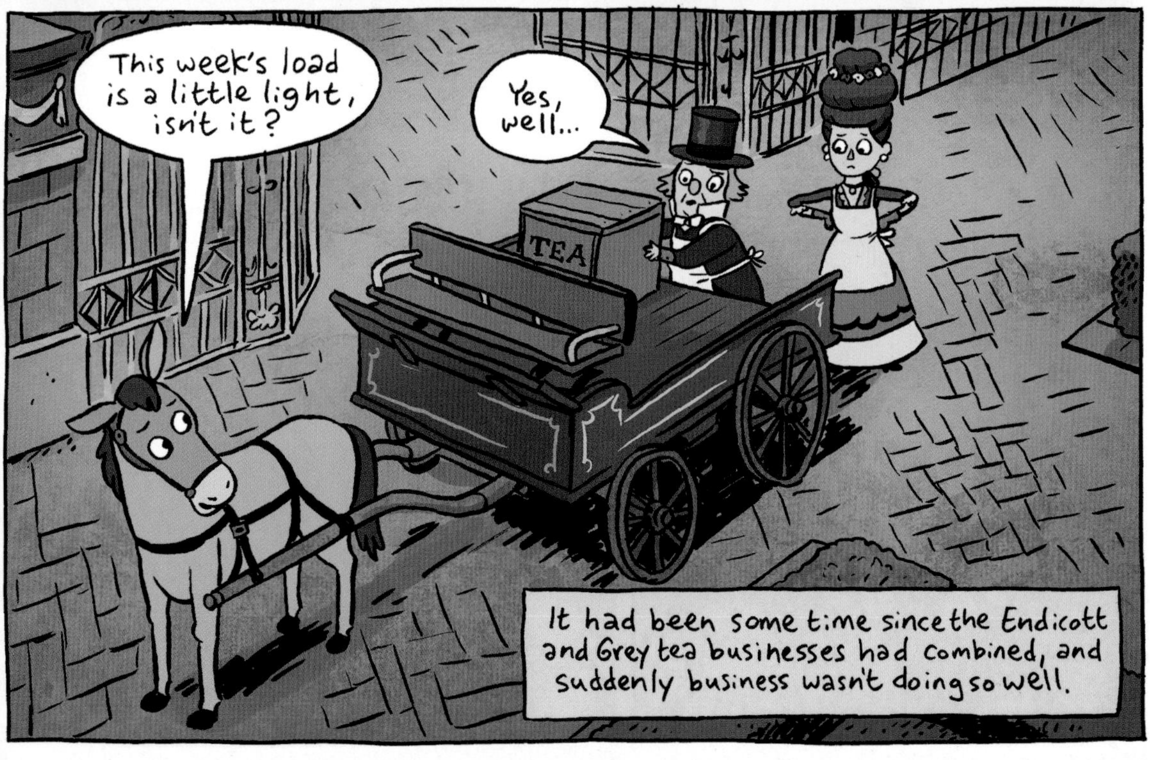
This week's load is a little light, isn't it?
Yes, well...
TEA
It had been some time since the Endicott and Grey tea businesses had combined, and suddenly business wasn't doing so well.

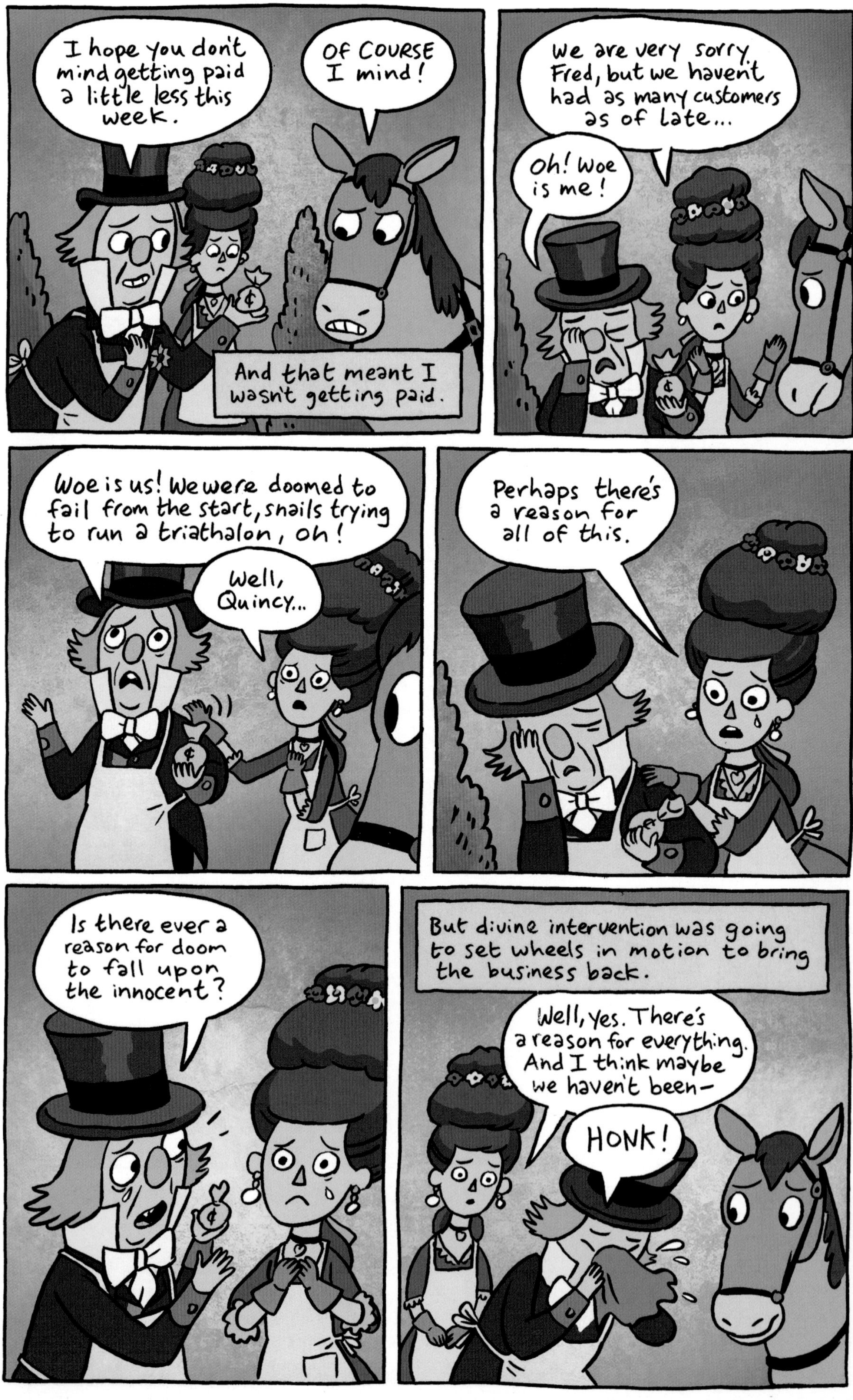
I hope you don't mind getting paid a little less this week.
OF COURSE I mind!
And that meant I wasn't getting paid.
We are very sorry, Fred, but we haven't had as many customers as of late...
Oh! Woe is me!
Woe is us! We were doomed to fail from the start, snails trying to run a triathalon, oh!
Well, Quincy...
Perhaps there's a reason for all of this.
Is there ever a reason for doom to fall upon the innocent?
But divine intervention was going to set wheels in motion to bring the business back.
Well, yes. There's a reason for everything. And I think maybe we haven't been—
HONK!

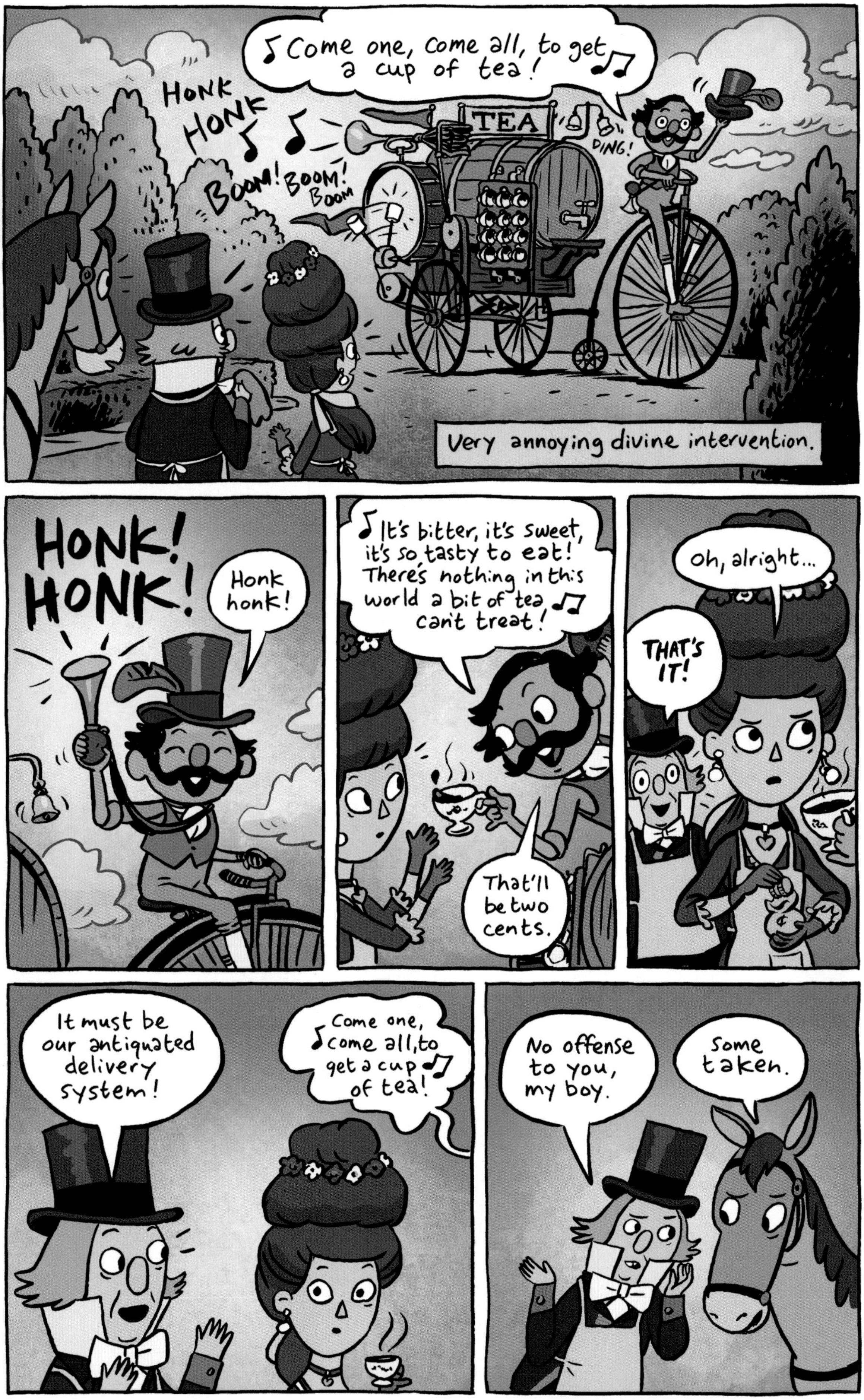
Come one, come all, to get a cup of tea!
HONK HONK
BOOM! BOOM! BOOM
TEA
DING!
Very annoying divine intervention.
HONK! HONK!
Honk honk!
It's bitter, it's sweet, it's so tasty to eat! There's nothing in this world a bit of tea can't treat!
That'll be two cents.
Oh, alright...
THAT'S IT!
It must be our antiquated delivery system!
Come one, come all, to get a cup of tea!
No offense to you, my boy.
Some taken.

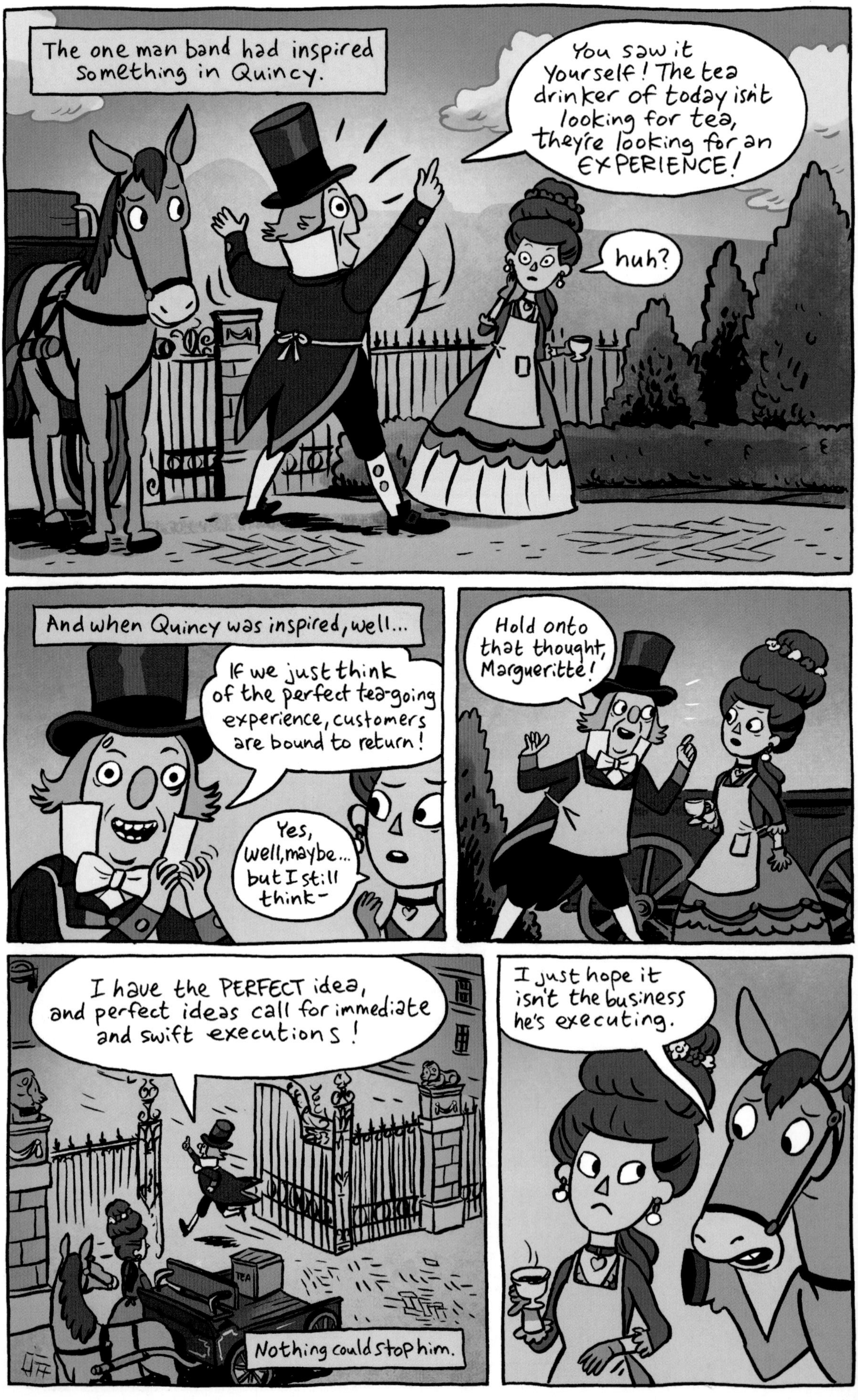
The one man band had inspired something in Quincy.
You saw it Yourself! The tea drinker of today isn't looking for tea, they're looking for an EXPERIENCE!
huh?
And when Quincy was inspired, well...
If we just think of the perfect tea-going experience, customers are bound to return!
Yes, well, maybe... but I still think-
Hold onto that thought, Margueritte!
I have the PERFECT idea, and perfect ideas call for immediate and swift executions!
TEA
Nothing could stop him.
I just hope it isn't the business he's executing.

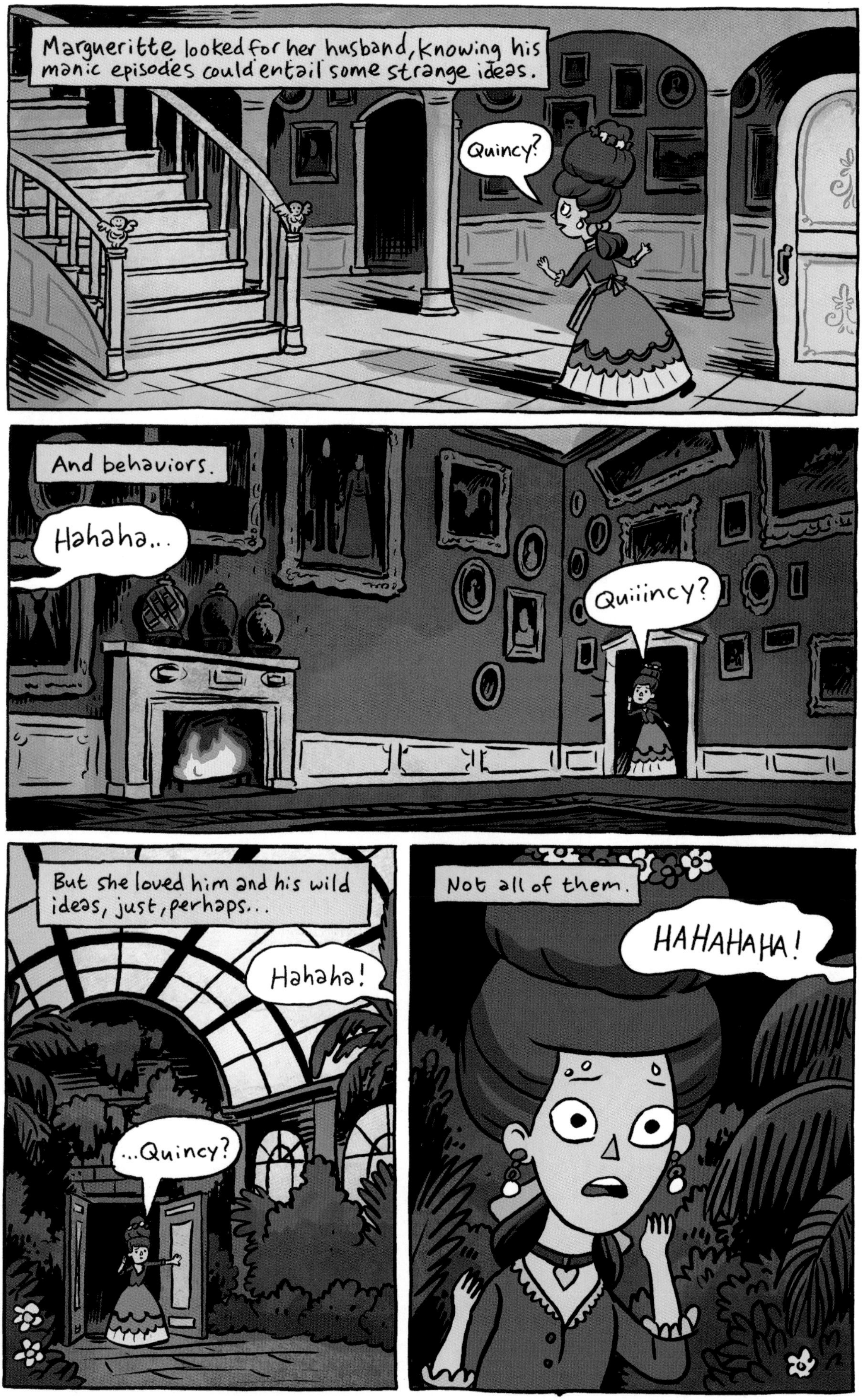
Margueritte looked for her husband, knowing his manic episodes could entail some strange ideas.
Quincy?
And behaviors.
Hahaha...
Quiiincy?
But she loved him and his wild ideas, just, perhaps...
Hahaha!
...Quincy?
Not all of them.
HAHAHAHA!

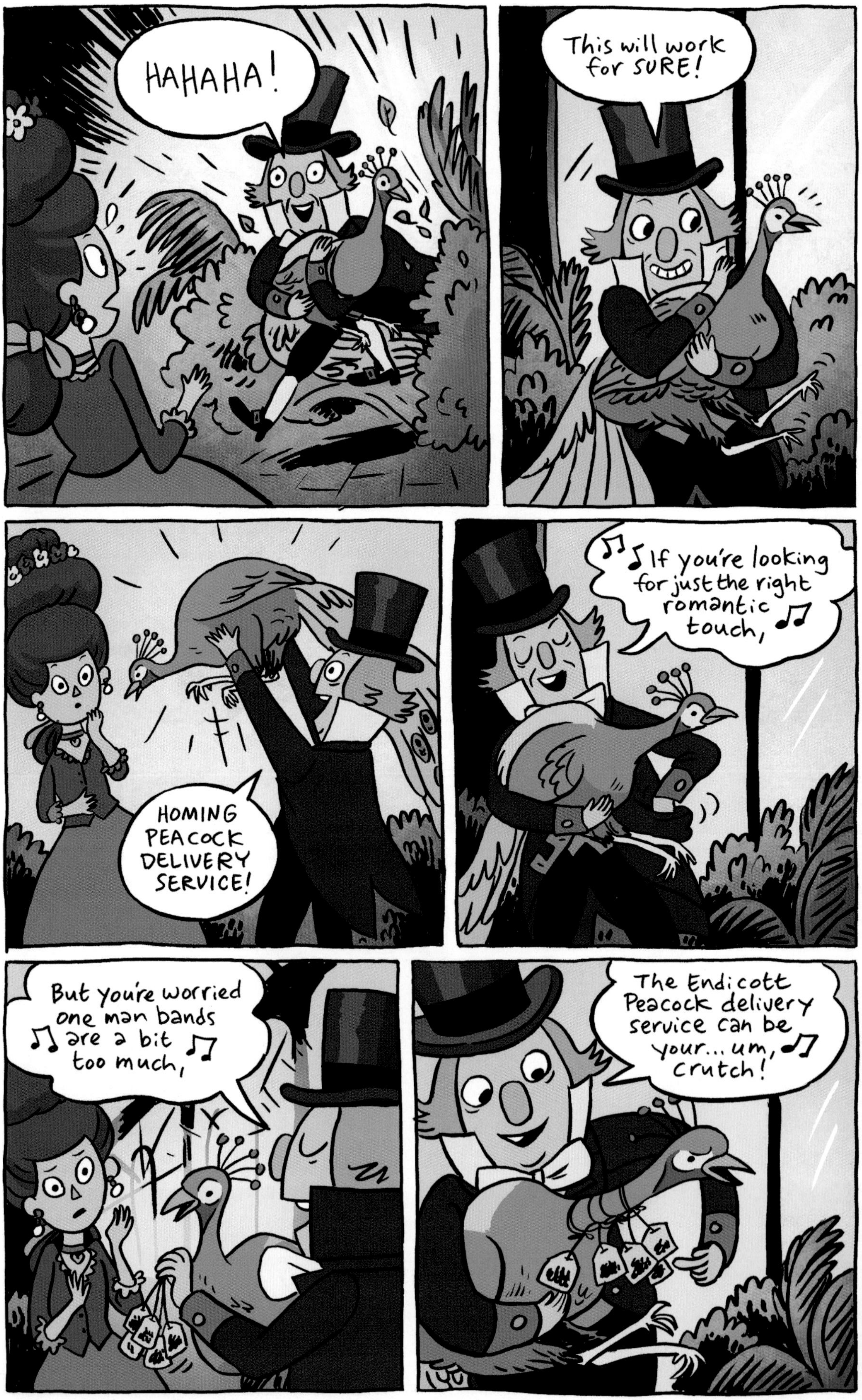
HAHAHA!
This will work for SURE!
HOMING PEACOCK DELIVERY SERVICE!
♫ ♩ If you're looking for just the right romantic touch, ♫
But you're worried one man bands ♫ are a bit too much, ♫
The Endicott Peacock delivery service can be your... um, ♫ crutch!

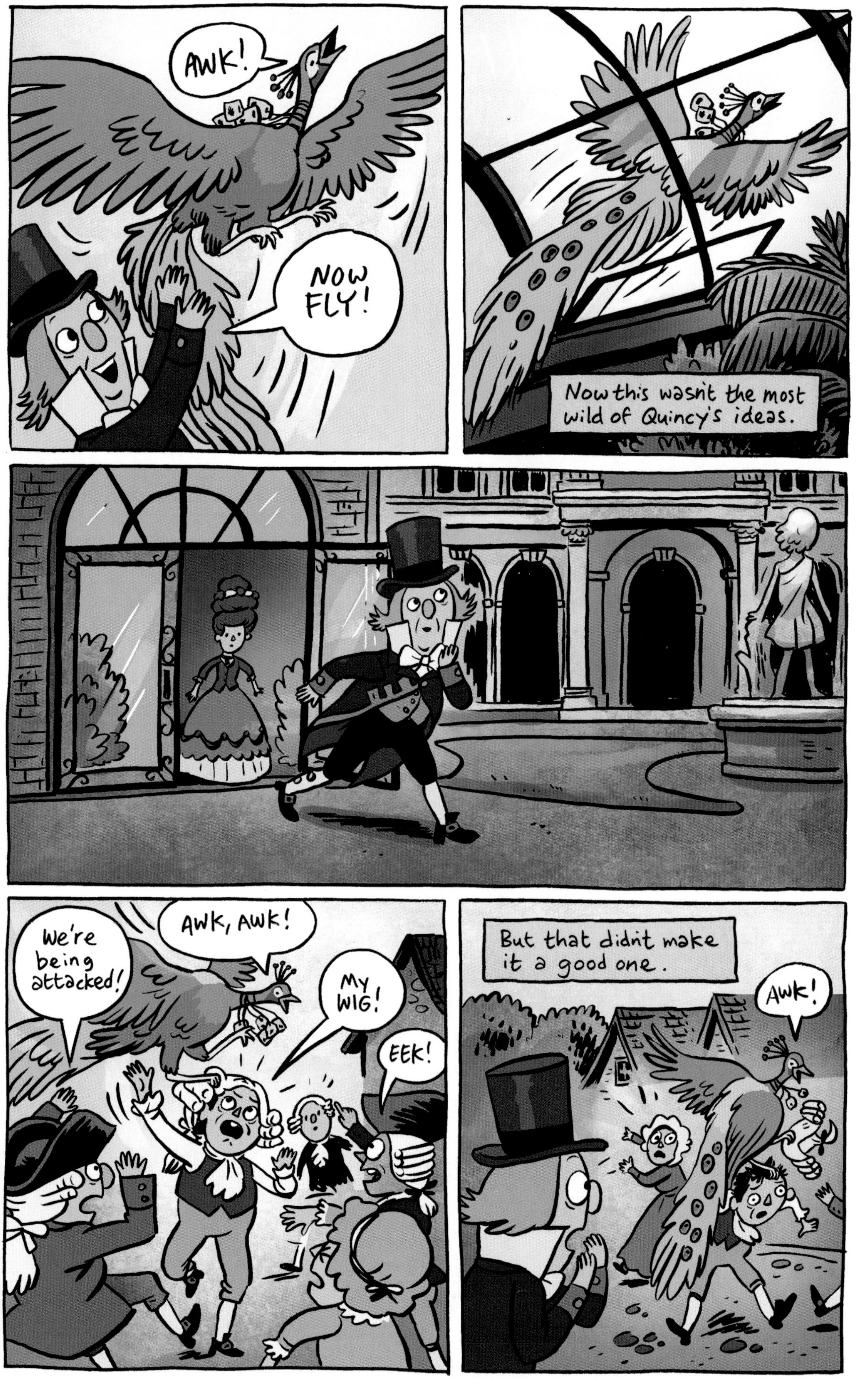
AWK!
NOW FLY!
Now this wasn't the most wild of Quincy's ideas.
We're being attacked!
AWK, AWK!
MY WIG!
EEK!
But that didn't make it a good one.
AWK!

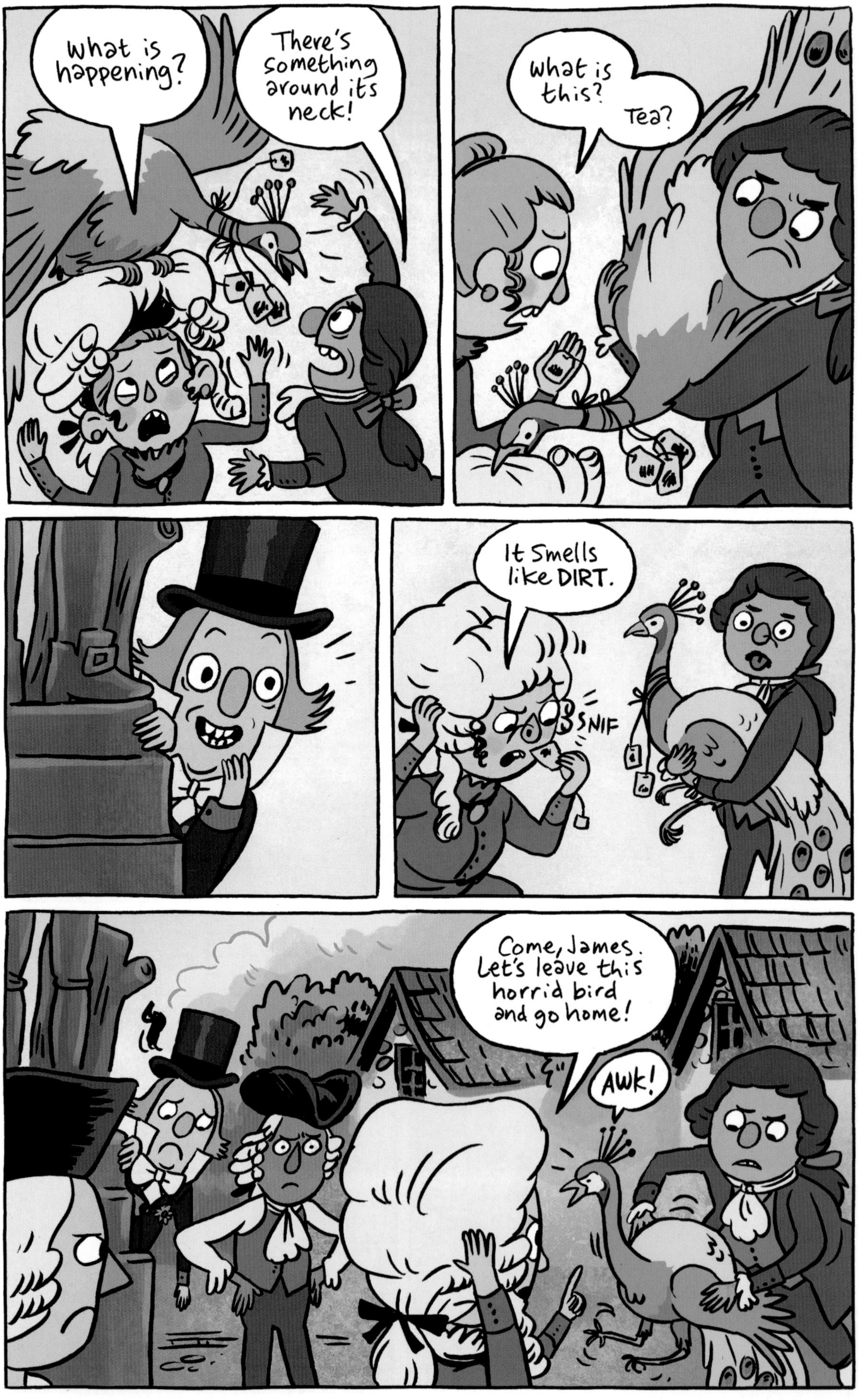
What is happening?
There's something around its neck!
What is this?
Tea?
It Smells like DIRT.
SNIF
Come, James. Let's leave this horrid bird and go home!
AWK!

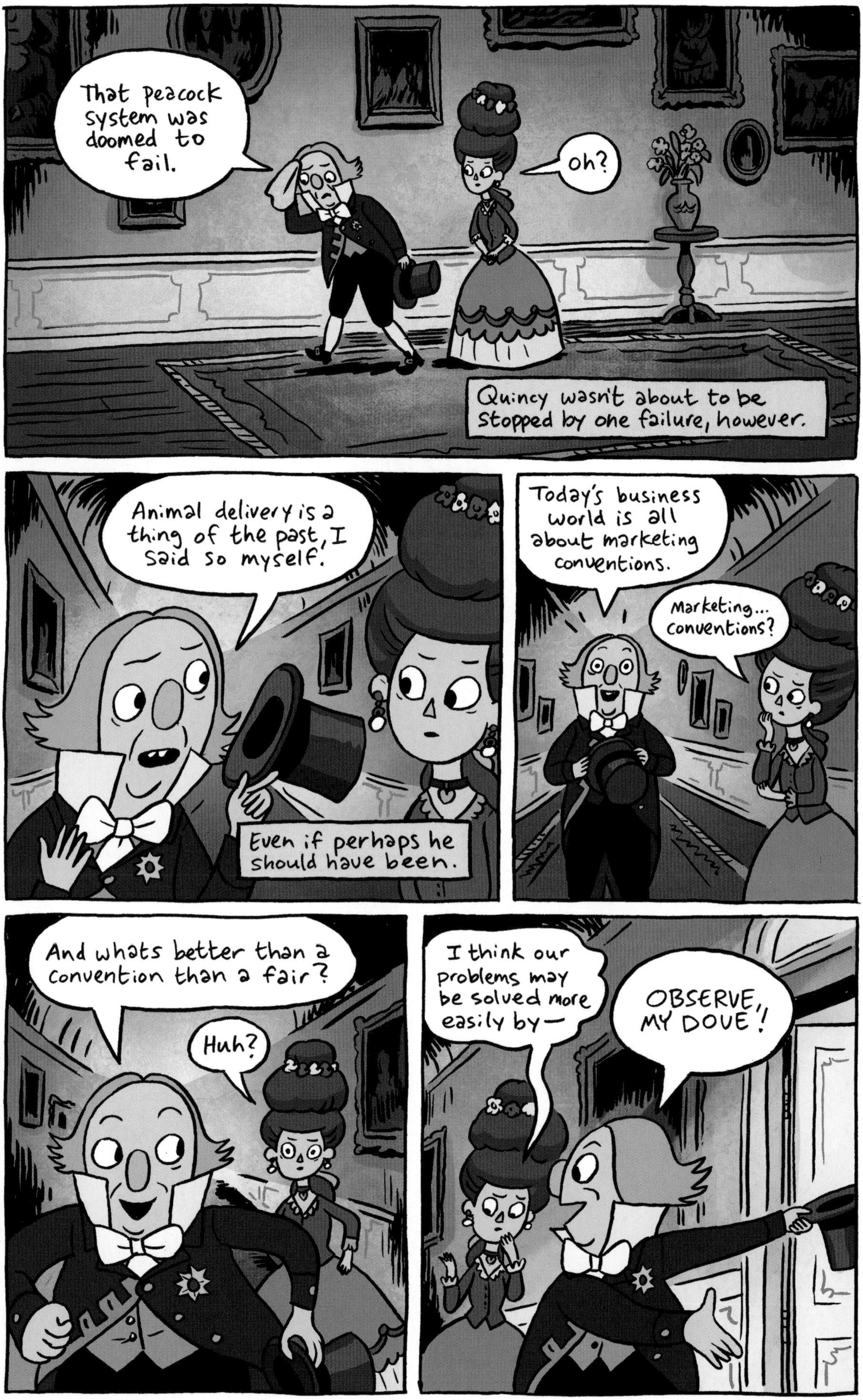
That peacock system was doomed to fail.
Oh?
Quincy wasn't about to be stopped by one failure, however.
Animal delivery is a thing of the past, I said so myself.
Even if perhaps he should have been.
Today's business world is all about marketing conventions.
Marketing... conventions?
And whats better than a convention than a fair?
Huh?
I think our problems may be solved more easily by—
OBSERVE, MY DOVE!!

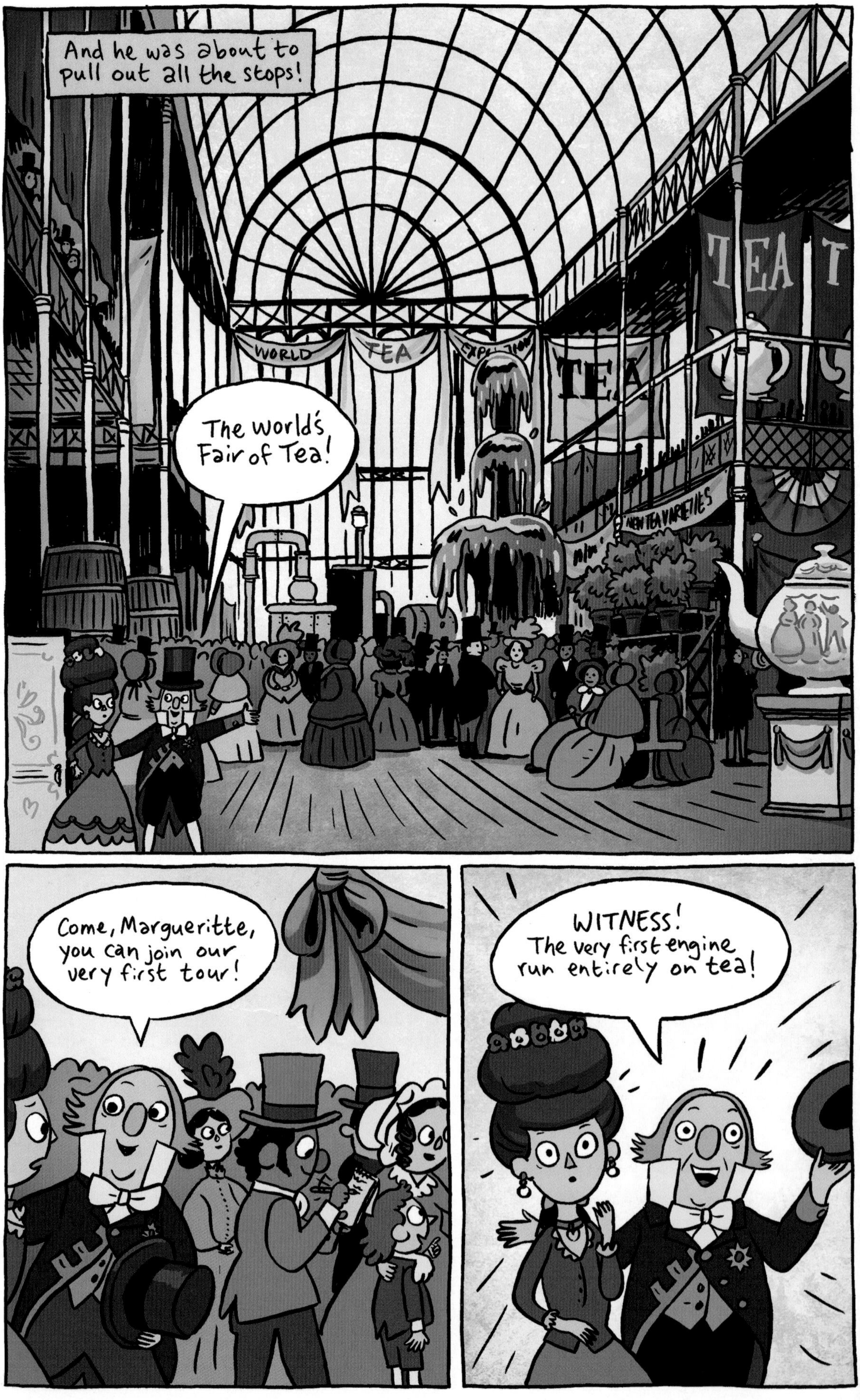
And he was about to pull out all the stops!
The world's Fair of Tea!
WORLD
TEA
TEA
TEA
NEW TEA VARIETIES
Come, Margueritte, you can join our very first tour!
WITNESS! The very first engine run entirely on tea!

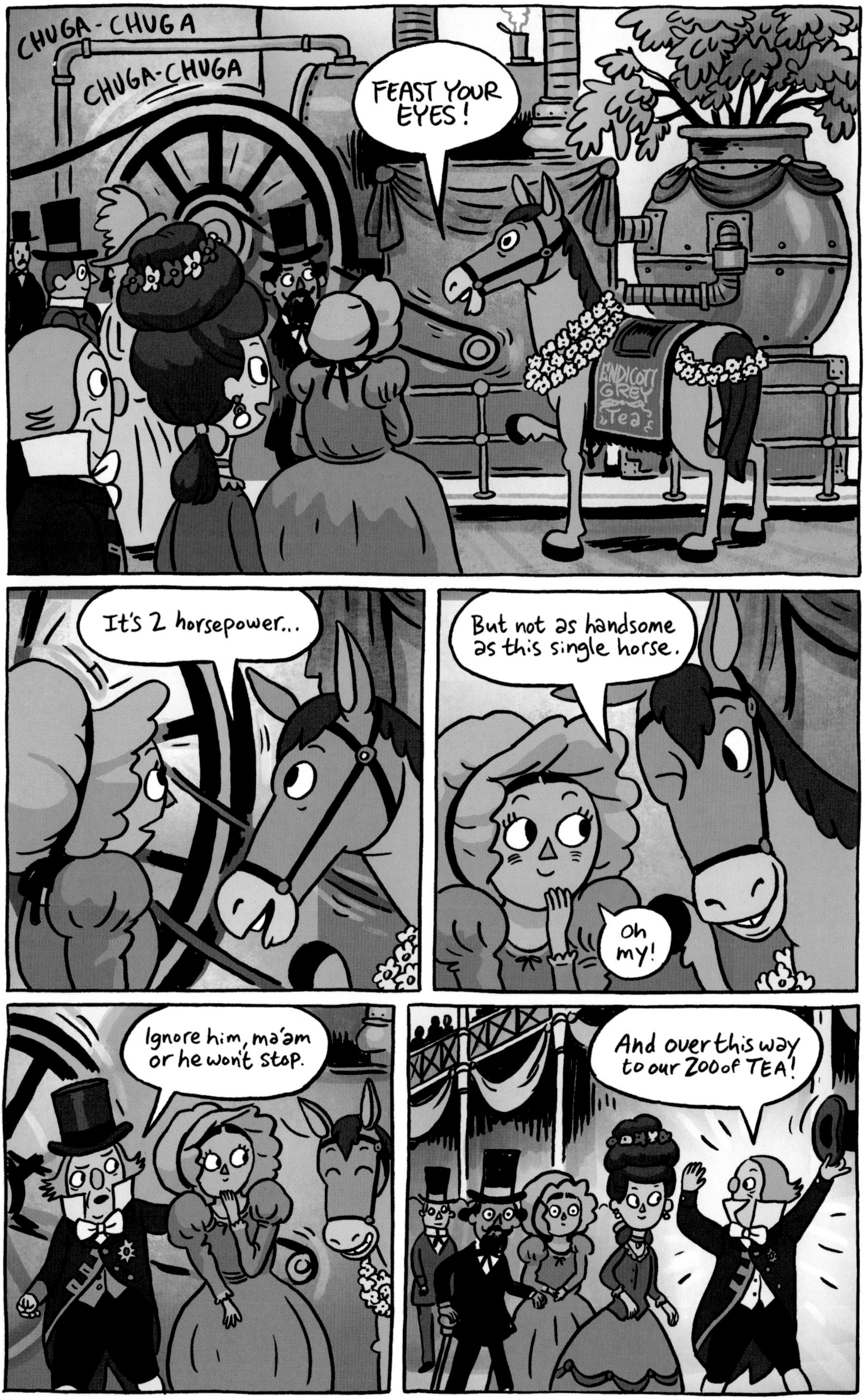
CHUGA-CHUGA
CHUGA-CHUGA
FEAST YOUR EYES!
ENDICOTT GREY Tea
It's 2 horsepower...
But not as handsome as this single horse.
Oh my!
Ignore him, ma'am or he won't stop.
And over this way to our ZOO of TEA!

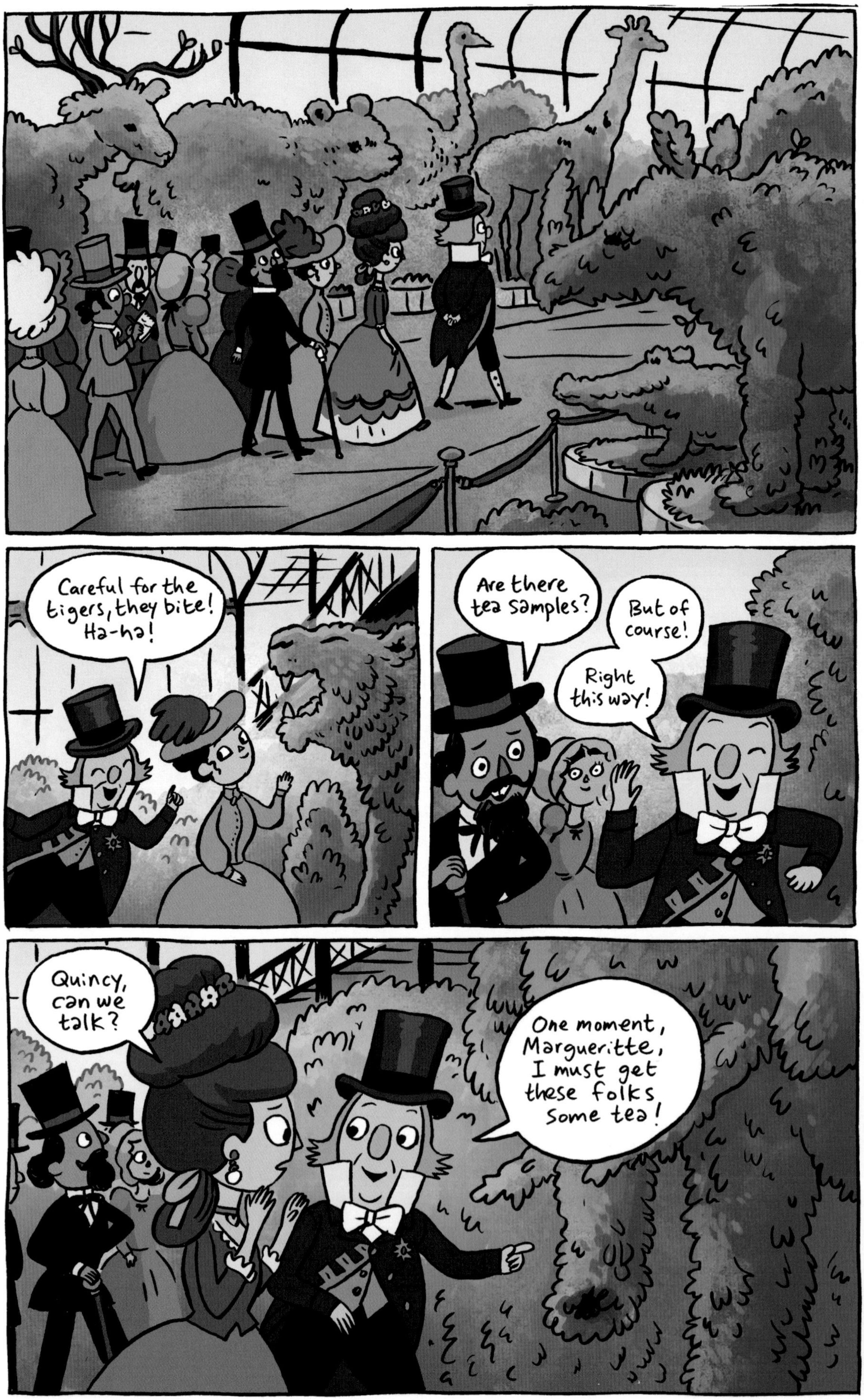
Careful for the tigers, they bite! Ha-ha!
Are there tea samples?
But of course!
Right this way!
Quincy, can we talk?
One moment, Margueritte, I must get these folks some tea!

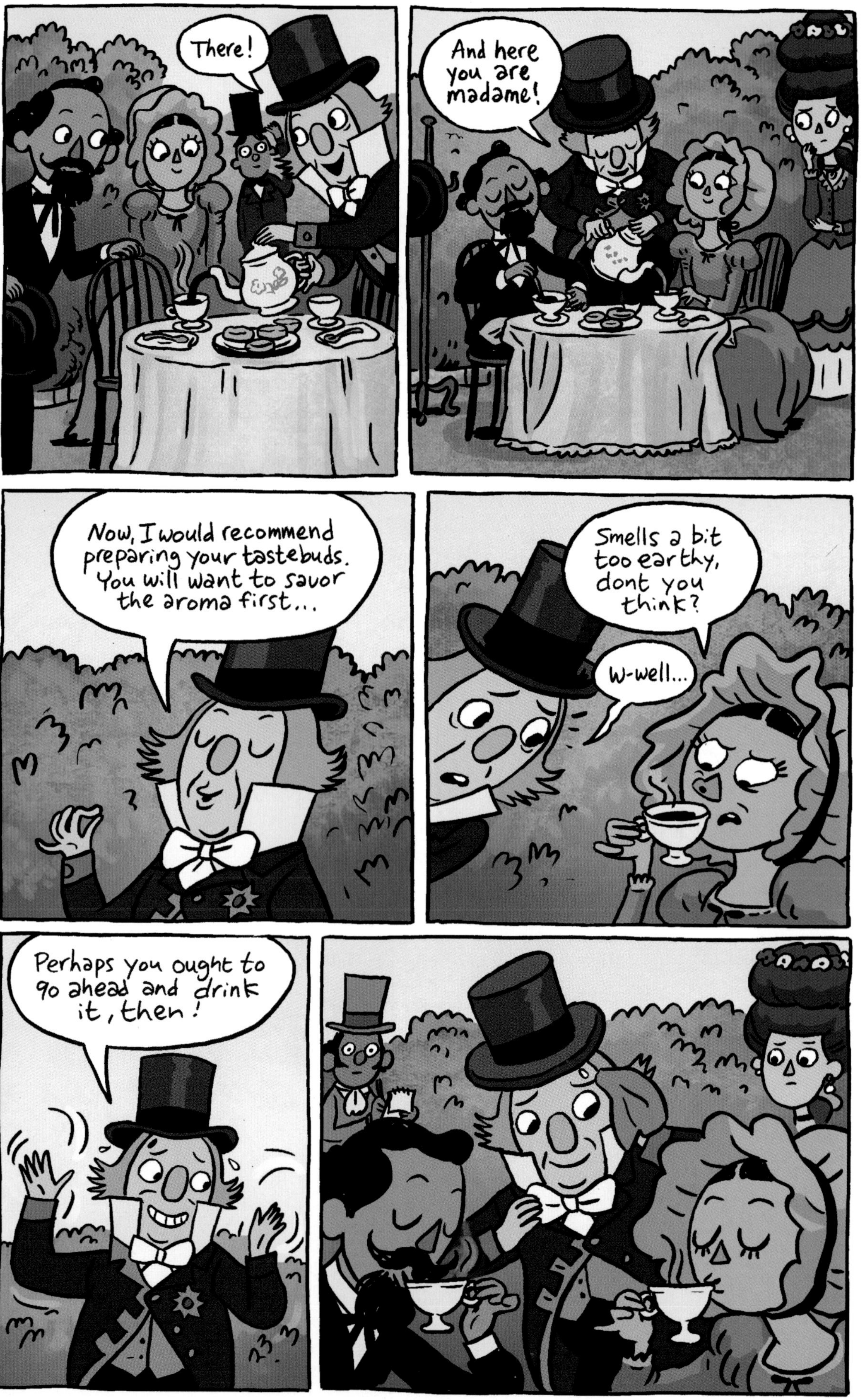
There!
And here you are madame!
Now, I would recommend preparing your tastebuds. You will want to savor the aroma first...
Smells a bit too earthy, dont you think?
W-well...
Perhaps you ought to go ahead and drink it, then!

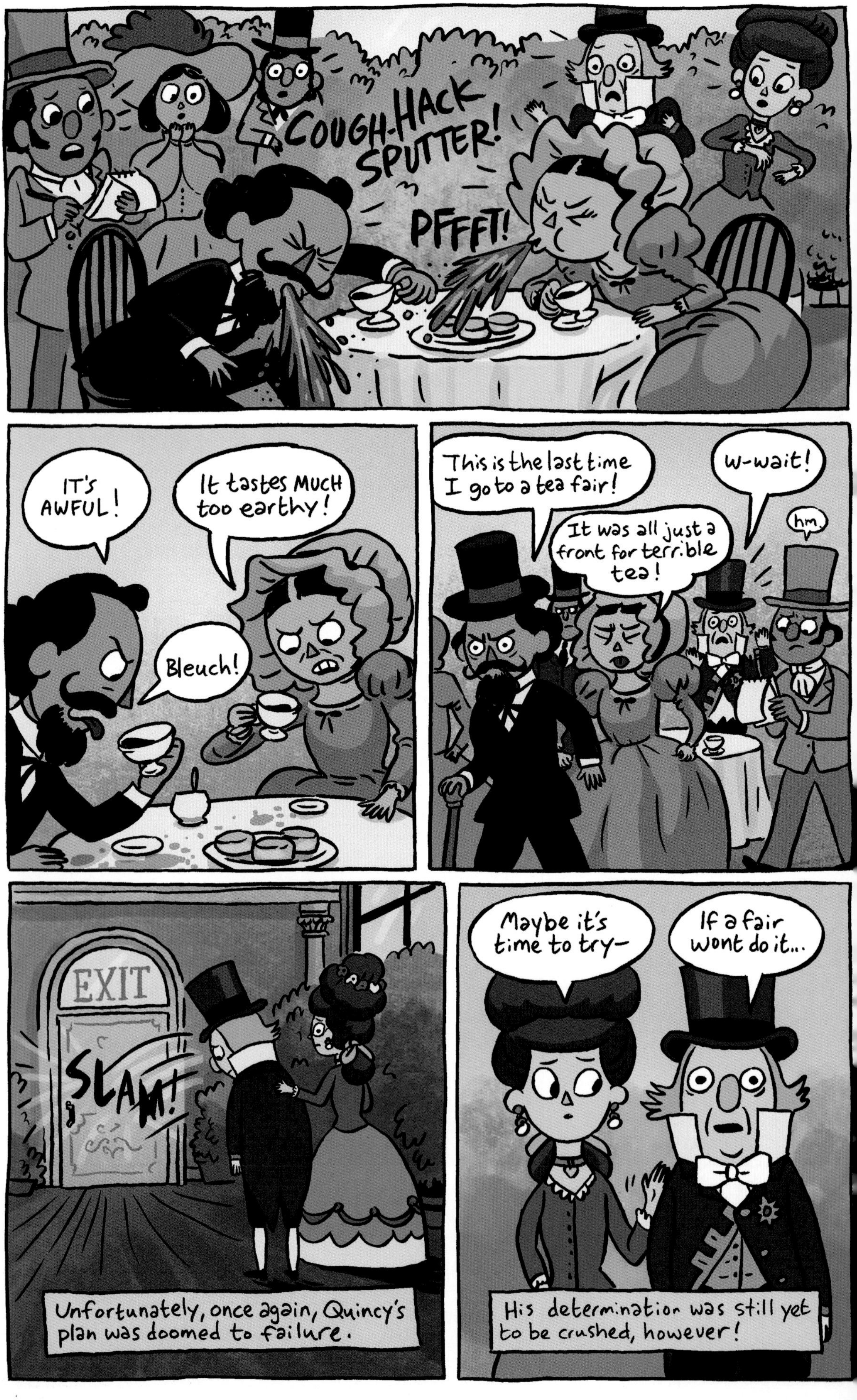
COUGH-HACK
SPUTTER!
PFFFT!
IT'S AWFUL!
It tastes MUCH too earthy!
Bleuch!
This is the last time I go to a tea fair!
It was all just a front for terrible tea!
W-wait!
hm.
EXIT
SLAM!
Unfortunately, once again, Quincy's plan was doomed to failure.
Maybe it's time to try–
If a fair wont do it...
His determination was still yet to be crushed, however!

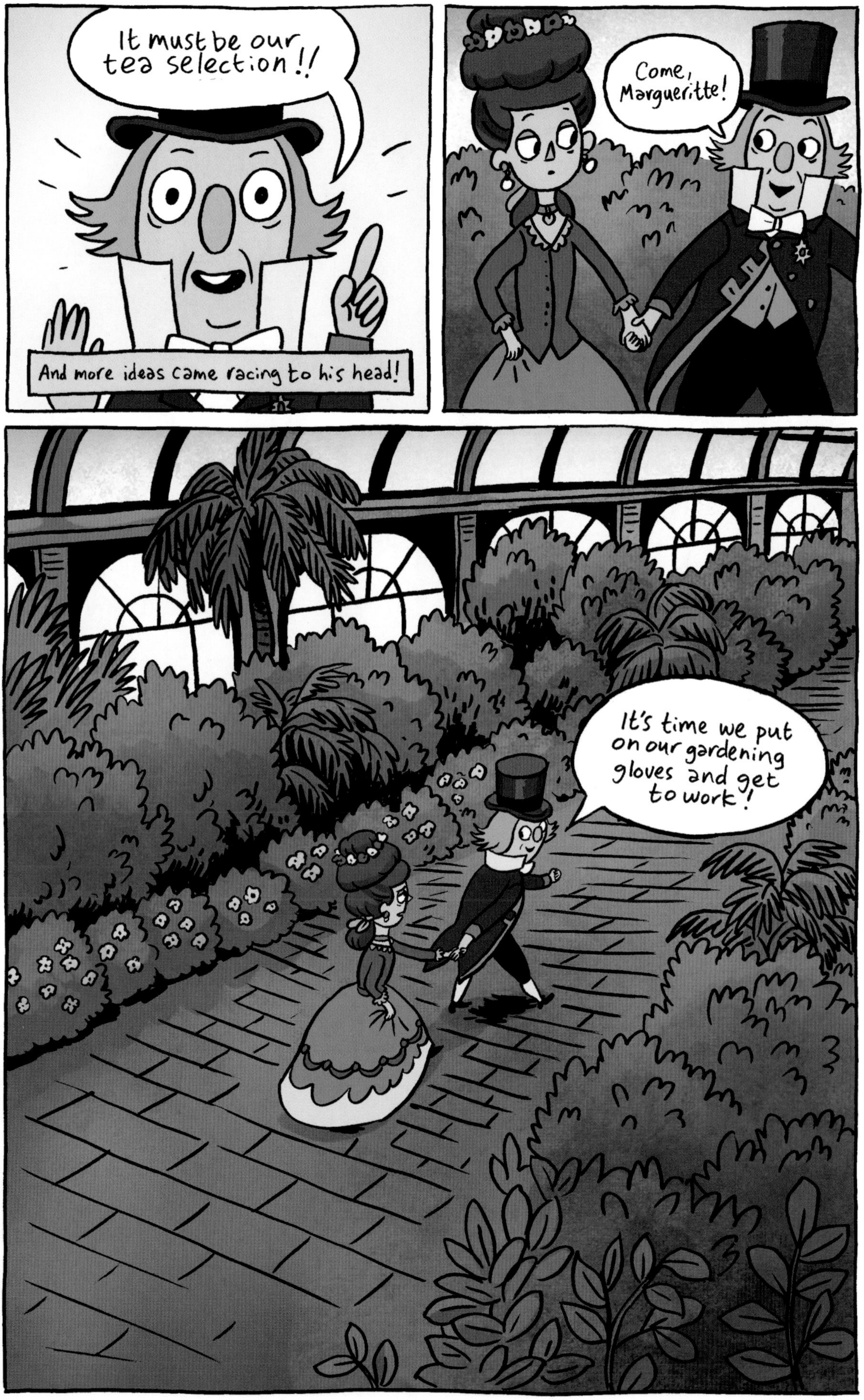
It must be our tea selection!!
And more ideas came racing to his head!
Come, Margueritte!
It's time we put on our gardening gloves and get to work!

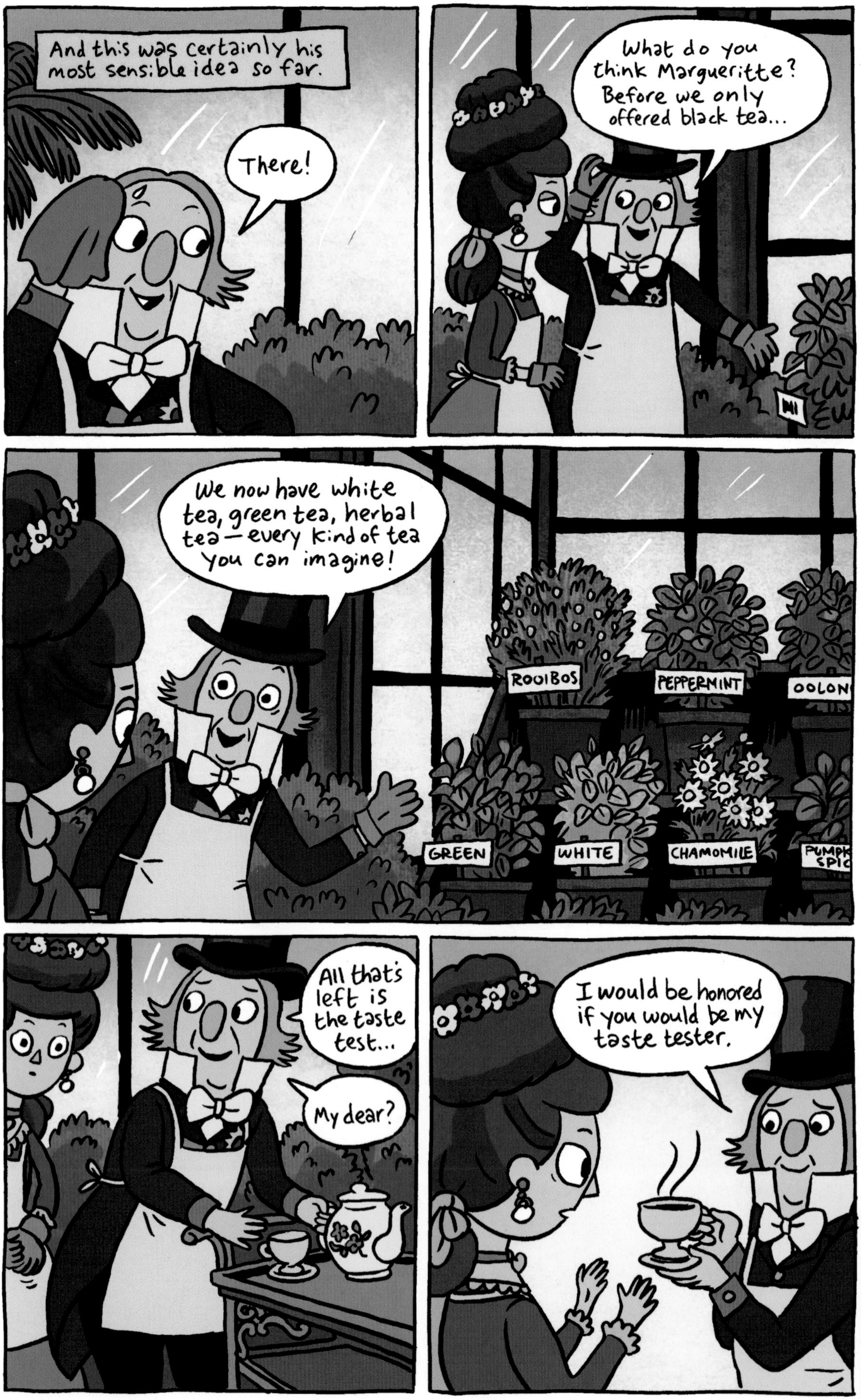
And this was certainly his most sensible idea so far.
There!
What do you think Margueritte? Before we only offered black tea...
We now have white tea, green tea, herbal tea—every kind of tea you can imagine!
ROOIBOS
PEPPERMINT
GREEN
WHITE
CHAMOMILE
All that's left is the taste test...
My dear?
I would be honored if you would be my taste tester.

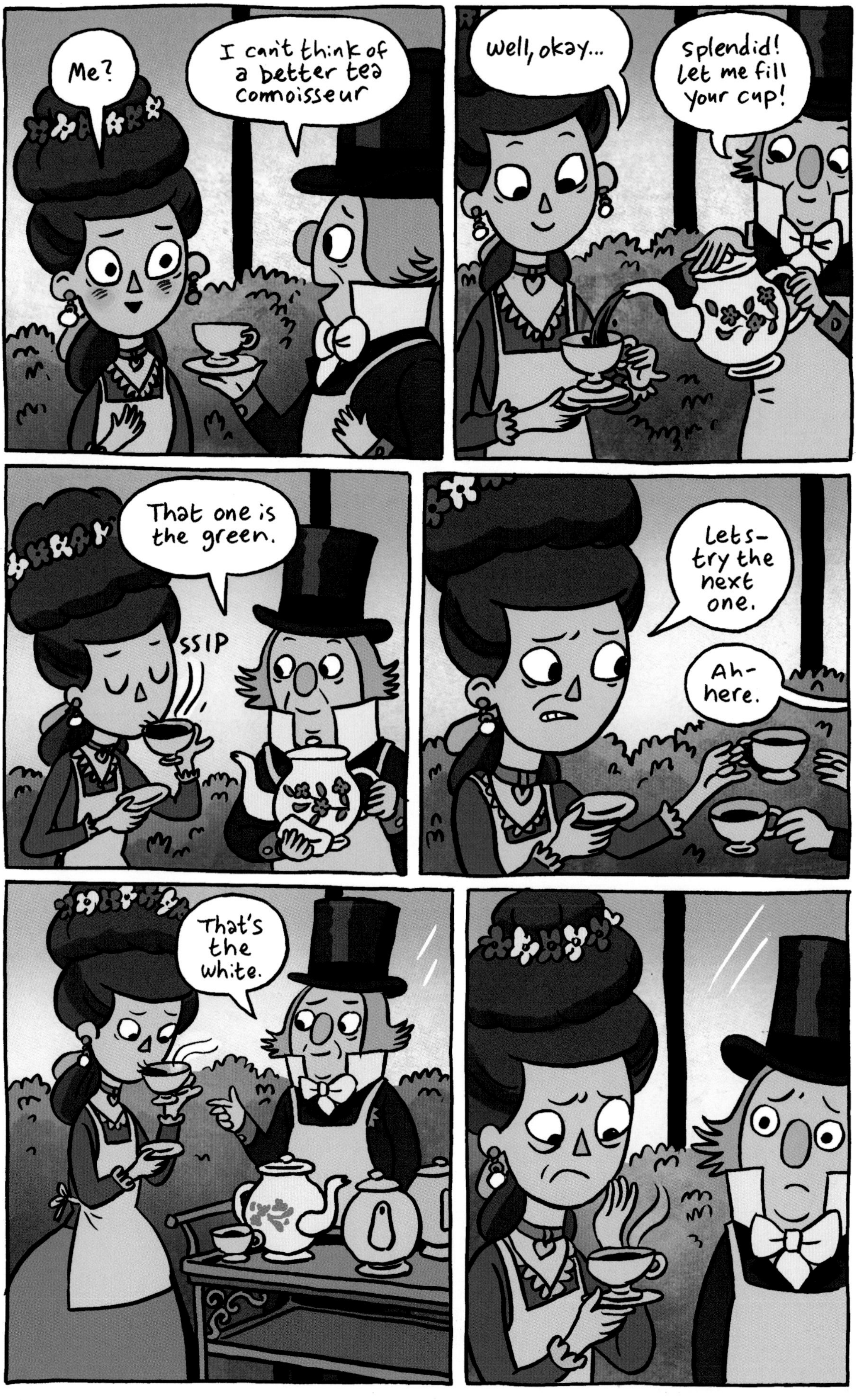
Me?
I can't think of a better tea connoisseur
Well, okay...
Splendid! Let me fill your cup!
That one is the green.
SSIP
Lets-try the next one.
Ah-here.
That's the white.

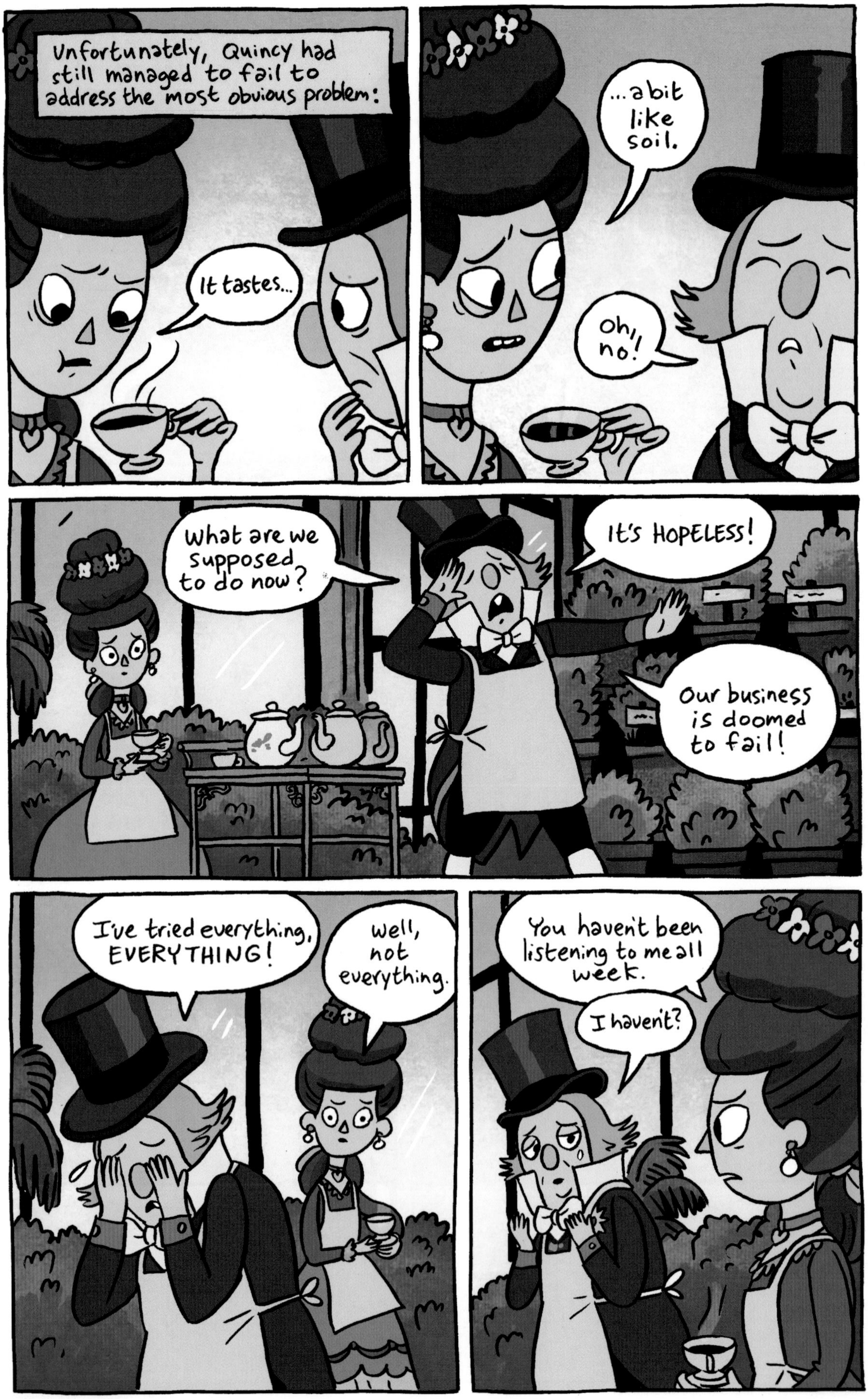
Unfortunately, Quincy had still managed to fail to address the most obvious problem:
It tastes...
...a bit like soil.
Oh, no!
What are we supposed to do now?
It's HOPELESS!
Our business is doomed to fail!
I've tried everything, EVERYTHING!
Well, not everything.
You haven't been listening to me all week.
I haven't?

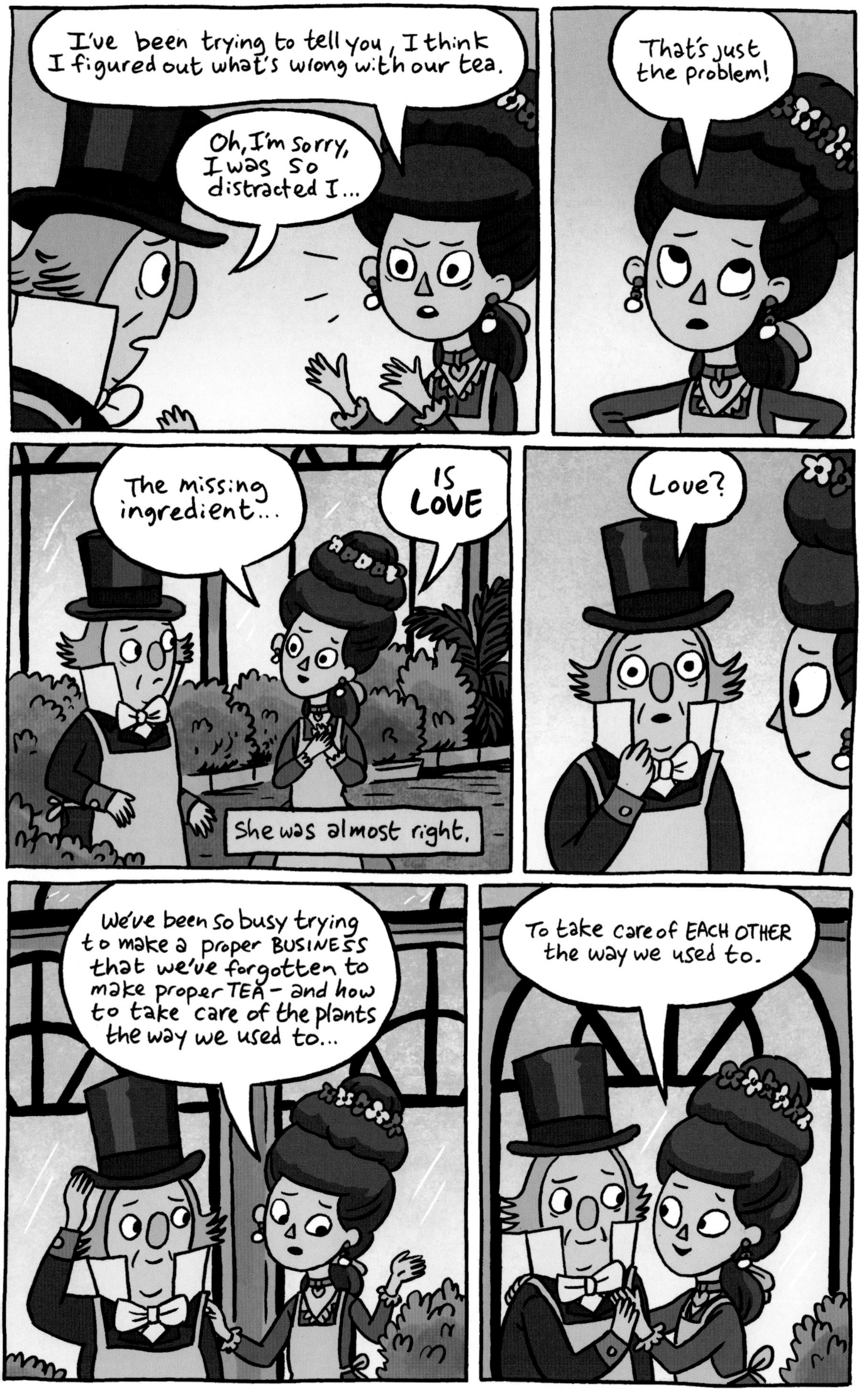
I've been trying to tell you, I think I figured out what's wrong with our tea.
Oh, I'm sorry, I was so distracted I...
That's just the problem!
The missing ingredient...
IS LOVE
She was almost right.
Love?
We've been so busy trying to make a proper BUSINESS that we've forgotten to make proper TEA - and how to take care of the plants the way we used to...
To take care of EACH OTHER the way we used to.

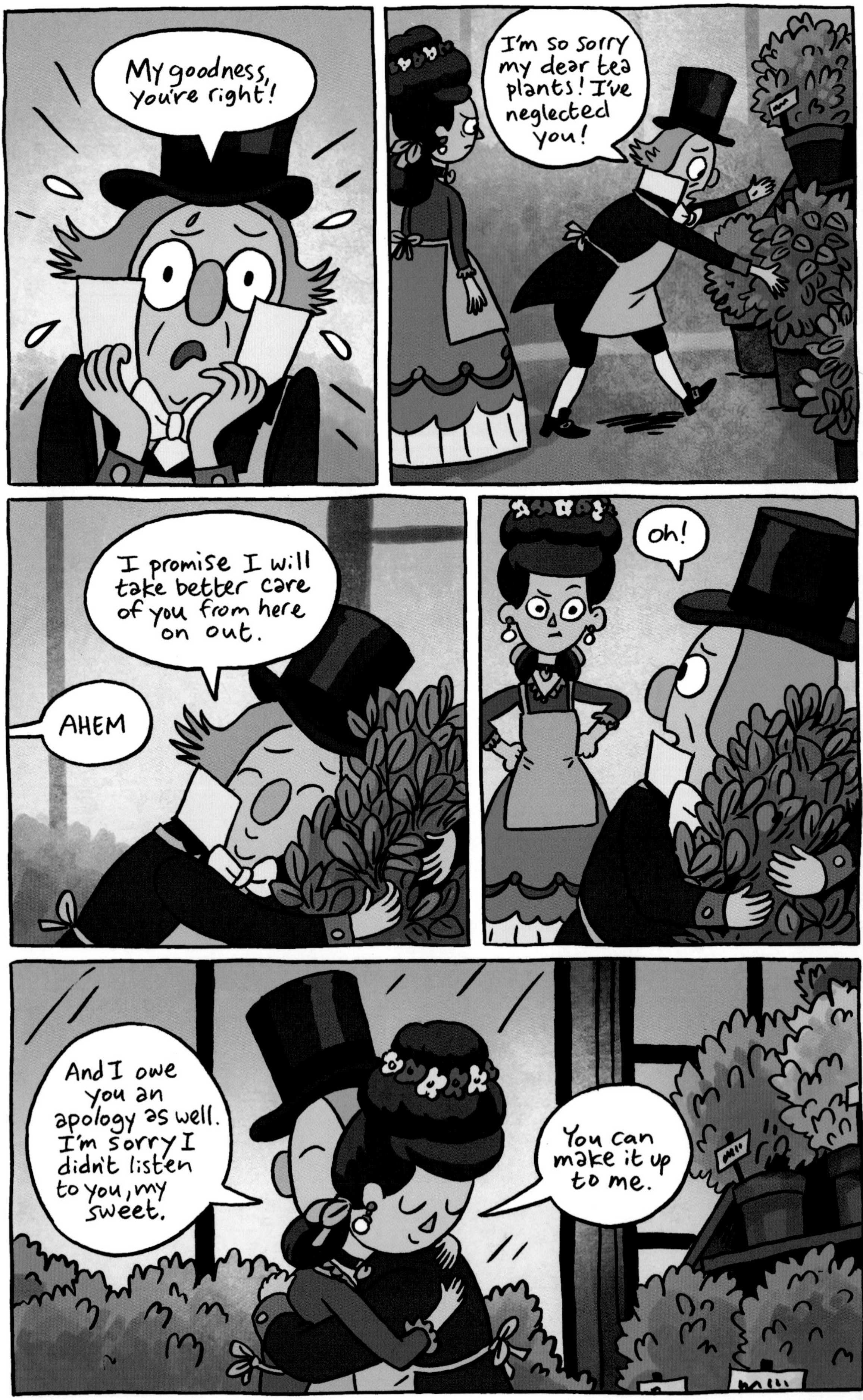
My goodness, you're right!
I'm so sorry my dear tea plants! I've neglected you!
I promise I will take better care of you from here on out.
AHEM
Oh!
And I owe you an apology as well. I'm sorry I didn't listen to you, my sweet.
You can make it up to me.

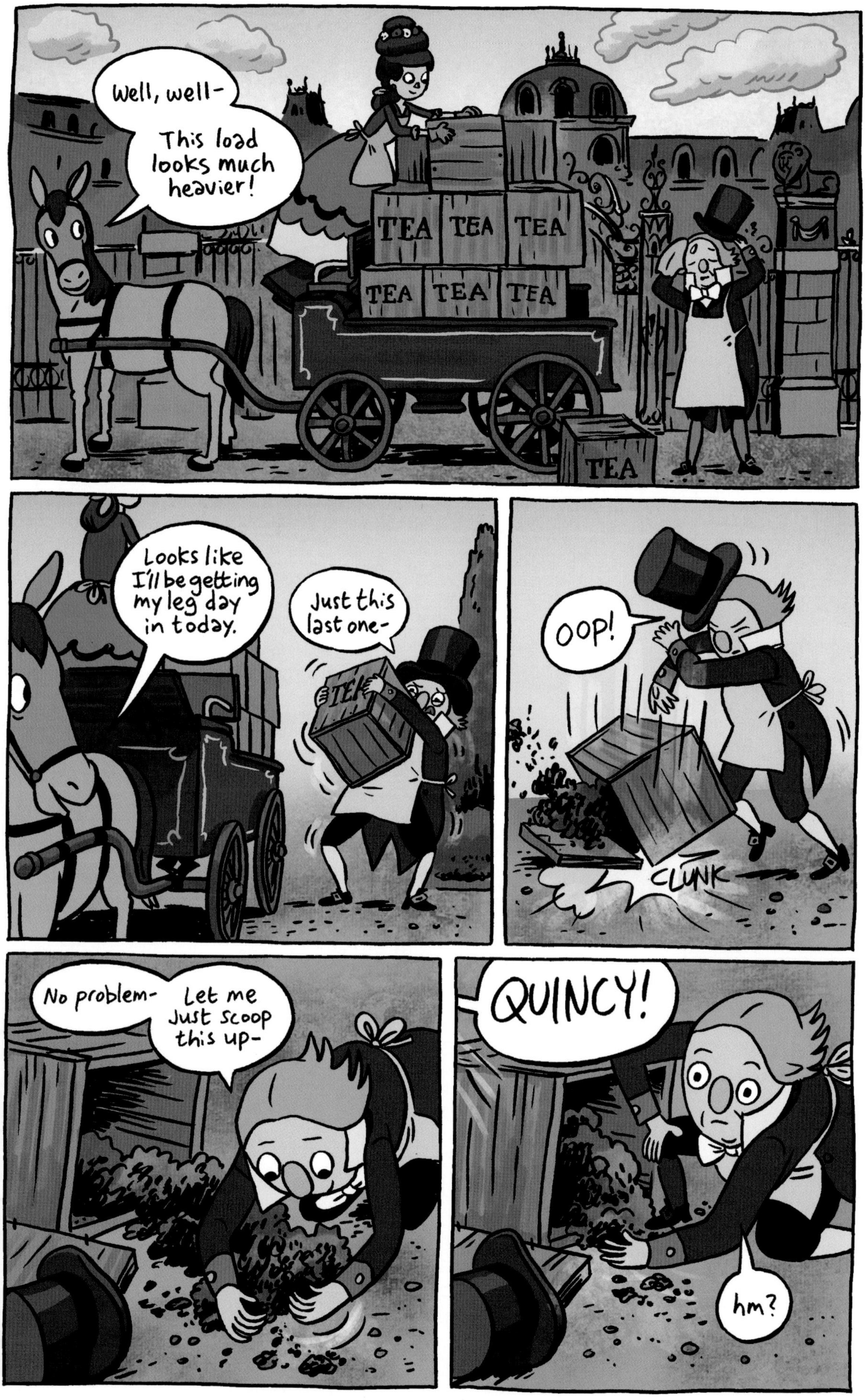
Well, well-
This load looks much heavier!
TEA TEA TEA
TEA TEA TEA
TEA
Looks like I'll be getting my leg day in today.
Just this last one-
TEA
OOP!
CLUNK
No problem-
Let me just scoop this up-
QUINCY!
hm?

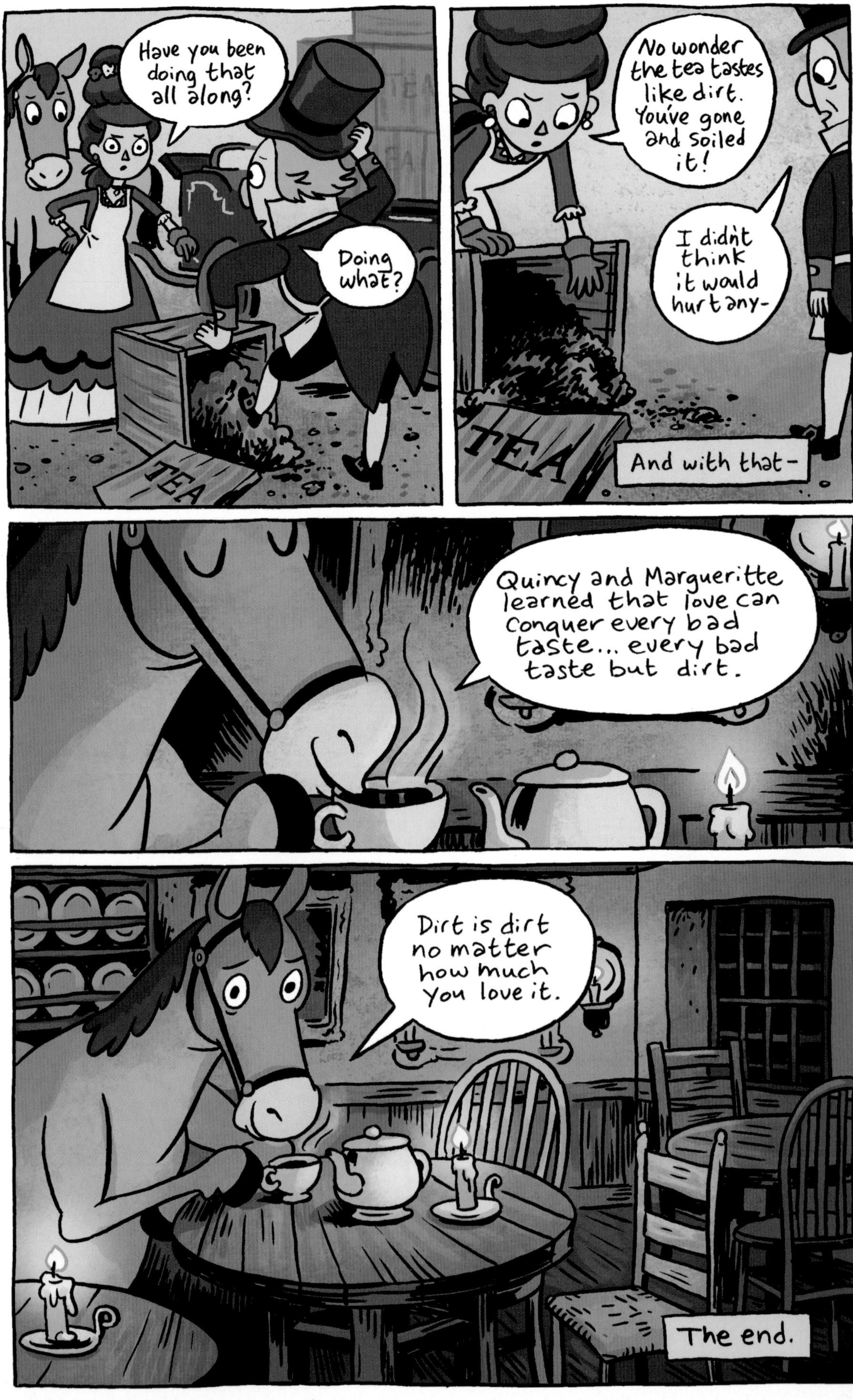
Have you been doing that all along?
Doing what?
No wonder the tea tastes like dirt. You've gone and soiled it!
I didn't think it would hurt any-
And with that-
Quincy and Margueritte learned that love can conquer every bad taste... every bad taste but dirt.
Dirt is dirt no matter how much you love it.
The end.

Cover Gallery

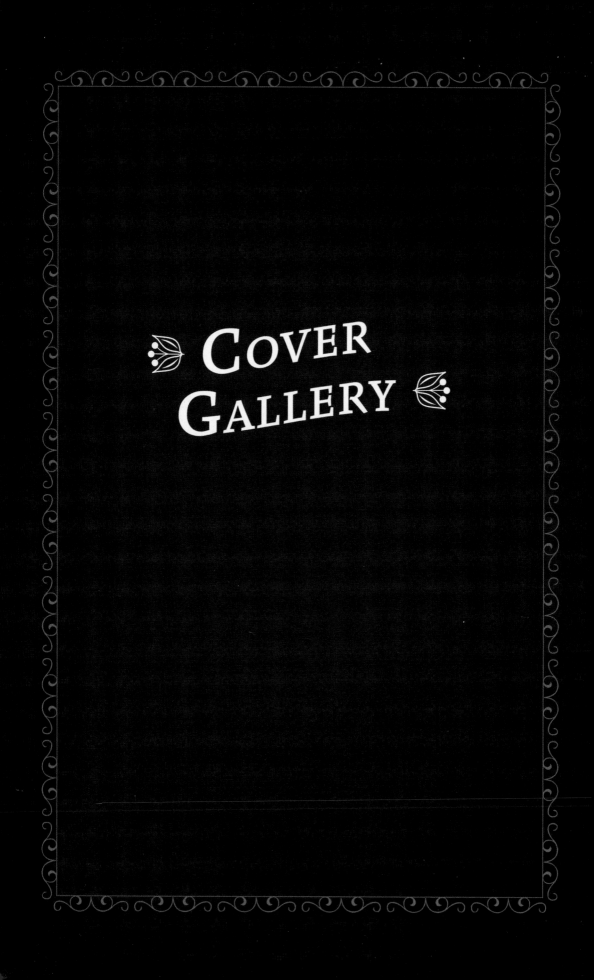

ISSUE SEVENTEEN COVER
JESSE TISSE

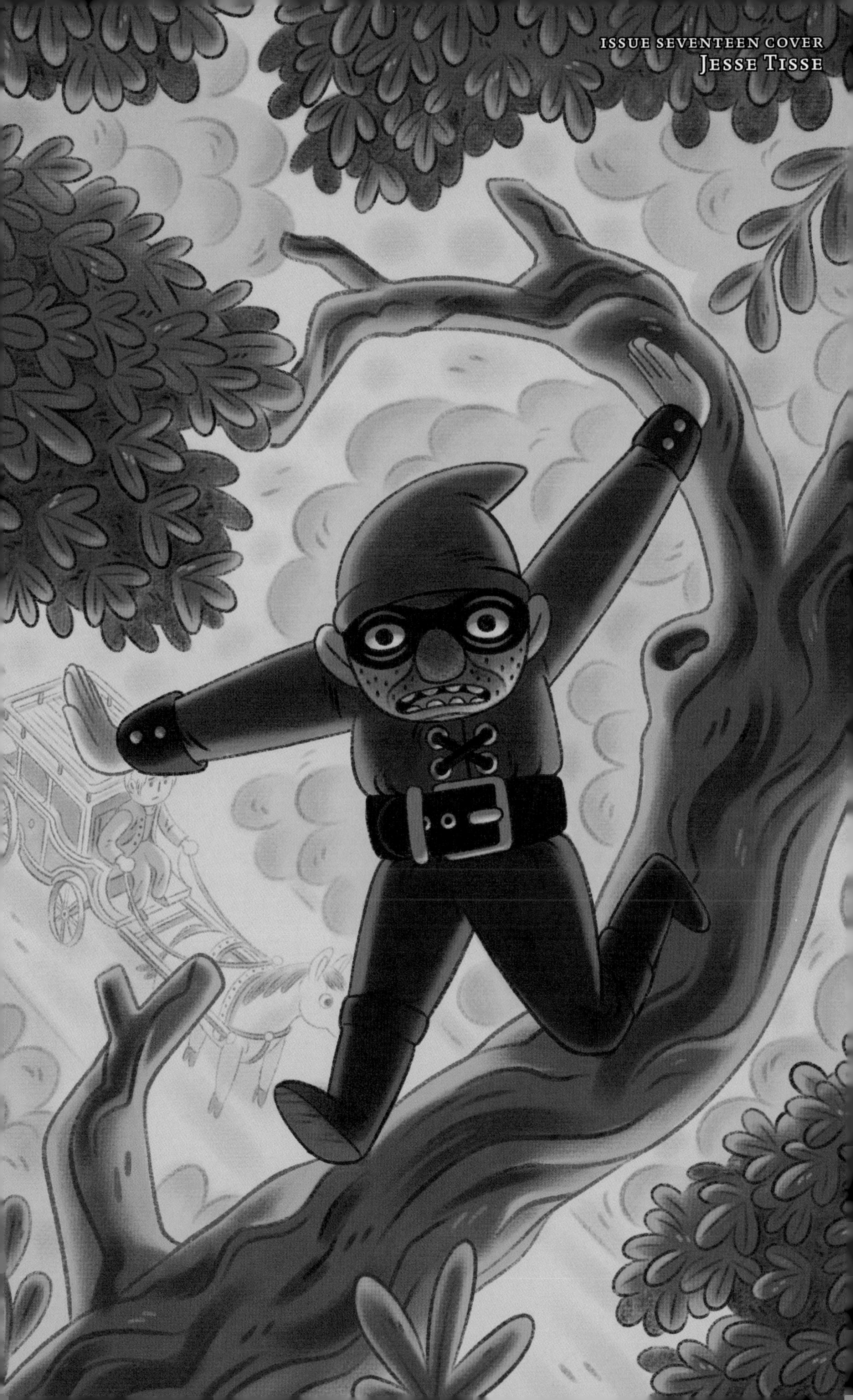

ISSUE SEVENTEEN SUBSCRIPTION COVER
Kyle Smart

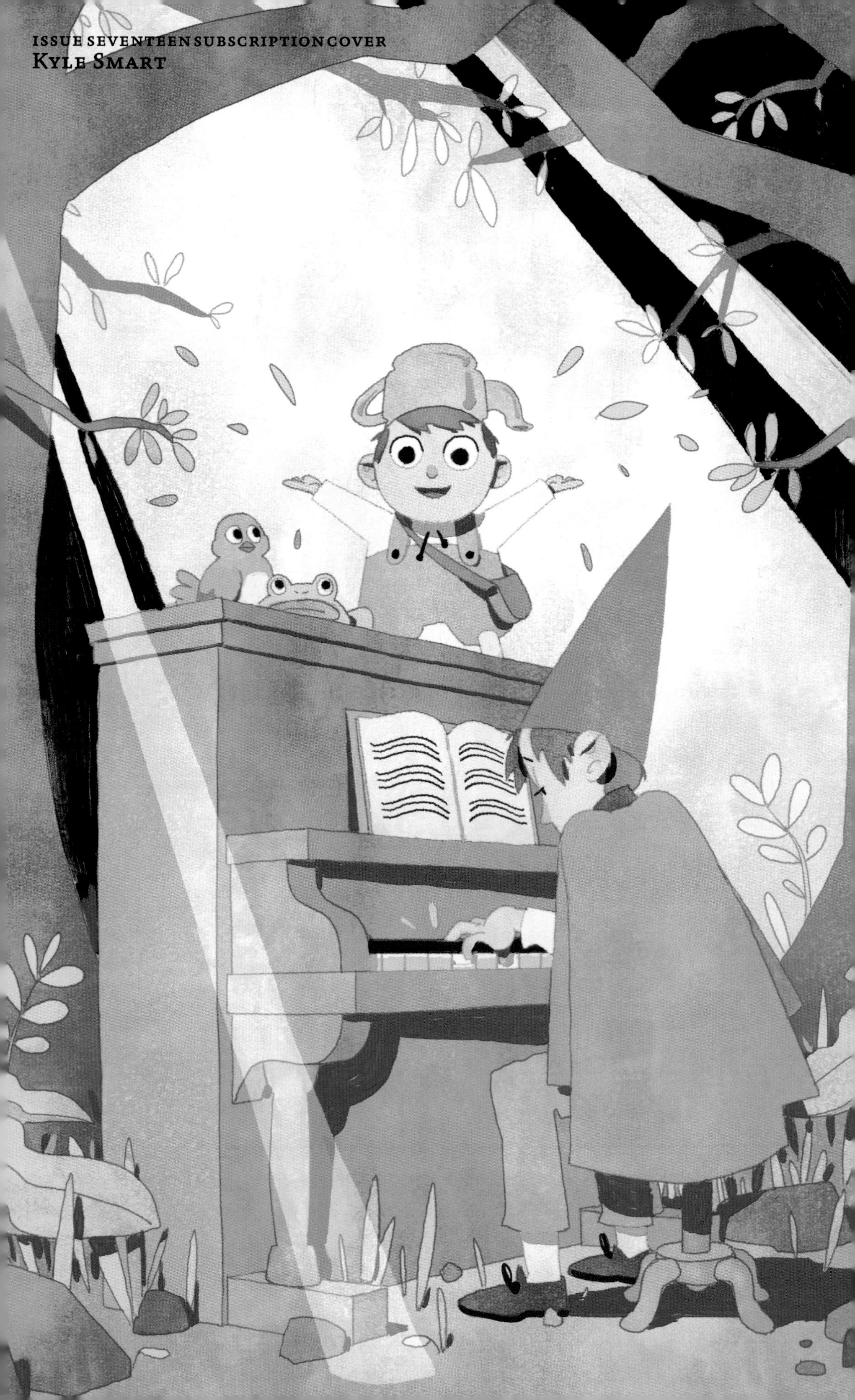

ISSUE EIGHTEEN COVER
KIERNAN SJURSEN-LIEN

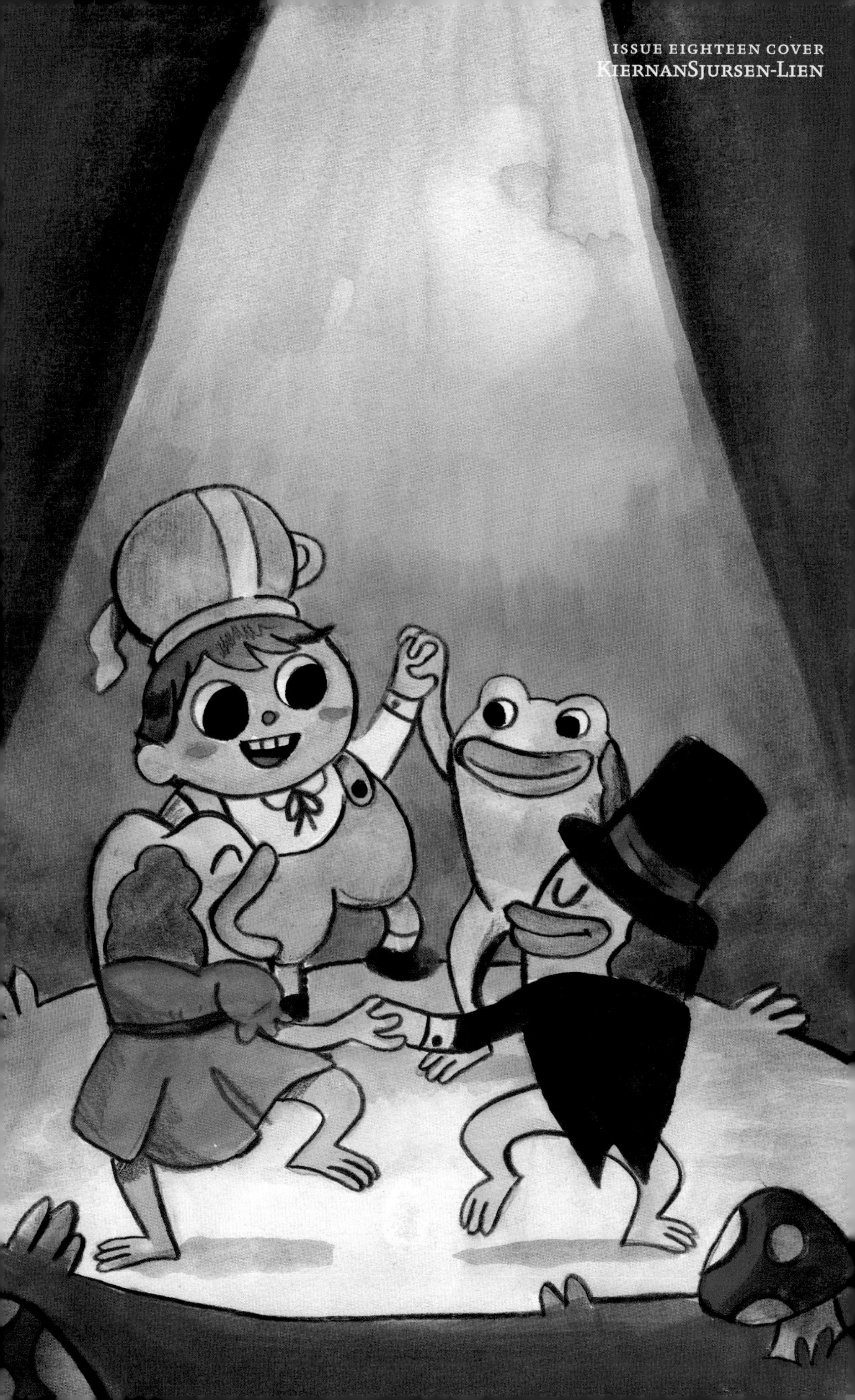

ISSUE EIGHTEEN SUBSCRIPTION COVER
HAYDEN SHERMAN

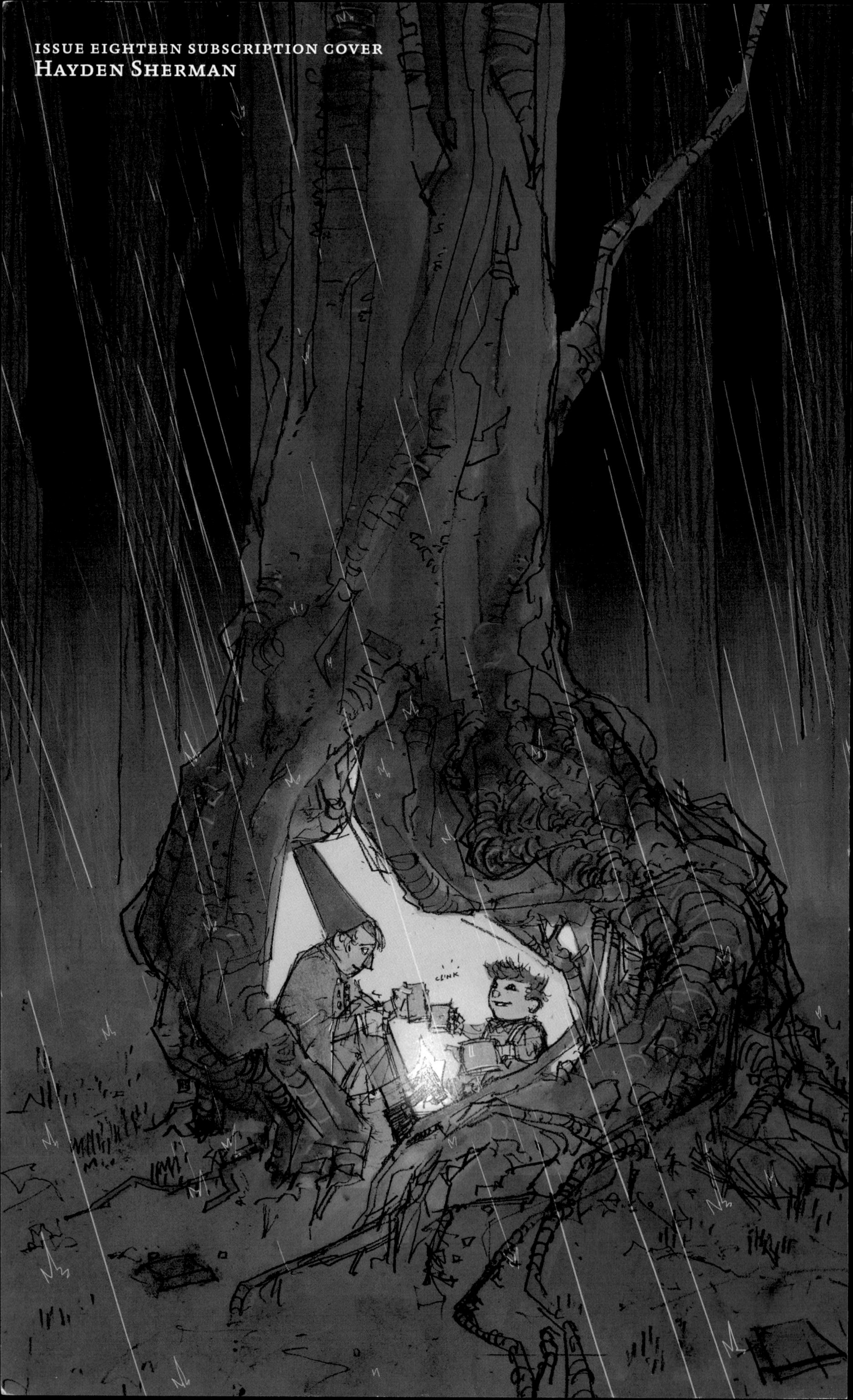

ISSUE NINETEEN COVER
DIIGII DAGUNA

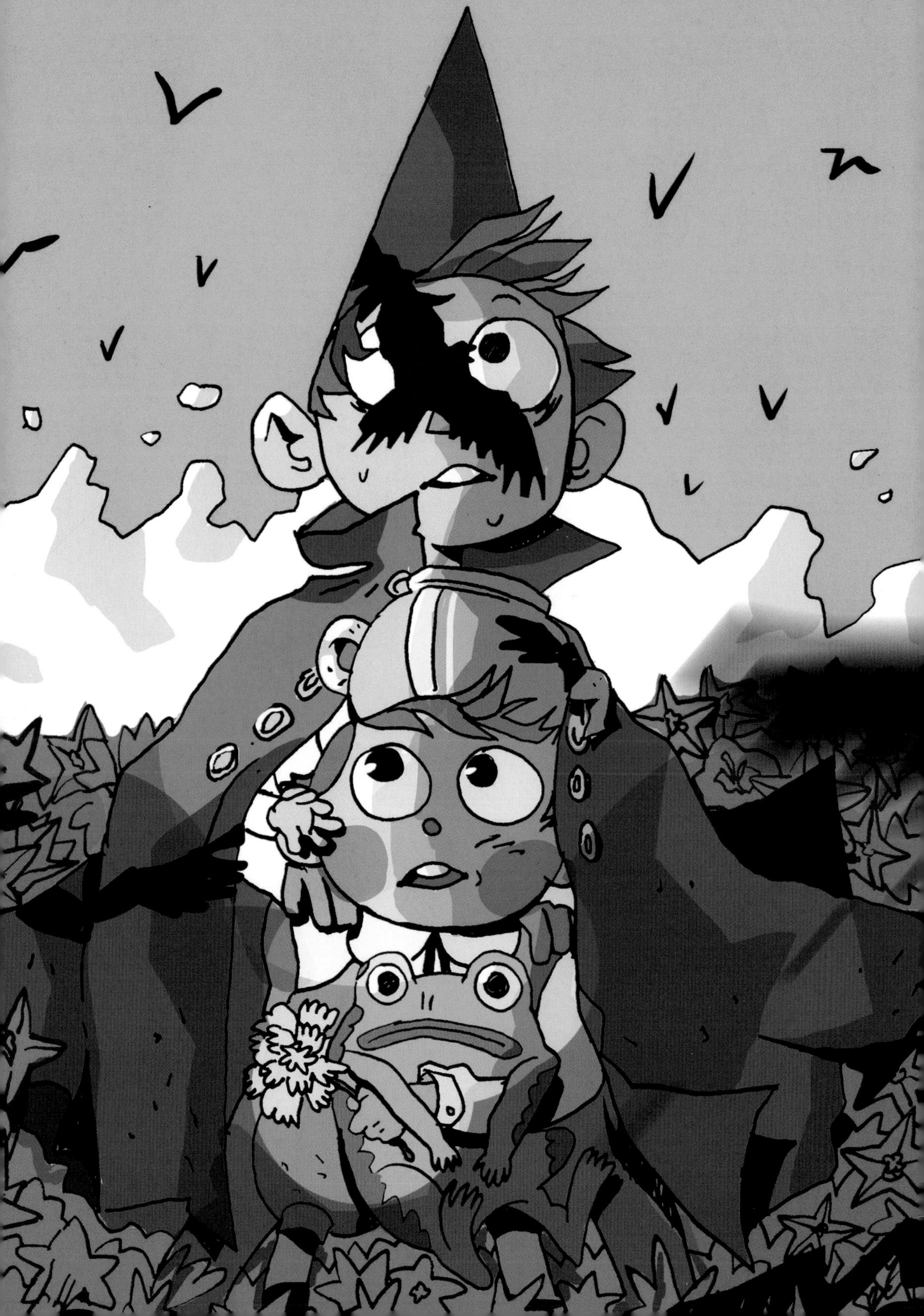

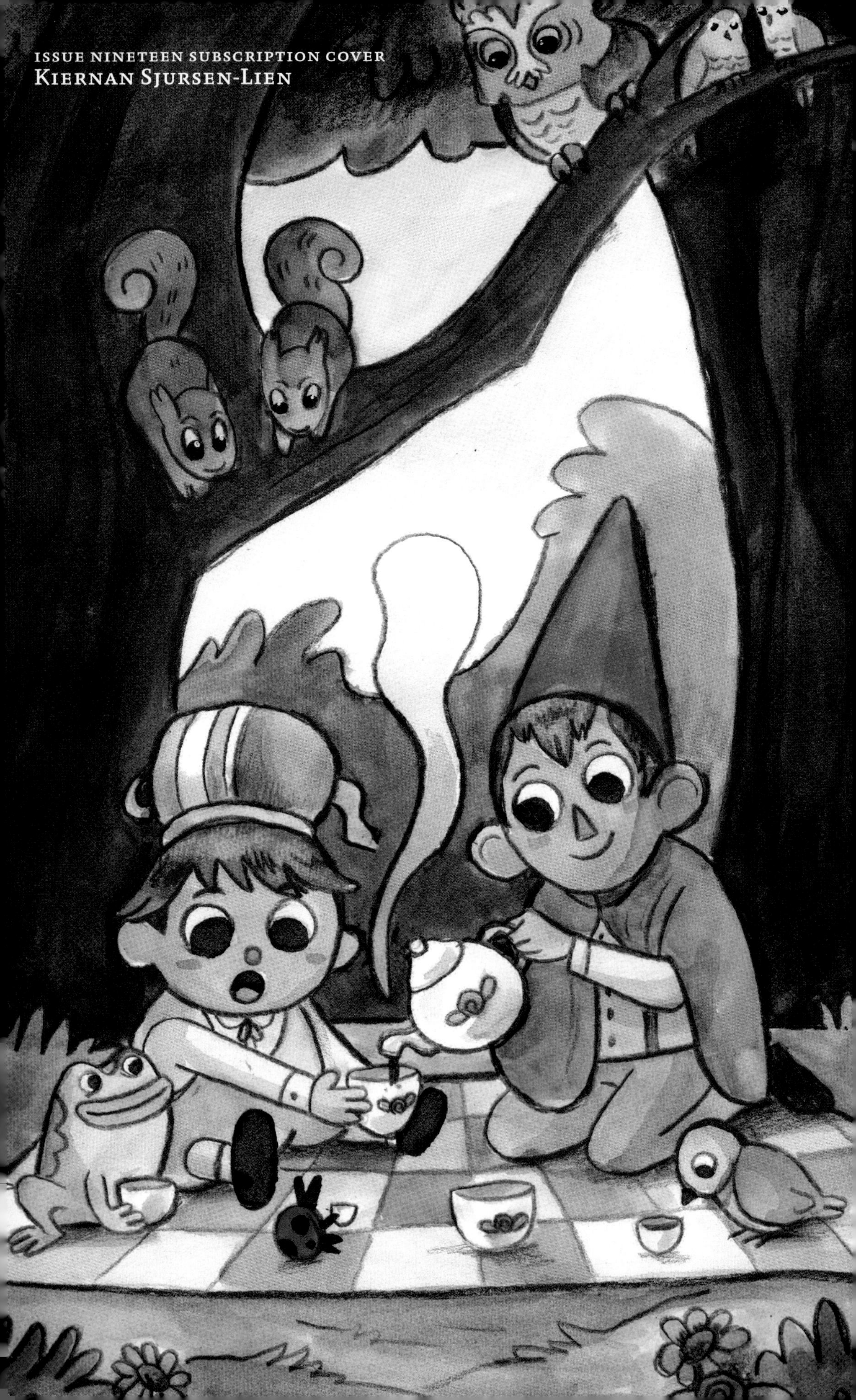

ISSUE NINETEEN SUBSCRIPTION COVER
Kiernan Sjursen-Lien

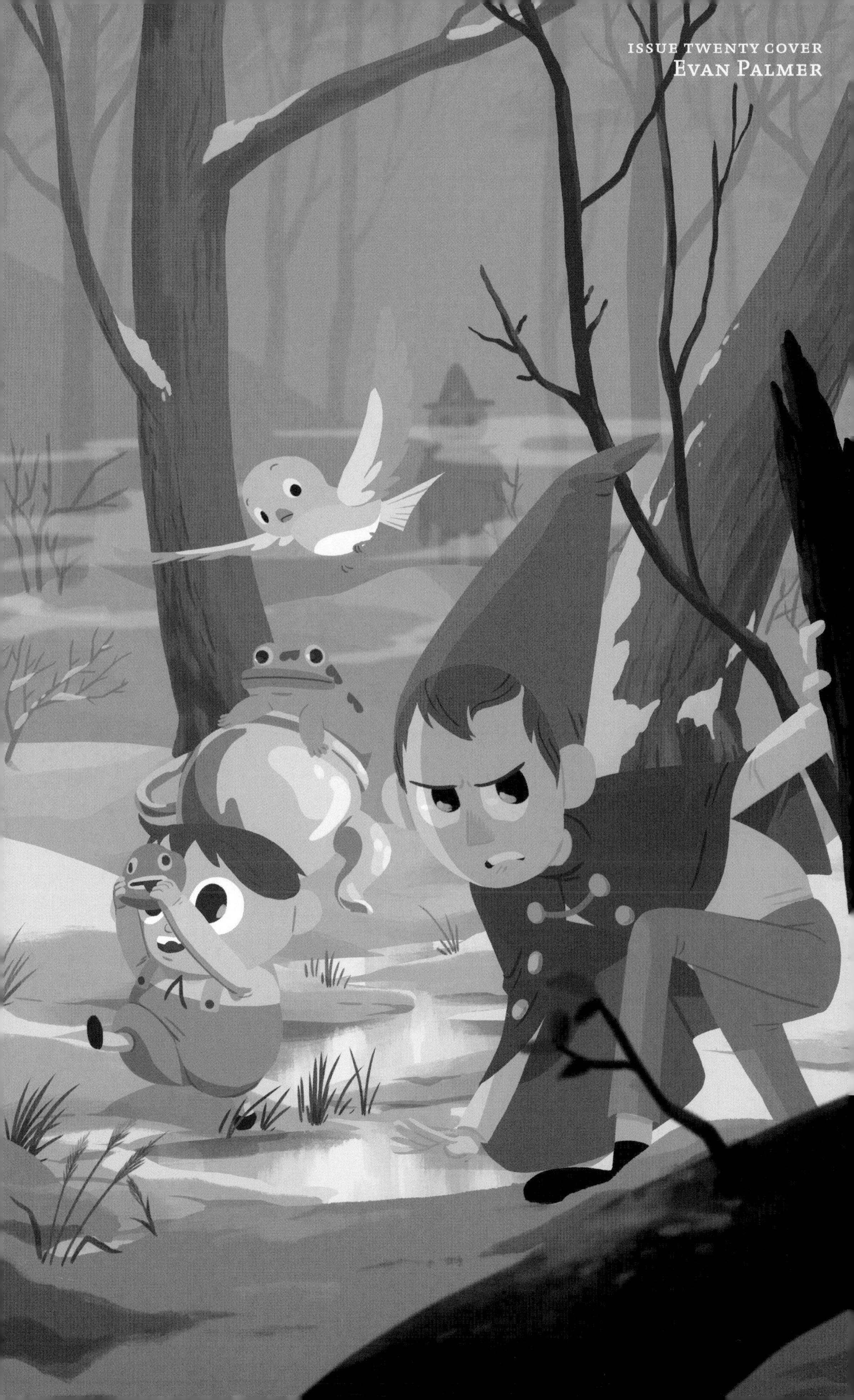

ISSUE TWENTY COVER
EVAN PALMER

ISSUE TWENTY SUBSCRIPTION COVER
MEG OMAC

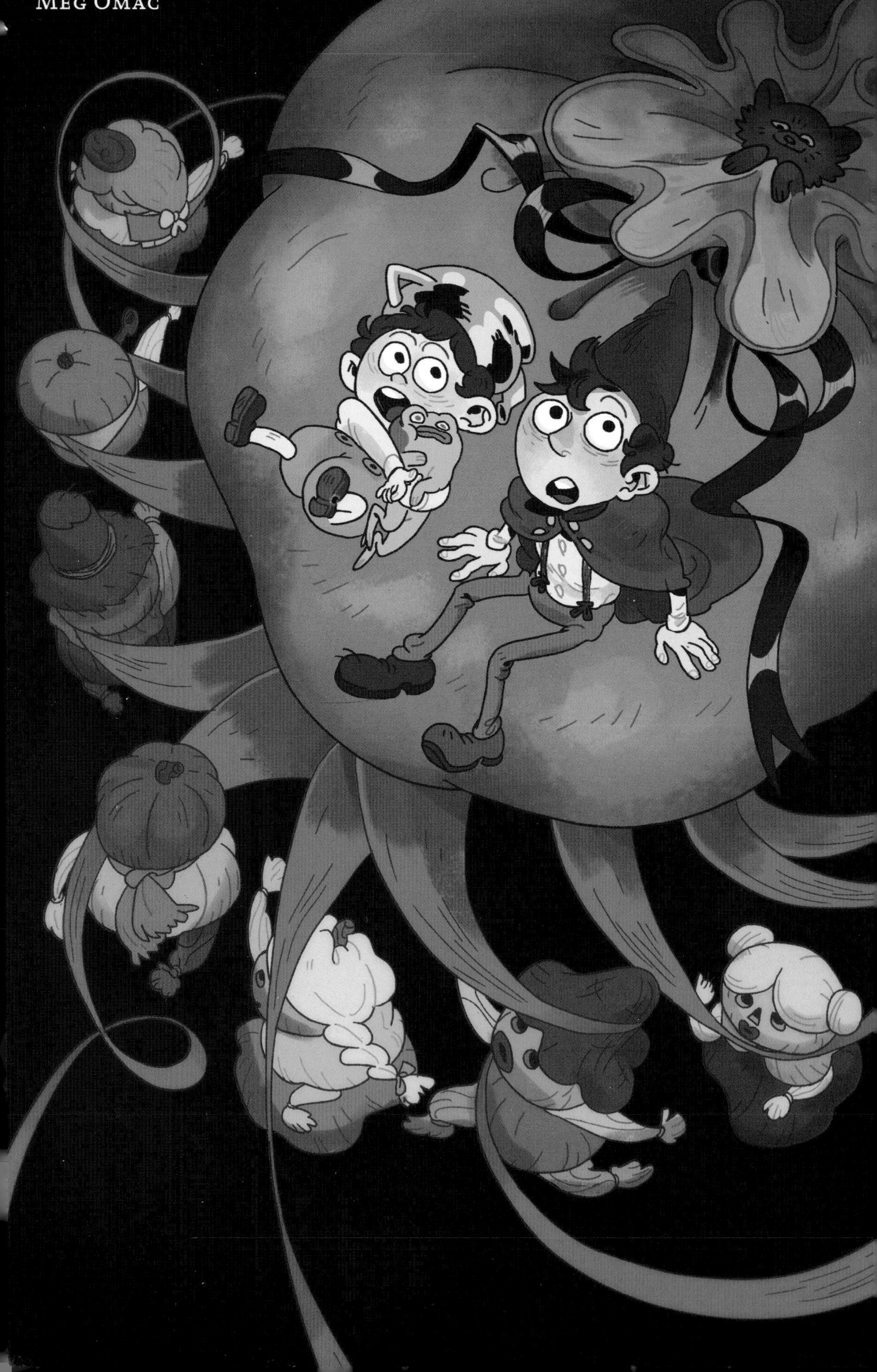